TURNING POINT

SUSAN LYNN PELLETIER

Copyright © 2021 by Susan Lynn Pelletier

All rights reserved. No part of this publication may be reproduced, distributed, or transmitted in any form or by any means, including photocopying, recording, or other electronic or mechanical methods, without the prior written permission of the publisher, except in the case brief quotations embodied in critical reviews and other noncommercial uses permitted by copyright law.

ISBN: 978-1-63945-227-9 (Paperback)
        978-1-63945-228-6 (Ebook)

The views expressed in this book are solely those of the author and do not necessarily reflect the views of the publisher, and the publisher hereby disclaims any responsibility for them.

Writers' Branding
1800-608-6550
www.writersbranding.com
orders@writersbranding.com

ACKNOWLEDGEMENT

To Tom, for giving me the idea for this story, I hope you're smiling down from heaven.
To all the Oxford Middle School staff that encouraged me to get started.
    I am grateful to Christ Church in Westerly for allowing me access to the church and answering all my questions.
    My appreciation: to Linda and Mike Colby for sharing your cancer story with me.
    A thank you goes to Ocean House and its staff; for giving me an exclusive tour of its facilities.
    A thank you; to my niece Michelle who arranged for Dharmendra Acharya to take the back cover picture of me.
    To Stephanie Jarvis Campbell: editor extraordinaire whose advice and proof-reading provided unmeasurable help.
    To Jan and Karen: who came to my rescue when I needed them. I appreciate and thank them for their time and expertise.

DEDICATION

This book is dedicated to:

    My husband, Gaetan, who for over forty years, has been the love of my life.

    My children: Juliane, Timothy, and Nicholas and their spouses, for all the support and encouragement you have given me.

    My grandchildren: they have brought a smile to my face and joy into my heart every day.

    My sisters and brother: who have shared life's journey with me.

    And to Jan, no words can express how much your friendship means to me. Without you I wouldn't know Westerly, Rhode Island and all its charm.

Turning Point

VARVARA HAROUTUNIAN
B. 1905
M. 1922 JEAN LEBLANC (1885-1957)
M. 1922 JEAN LEBLANC (1885-1957)
1965 MICHAEL TRUDEAU
1966 MAVERICK TALBERT

IRENE LEBLANC
B.1923-1980
M. 1945 LESLIE CLAYTON (1922-1980)

    JAN CLAYTON
    B. 1946
    M.1965 TIMOTHY ST PAUL

        VICTORIA ST PAUL
        B. 1966
        M.1985 MARC BURSELL

            ANGELIQUE BURSELL
            B. 1986
            M.2009 YVES HAROUTUNIAN

                VARVARA HAROUTUNIAN
                B.2007 (VARI)

            MARC BURSELL
            B. 1988

    ELIZABETH CLAYTON
    B. 1948
    M.1967 REGINAL GREEN

        NICHOLAS GREEN
        B. 1968
        B. 1987 SAFYIA SMITH

            MICHELLE GREEN
            B. 1987
            M.2006 KEITH GEORGE

                KAYLA GEORGE
                EMILY GEORGE
                B.2007 (TWINS)

            JENNIFER GREEN
            B. 1988
            M.2011 ABDURAHMAN PELLETIER

                ERIN PELLETIER
                B.2013

        MARYANN GREEN
        B.1970
        B.1990 KENNETH LAMPREY

            COLBY LAMPREY
            B.1990
            MATTHEW LAMPREY
            B.1992
            NOAH LAMPREY
            B.1995

Susan Lynn Pelletier

KAREN CLAYTON
B.1950
M.1968 RONALD MARTIN

    KAREN CLAYTON
    B.1971
    M.1993 BRIAN CHASE

        JOHN CHASE
        B.1995

    JAMES MARIN
    B.1973
    M.1993 BRITNEY EKMAN

        JULIANE MARTIN
        B.1996

    ALISHA MARTIN
    B.1994

PETER CLAYTON
B.1952
COMPANION-CHARLES WENTWORTH III

RICHARD CLAYTON
B.1954
M.1976-CHRISTINA JALBERT

    WILLIAM CLAYTON
    B.1978
    M.2001 FIAZA SAID

        COREY CLAYTON
        B.2002
        PATRICIA CLAYTON
        B.2004

AURELE LEBLANC
B.1925
D.1944

BERMONT LEBLANC
B.1927
M.1948 SASHA RUTHKEVITCH

    JEAN MARIE LEBLANC
    B.1950
    M.1969 YVETTE COTE'

        JOSHUA LEBLANC
        B.1970
        M.1990-JOAN BENE'

            REBECCA LEBLANC
            B.1991
            RACHAEL LEBLANC
            B.1994

Turning Point

LEO LEBLANC
B.1952
M.1974-JACQULINE
    GIBBONS

DAVID LEBLANC
B.1974

NICHOLE LEBLANC
B.1072

AMY LEBLANC
B.1975
MEGAN LEBLANC
B.1977

Angelique's hands were sweating as she gripped the steering wheel and drove south on I-95. Glancing in the rearview mirror, she checked on the sleeping child strapped snuggly in her car seat. She rolled her tense shoulders backward to try to relieve some of the stiffness, and then taking a deep breath of air, she settled down for the ride ahead.

She was going home, and with a sigh, Angelique realized how she longed for this moment and yet dreaded the upcoming confrontation with her mother, whom she hadn't to spoken to in the past three years. There was a lot of history that led up to the estrangement and the time had come for it to end. Her thoughts drifted to her great-great-grandmother, Varvara, the matriarch of the family, who at age 104 had sent out the request for the whole family to come home for the Easter weekend. No one ignored a command from Mémère. Angelique admitted to herself that she owed a lot to the grand lady who was her great-great-grandmother. Just about everything in her life revolved around the lessons she learned from Varvara. Now Varvara was going to record her life's story and wanted Vari to be among the children listening to it.

The approaching exit brought her thoughts back to the present as she quickly left the highway. With only a short distance left, she crossed Route 1 and drove toward Watch Hill. She could smell the strong scent of salt on the air, and the seagulls were calling out their welcome.

Coming over the rise, the vista of Watch Hill within the town of Westerly, Rhode Island, spread before Angelique with the vast blue Atlantic in the background. She never got over the pleasure of seeing the ocean. As she drove past the harbor, she marveled at its stark emptiness. She envisioned what it would look like in just a few months, when it would be filled with yachts and fishing boats. She drove down Bay Street, noticing that most of the stores were still closed. As she passed Puffin's, she reminded herself she needed to go there in search of a birthday present for Mémère and was glad to see that it was open. Continuing on, she drove past the Flying Horse Carousel, built in 1876 and a registered National Historic Landmark. It was still all boarded up, but soon the horses would return and children's laughter would again be heard coming from inside the carousel. As Angelique continued up the road, the driveway to the family's home, Seagull's Perch, appeared with its large arborvitaes on each side. They always appeared like large green welcoming arms. Her tires rumbled as she drove over the seashell driveway and made her way to the parking spaces next to the large three-car garage. She had grown up in the apartment above it.

Angelique pulled into a parking space and paused to contain the feelings that only the old family home could create. The large, beautiful, white mansion was positioned high on a bluff; its many windows provided spectacular views of the Atlantic Ocean. Surrounded by large wraparound porches, it gracefully stretched out in historic grandeur. The morning sun's rays made each glass pane twinkle like diamonds. It was built in the mid- 1800s by Angelique's ancestor who was a sea captain and merchant. The home had three stories and twenty rooms, twelve of them bedrooms. On top of the mansion was a glass-enclosed widow's perch. Angelique remembered the numerous times she and her cousins ran through the many hallways and bedrooms during the family holidays and long summer vacations she had spent in the old house. She smiled to herself and looked at the small girl in the back seat. Strong feelings of love for her daughter stirred in her stomach.

Gracefully exiting the car, she opened the back door and helped her daughter out. Holding the little girl's hand, she walked up the stairs to the spacious wraparound porch. White wicker furniture with bright yellow and blue cushions was scattered in carefree abandonment across the spacious covered porch. Memories of lost conversations and long games of Hand and Foot with cousins skittered through her thoughts, but were interrupted when the door opened to reveal a tall, thin woman.

Victoria. She wore her hair pulled back and tied up with a ribbon, looking more like a 25-year-old than a grandmother in her forties; she was dressed in black leggings and a bright yellow top that was cinched at the waist with a wide leather belt. She obviously had just finished her morning dance routine. The woman looked from Angelique to the little girl, who was now hiding behind her mother's leg, and there was a brief softening in Victoria's eyes when they fell on the child, but the tone wasn't soft when she addressed Angelique.

"So, you decided to come home."

"Hello to you, too, Mother."

"Don't use that tone of voice…"

The pending argument was interrupted by the arrival of a tall, attractive man dressed in a t-shirt and jeans. Coming behind him were three small dogs yapping, with excited woofs, their tiny feet sliding to a stop in front of Angelique and her daughter Vari.

"Uncle Marc!" Vari jumped up and down with her arms raised. "Uppa! Uppa!" In one swoop, Vari was tossed high in the air, bubbling giggles echoing around the great entrance hall. The dogs, wanting in on the fun, ran around in circles, alternating between high jumps in the air and their own form of yapping laughter.

"I'm glad you made it. How was the ride?" Marc asked Angelique. "Did you hit the traffic in Providence?"

"Well, come inside." Victoria said. "You two always did stick together."

"Yes," replied Marc. "Mother, let's not start arguing. I think you'd like to meet your grandchild." Still holding Vari in his arms, he turned and said, "Mother this little munchkin is Vari. Vari, this is your grandma."

Vari peeked around Mark's shoulder and gave a cherub smile. She greeted Victoria with a quiet hello.

"Well, hello to you, too," replied Victoria as she looked at Vari for the first time. Her features softened as she gazed at her granddaughter.

The two siblings exchanged understanding looks. They had several conversations about Vari and their mother meeting and how it would go.

Standing in the foyer, Angelique looked around her old home. The main floor consisted of the grand entranceway, where they were standing; its main feature was the curved grand staircase and black-and-white marbled floor. The stairway was a favorite amongst the children; on every floor there was a section that was open and you could either look up to the third-floor ceiling or down to the first floor. There were many family pictures of children's faces looking over the railings on every landing.

Throughout the house you could see a continuous run of crown molding circling the ceilings. Ornate moldings could be found on the doorway and windows' trim, giving the house an air of elegance. She glanced off to the left to where the formal dining room was. She let out a sigh of relief, noting that nothing had changed. It was decorated in Victorian style with a twelve-foot ceiling, floor-to-ceiling windows and a beautiful hardwood floor. The room was extremely attractive with its delft blue walls and fancy white trim. An ornately carved white marble arched fireplace stood along one wall with glass cased china closets on each side. The room was furnished with delicate Victorian furniture and a blue Oriental carpet-covered floor. Switching to the right of the foyer, she glanced into the library/office. It, too, had not changed; its walls were covered from floor to ceiling with shelves of books, and a large oversized oak desk was centered in the middle of the floor. Black leather furniture gave the room a rich masculine feel, and the oak fireplace in the corner always gave the room a touch of warmth. She knew every inch of the house, for she had lived in one part or the other for most of her life. Just thinking of it made her anxious to see it all again. It had been a long three years, and she was glad to finally be home.

Marc interrupted her thoughts, asking her to join the rest of the family that was gathered in the great room.

"I need to get my things from the car," said Angelique.

"I'll help later, Angel," Marc said. "Come say hello to everyone. They've been waiting to see you." He started walking, with Vari on his shoulders, and Angelique had no choice but to follow. Victoria did the same.

The back of the house, which faced the ocean, contained the family room and great room. These two rooms had panoramic views of the ocean, and on a clear day, you could see Block Island and parts of Long Island. News of Angelique's arrival traveled fast through the house, and a calliope of noise spilled out of the family room. When Victoria and Angelique entered the great room, a hushed silence fell upon the family as they watched and waited to see what would happen. Then, from the other side of the room, a voice spoke out.

"Angel, I'm glad you accepted my invitation."

Tears filled up Angelique's eyes as she gazed at the woman slowly being pushed to the front of the group. Her great-great-grandmother, the matriarch of the family, was now sitting in a wheelchair. That was new— when Angelique had last seen her, she was still strong, vibrant, and dancing. Now, as Angelique looked, she saw how fragile her great-great-grandmother had become. Varvara was once a tall woman, but it seemed a small portion of her had disappeared. She looked so tiny sitting in the chair. Angelique noticed that her once strong hands now were covered with paper-thin skin that exposed the blue veins underneath, giving them the appearance of being delicate and fragile.

Angelique leaned close and kissed her on both cheeks. Her great-great- grandmother was savvy and they had kept in touch through e-mail, video chatting, and texting but that couldn't compare to being in the same room and being able to hug and kiss her. Thinking back, Angelique realized that lately

Varvara had only used texting to communicate with her. Obviously, hiding her weaken condition.

"Welcome home, Angel. Thank you for coming. Now, Marc, put that child down so I can greet my namesake."

Gently placing Vari down in front of the wheelchair, Marc stepped back. "Vari, come say hello to Mémère', who I told you we were coming to see," Angelique said, standing behind her daughter.

Varvara looked at the small child and reached out to touch the dark curls that surrounded her cherub-like face.

"Are you the ballerina in my pictures?' Vari asked in a whisper.

Looking up questioningly at Angelique, who nodded, Varvara answered, "Yes."

"My ballerina is young and you're old," Vari said.

This brought a few gasps and some laughter from the family that had gathered behind Varvara in the great room.

"I was young once, many years ago." Chuckling, Varvara wiped a tear from her eye with her handkerchief and commented that Vari must take after her.

"And what is your name, may I ask?" Varvara said to Vari.

"My name is Varvara Jan Haroutunian," answered Vari proudly. "That's my name, too!" said Varvara.

At this statement, Vari made a funny face and looked questioningly at her mother.

With laughter, Angelique nodded, saying, "You are named after her, Vari!" Vari again made a funny face, but, like most two-and a half-year-olds, had lost interest in the conversation. She had spotted the dogs sitting near the windows and wandered off to pat them.

Varvara began looking very tired and, nodding to the nurse, she slowly was wheeled out of the room. "Angelique, come see me tomorrow morning after practice. Please bring the child with you," Varvara's voice from the hallway.

Everyone started talking at once. Angelique's grandparents came forward and hugged both Angelique and Vari.

"I'm so glad you have come home," said Jan.

"Who is this girl? Do I know you?" asked Tim as his eyes twinkled with laughter.

"Gampa Tim. It's me." Vari shouted.

"How can you be Vari, she's just a little baby," teased, Tim. "I growed-up." Vari said.

Laughter at the exchange came from the rest of the group. Greetings from cousins and hugs and kisses from Aunt Sasha and Uncle Bermont made Angelique feel at home. Vari had been playing with the dogs until she noticed that in the corner was a toy box around which sat several children. She ran over and sat down and joined in to play with a girl with blonde hair. Angelique noticed familiar sounds coming from the kitchen, just off the great room: She walked over and saw the familiar scene of her aunts, Karen and Christina, preparing lunch. The only thing different was the kitchen had been completely renovated with new stainless steel appliances, a five—burner gas stove, black granite countertops, and a center island that held a microwave, a warming drawer and, in its corner, a small wash sink. Both aunts stopped what they were doing and engulfed Angelique in warm welcoming hugs and kisses.

"Lunch will be ready in a few minutes. It's good to see you back home, Angelique!" Aunt Karen said as she quickly gave Angelique another kiss and went back to working on lunch.

Angelique continued to look around her old home. Off the kitchen, the porch had been converted into a breakfast nook and sunroom. She glanced over to check on Vari, who was still playing with the other children in the corner, and she hadn't noticed that Marc had come up behind her.

"It's amazing how fast little ones adjust to their surroundings," Marc whispered into Angelique's ear. "I need to talk to you as soon as possible. Can you meet me after we eat?"

"I need to get my things from my car. Why don't we meet out front on the porch?" without waiting for an answer she asked, "How long has Mémère been in the wheelchair? All the times we talked on Skype she was at her desk, and when we went out to eat for Vari's second birthday, she was walking with just her cane. It's just a little unnerving to see her in it. It makes her look old."

"Ever since she had pneumonia she has had trouble, but she caught a cold last winter, and since then she seems to get tired very easily. What can you expect? She's almost one hundred and five."

Over the next hour, Angelique reacquainted herself with the family. Though she had kept in contact with several members over the last three years, she wasn't up to date with all the family news. From the many cousins and her aunts and uncles, she soon learned about the changes that had happened since she had been gone, including a few new cousins that had been born. This news was received with interest because, not only did she love babies, but also they would provide playmates for Vari. Leaving the great room, Angelique quietly walked down the hall and stepped out onto the porch. She found Marc pacing back and forth and overheard him talking on his cell.

"I haven't told her yet. She just arrived. You need to be patient. Yeah, I know you've been waiting a long time." Noticing Angelique, he said, "Got to go," and quickly hung up.

"Marc, who were you talking to?"

With a guilty look on his face, Marc tried to appear nonchalant, but he failed.

"Who were you talking to?" Angelique, now agitated, repeated.

"Now, don't get angry with me. I didn't want you to find out this way. I was going to…"

"Just stop it, Marc, and tell me."

"Yves is in town. He's looking over Tempest and Belle Rose. He wants to see you!"

Angelique stared at Marc, as her face showed astonishment and then anger. Red-faced, she stamped her foot and angrily shouted. "Well, I don't think I want to see him. He walked away from me. He's the one who said he didn't want me! He can't just decide he's changed his mind and expect I would welcome him back into my life!"

"There were circumstances, Sis."

"Circumstances,' she scoffed! "What circumstances?"

Three years ago. She believed Yves was the answer to all her dreams. That summer, graduating from Johnson & Wales University, and traveling to France to visit her great-uncle's home. Just thinking about Bellaire, her uncle's estate, extracted an aah! It was a horse breeding and equestrian training center in Normandy. Back then, she had two loves-dancing and horses. Detailed plans were made to spend the next twelve weeks learning all she could from the trainers and breeders that worked there. She also was training for a dressage competition and needed some help on a routine. At the end of the summer she was to audition for the "'Ecole Françoise," the French School of Ballet.

She had arrived at Bellaire in June. She could hardly keep her excitement of being in France for the first time in check. She landed at the Paris airport and was met by her Aunt Sasha and Uncle Bermont. Arriving late in the evening, she didn't see much of her surroundings as she was driven to Bellaire. Even though she was on vacation, she kept up her daily routine. Rising early, she made her way out to the barn to the dance studio. It was a family tradition; ballet was in their blood, so when entering the studio, she wasn't surprised to find it was already occupied with her cousins Becca and Rachael. Coming up behind her were her Uncle Bermont and her Aunt Sasha. As greetings were exchanged, all were going through the motions of warming up and stretching. Rachael stepped over to the stereo and started the music, Tchaikovsky's Swan Lake. All began working at the barre on the ritualized routine. From infancy, girl or boy, all children were taught plies in first position, grande plies followed by repetitions in second, fourth, and fifth position, relevés, pirouettes, tendus, échappés and more. This was the start to each day and was danced with finesse and grace by all.

An hour later, mopping her brow with her towel, Angelique left the barn and turned to head back to the house. Catching her breath in surprise and wonder, Angelique couldn't help but stare. Coming toward her was the most beautiful man she had ever seen. He was leading the mare, Belle Tara, in from the exercise ring, taking her back into the barn. What prompted Angelique to stare was his face. He had a large forehead with arched eyebrows, strong cheekbones, and a slight cleft in his chin. His nose was long and slightly bent, and his lips were full. The most striking feature was his eyes. They were a soft brown color with flecks of gold and were surrounded with beautiful, long, curly eyelashes. Their color reminded her of the after-dinner cognac that her Uncle Bermont had, and, like cognac, seeing this man gave her a warm feeling in her stomach. His hair was a rich chestnut brown, and his bronzed skin glistened as the sunlight reflected off his broad shoulders. A strong muscular chest, lightly covered with hair, tapered down to a slim waist. His legs were long and muscled. The muscles in his arms bulged as he controlled the excited mare. Everything combined made an exciting specimen of a man.

"Hello," he said in a deep, rich voice as he guided the horse away from the group of girls.

"B… bon… Bonjour," Angelique stuttered. The words were barely out of her mouth before he disappeared into the barn. Walking back toward the house through the gardens, Angelique was joined by her two cousins, who chuckled as they listened to her muttering to herself. "Stupid. … Bonjour … Dumb! What an impression I made. Who is he….?

Angelique put her thoughts into words and, turning to her cousins asked, "Who is he?"

"Yves is the new trainer Grand-Papa hired last fall. He is actually connected to the family, the great-grandson of Varvara's uncle," Rachael quickly informed Angelique. "He studied under the famous trainer Willi Schultheis and is wonderful with the horses. He even rode Grand-Papa's Mystique Rose!" Rebecca added. "Grand-Papa was pleased as he had broken his arm and couldn't exercise Mystique Rose himself. Yves is the one who will be working with you this summer."

"Isn't he gorgeous?" piped up Rebecca. "We are all gaga over him."

Angelique was suddenly startled out of her reverie when she saw snapping fingers in front of her face.

"Earth to Angel, Earth to Angel! Where did you drift off to?" asked Marc. "Reviewing the past," Angelique said, shrugging her shoulders.

"You dwell too much on the past! Put it behind you and move on. You can't change it! It was what it was."

"I can't forget the past! Why don't any of you understand? I had everything, and then mother's interference and Yves' compliance destroyed it all. I have had almost three years of struggle. Having Vari all by myself was not easy, and I'll not forget that!" Her eyes glared at Marc.

"Yes, I know, but she is also part of the future, and she deserves to know her dad. Angelique, talk to him; at least try to work through the problems. You aren't happy and neither is he. I miss my smiling sister, Angel."

Marc's words made Angelique stop yelling, and she sadly smiled back at him. She knew that Marc and Yves had business dealings together, but the siblings had usually avoided discussions about Yves when they were together. Now that Yves couldn't be avoided, she took a deep breath and asked.

"How has he been and why is he here?"

"He has a slight limp from the accident and sometimes has to walk with a cane. There was some damage done to his left eye, and he sometimes has to wear an eye patch over it. All in all, he has healed better than expected. In the beginning, they didn't believe he would live at all."

Angelique had learned of Yves accident just before she returned to the States. She had gone to the hospital for one last plea, but Yves had refused to see her. She had told no one about the visit. She had been told by Marc the complete story. How three years ago, Yves had been kicked by a horse and had shattered his femur. During a horse competition, he had observed a child that had wandered away from her mother and had entered a horse stall. Yves had acted quickly, jumping into the stall. He got between the child and the startled horse and been kicked in the process. He also took a glancing blow to his head. For months doctors thought he wouldn't ever walk again.

Angelique asked again: "Why is he here now, Marc?"

Marc explained that Yves was doing business with him, that they were meeting tomorrow so he could look over two horses, Tempest and Belle Rose. "Uncle Bermont thinks that breeding his stallion Royal King with Belle Rose would have great results. We have been planning on several matches between their horses and ours. We want to see what comes from putting their Morning Star with Tempest."

Angelique remembered Morning Star, a beautiful black foal with long legs and lots of spirit, from her stay in France, "Is she still full of mischief and does she still run like the wind?"

"Yes, to both questions," answered Marc. "Yves has come here every spring for the past two years. We are trying to establish a strong line of racehorses. We have talked often, and you are always brought into the conversation. He wants to talk to you. He still has feelings for you. Yves knows that he made mistakes. I wish you could listen to what he has to say."

Angelique stood glaring at Marc before she could gather her thoughts. "I have reasons to be angry with him, and there is nothing he could say that would change that!"

"Don't dwell on the past so much that you can't have a future! Think of Vari, if not yourself. She needs her daddy. I know that you still love him, and I believe he still loves you. Give yourself and him a chance. Talk to him!" Marc said as he took a deep breath.

Angelique's sea green eyes glittered with fire at Marc. She knew he was right, but she hated to be pushed. "Listen, you don't have to lecture me about this. I have heard what you have to say, Marc, and I understand your position." Angelique stopped, as if struggling with herself, and then admitted, "I still love him." She shrugged her shoulders. "I just don't know how to put the past behind me. There is so much between us, good and bad!"

"Give it a chance, Sis. Just listen to him. But for now, come on. We'll get all these things in your room and see what the others are doing!"

Walking side by side, they entered the house. After putting Angelique's things in her room, they went down to the great room. They found most of the family watching TV or playing cards. Vari was sitting on the floor playing with the dogs. Angelique enjoyed the afternoon and evening spent sharing in conversations and catching up with her family. More and more, she realized just how much she missed the familiar laughter and teasing that went on in any large family gathering. All the while, her thoughts were on Yves and how she would handle seeing him again.

Yves was staring at the phone he held in his hand. He felt as if the air had been sucked right out of him. He had heard her voice in the background while talking to Marc and it brought back all of the past as if it had happened yesterday. His thoughts went back to that first day.

He had been working in the training ring with Belle Tara and was returning her to the stables and noticed the young woman in the barn's doorway. He knew who she was from the family's excited chatter over the last week. She was petite in size; she didn't look more than fifteen. Not quite five feet, she had a small frame with curves in all the right places. Her long, curly hair was clipped back at the nape of her neck, but wisps of curls were escaping around her elfin face. Her hair was a rich deep auburn. Yves was surprised at the yearning he felt to run his fingers through those curls. She had the sea green eyes that many in her family possessed, and right now they were staring right at him. Something was said from behind her and she laughed. At the sound of that laughter, Yves felt something stirring deep inside him, a sense of need, wanting. He continued toward the barn and said, "Hello," to her as he walked past.

He couldn't get her off his mind all afternoon as he went about his chores. He was finishing checking all the equipment in the tack room and was exiting the barn when the sound of a haunting melody drifted out of the dance studio. The music was like a warm blanket, its sound bringing a calming effect to everything that heard it, whether it be man or horse. Stepping back into the barn, Yves found himself drawn like a magnet to the doorway to see who danced there. He wasn't surprised to see that it was her.

She had point shoes on and was gracefully moving about the room. Sometimes her feet barely touched the floor before she was leaping up into the air. The beauty of the dance was stirring feelings inside of Yves that he had never felt before. There was a wanting of something intangible deep inside him. He was entranced by the scene before him.

Angelique felt that she was being watched. She stopped dancing and turning toward the door, found Yves standing there. She nervously inquired, "Do you need something?"

Yves replied, "No. I was just drawn to the music. You have magnificent talent. Angelique, are you as good on your horse as you are in the dance?"

Angelique bristled and replied stiffly, "I don't know how to answer that. I'll just wait for your opinion after you see my routine!"

Yves nodded. He had already been told by her uncle that he was going to train and teach Angelique while she was at Bellaire. He had already settled her horse, Midnight-Magic, in his stall. "Why don't we meet tomorrow to run through everything and set up a schedule that suits both of us?" Yves said.

"I'm going out with my cousins and Aunt Sasha in the afternoon, but I'm available after breakfast," Angelique said hesitantly.

"'Til then," Yves replied.

Yves thoughts were brought back to the present with the ringing of his cell phone. It was Marc on the other end.

"You're coming tomorrow after lunch!" "Thanks, Marc,

"I'll see you then," Yves nervously replied. He was sure the night would pass slowly, but just the thought of seeing Angelique the next day lifted his spirits and he whistled to himself. At least now, he had a chance to win her back.

On Saturday morning, Angelique watched as the sun rose, creating brilliant pink and purple clouds with golden rays stretching out which had caused a slight headache. Dressed in her workout clothes, she went down to the great room. On entering, she discovered that a large group of the family was already there warming up. Ballet always brought her release from any tension, and by the end of the routine, she was feeling better.

After eating breakfast, Angelique with Vari, made their way to Varvara's room. Varvara was waiting for her and gracefully motioned her to sit down in a chair that was part of the little seating area in the corner of the room.

"You are well?" Varvara's voice was still strong and clear.

"Yes, I am." Again, Angelique leaned over and gave kisses to both sides of Varvara's face. She noticed, again, how paper-thin Varvara's skin looked. The veins in her delicate hands with their long fingers were showing right through the skin. Angelique's image of her was always of strength, and now her great-great-grandmother seemed to be so frail.

"I know that I pressured you to come home and stay here while I do the documentary of my life," Varvara said. "For so many years, so many members of the family have been asking me to tell the story. Now, it's time, and I wanted you and Vari to be here. That wasn't the only reason I wanted you to return. I have not interfered with the decisions that you have made with your life. I am very proud of what you have accomplished all by yourself, especially how well you have raised Vari. But … there is always a but … no?"

"Angelique, I want you to mend the rift between you and your mother. I know that she interfered in your life, but she did have your best interest at heart. She hasn't had it easy these last three years. Her guilt and your estrangement have taken their toll on her. Facing her alcoholism and drug abuse were some of the good things that came out of it. I love both of you. The time has come for you to talk to her, clear the air, forgive her, and move on. And while we are on this subject, don't let your pride cost you to lose the chance at love. Go see Yves this afternoon and heal the gap."

Angelique looked both surprised and questioning at Varvara.

"Surprised, that I knew about you going to see Yves?" Varvara continued. "Not much happens in this house that I don't know about. Vari needs a father but more than that, you deserve to have him back in your life. Very few people find the kind of love you two had found in each other. Don't lose it."

"I will try, Mémère," Angelique replied. She couldn't help being a little agitated over Varvara's advice. Mostly because she knew her great-great-grandmother was right."

"That's all I ask."

Angelique was mulling over Varvara's advice as she left the room. Deep in thought and getting angry as she reviewed in her mind some of the reasons she was estranged from her mother, she walked straight into Marc out in the hallway.

"Whoa! Who set you on fire?" asked Marc. Then worried he asked, "Are you all right?"

"I'm fine!" answered Angelique, a little sarcastically. "No, I'm not! You all think you know what's best for me. I'm not sure any of you even care what my thoughts or feelings are about Yves. It's 'you should do this or you should do that!' Interference is what caused this whole mess in the first place, and you're all still doing it!"

Marc backed off. "I'm sorry, Sis. Do you still want to go to the farm?" "Yes, I'm still going to the farm, but don't expect it to be a kiss-and-make-up scene!"

Both started down the hall as they discussed when they would leave. "I want to get Vari down for a nap after lunch and Mother, believe it or not, offered to watch her this afternoon. I haven't quite adjusted to this new mother." Angelique shrugged her shoulders. "She is so different than how she was three years ago."

"A lot has changed. Especially since she came back from rehab, but I think the new man in her life made the biggest difference. Wait till you meet him. I like him and I think you will too."

"We will have to wait and see, but for now let's plan to leave here around one," Angelique said.

Driving toward the farm later that day, Angelique's stomach was doing flip—flops. She was so nervous that it felt like a whole army was doing battle inside her. As she looked out the car window, her eyes lighted on Yves as he leaned on the railed fence beside the barn. "He hasn't changed much," she thought, as her eyes travelled down the length of his body. Maybe he was a little leaner. Her heart leapt at the sight of him, for even though she was angry, she still loved him. As she exited the car, he came forward to greet her.

"How are you?" "I'm sorry…"

Both tried to talk at once.

"You go first," said Yves.

Standing stiffly with her arms folded, Angelique asked again:

"How are you?"

"I'm recovering."

"I'm glad you're better."

"I'm glad that you agreed to meet me. Angel, I'm sorry about the decisions I made in the past."

Angelique looked back at Yves with pent—up frustration and anger.

"Do you think that a simple apology is going to erase the last three years? I don't think so! So much has happened, so many mistakes, too many misunderstandings. I'm sorry." Angry tears threatened to over flow from her eyes as she lashed out at Yves.

Yves looked shaken as he observed Angelique's tears. He realized how much hurt she still felt and said, "I agree we can't go back and fix the past, even though with all my heart I wish I could. I know I can't, so … he hesitated, unsure if he should continue. Then he asked, "Do you still love me?"

Startled, Angelique looked questioningly at Yves' face. For Angelique, it seemed as if the world stopped. No sound or movement could be heard or seen. It was as if the whole world was waiting in anticipation for her answer.

"What kind of question is that? Do you think that loving you absolves all the hurt and pain you caused me?" she finally replied. "I don't care if what you did was with good intentions! It was wrong. What about me? Didn't you think I was mature enough to make my own decisions? I was old enough to be your lover, but too young to know what decision I wanted for my life. You sent me away! You rejected me. I went through hell! I was devastated and my heart was broken. And then I found I was pregnant! You're angry because I didn't come running back to you and tell you about the baby. Why should I think that you would want our child when you already said twice that you didn't want me? I was dammed if I was going to give you another chance at throwing what we had away and breaking my heart again! It was your choice that caused all this, remember. I wasn't consulted."

Angelique stopped to catch her breath. Yves started to speak, but she stopped him with a look, and she held her hand up as she waved him away. She moved off to the fields to calm herself down. Her thoughts were all jumbled.

"Oh, how good it was to see him again."
"Can I forgive him?"
"Is it possible to get back what we had?"
"I can't believe how strongly I want to have him back in my life."
"Can I trust him?"
"Should I trust him?"
"What about Vari?"
"Oh, my God! What if he wants her?"

"Can I share her?" With these thoughts, she marched back to Yves and poked him with her finger in his chest and began to yell at him again.

"You know, it was I who sat scared in a bathroom as I watched the test strip turn blue. I was alone when I started cramping and bleeding and thought I was losing our child! I came home to America, because Marc said he would be there to help me. Without him I don't know if I would have made it. Where were you when my head was in the toilet for hours every morning? You're angry because you missed that? Tough! I gave birth to Vari alone. I was scared and I needed you and you weren't there. Marc was supposed to be with me, but she came early and he actually was with you in France. My grandma came to see me with Mémère. They helped me through the first few days. Still, I had to pull myself together, and I was the one who took care of Vari for the past two and a half years. All by myself! So if you think that I need your forgiveness and that the fact that I still love you is going to wipe away all that is in the past, you have another thing coming!" Red—faced, her green eyes sparkling in fury, arms stiffly crossed in front of her, she glared at Yves, waiting for his response.

Yves sat quietly across from her.

"I didn't realize … I didn't know … I know that words aren't enough, but I'm truly sorry for all you had to go through and for not being there. Yes, it was wrong of me to make those decisions for you. I didn't mean to trivialize anything that happened. All I can ask for is your forgiveness and give you a promise that I will never make a decision for you again. I also have paid for my mistakes. I have missed the first years of my daughter's life. I now see I can't blame you, but need to accept my responsibility for it. I guess my question is, can you ever forgive me for all that has gone on in the past, and do we have a chance at a future together? Will you give me another chance to recapture the feelings we had back then? Do you still love me?"

"Those questions aren't easy to answer, Yves! Yes, I will always love you, but that's not really what you're asking. I don't know if I can forgive you for all that is in the past. I don't know if we can regain that relationship we had back then. Oh … You have to be patient!" She paused, and looking into his eyes that were so filled with hope and said, "Yes, I will always love you."

Yves reached for Angelique and enveloped her in a loving embrace. His lips finally met hers. It started out as a gentle kiss, but soon changed to a deep and tender expression of his love for her. Angelique wasn't happy about the kiss, and coming up for air, Angelique pushed him away and stared into Yves' face. There were so many thoughts, feelings, and questions going through her mind.

"You need to take it slow. I am going to need time to figure out things. It's not going to be easy to repair our relationship and get back what we had. I'm going to have to learn how to trust you again."

"So, how do we find our way through the past so we can move forward? I would like to meet my daughter. I have missed so much! Can we meet today? I have so much time to make up."

Angelique thought for a moment. She always wanted Vari to meet Yves, but she said, "I know you have waited a long time, but I don't think today will work. It is already late and she goes to bed by seven." Yves face dropped and his eyes reflected his sadness at her decision. "I can see you are disappointed. Yves, she knows you're her daddy. I've told her everything about you. She wants to meet you. She is the only good thing that came out of that time. Having her is a great gift. How about we go for lunch tomorrow? You can come pick us up at noon. Vari loves pizza. We could go to the Mystic Pizza Shop."

"Thank you, Angel, I would like that."

They continued to talk with each other, sharing thoughts and ideas over the future they wanted. They fought and argued over issues, but did clear up a lot of the misunderstandings. They were interrupted by her brother Marc, who had kept busy taking care of the horses, and staying out of the way. "Hey, you two, I'm glad to see you two talking. It's a beautiful sight. Do you have any skin left, Yves? I could hear you from the barn, Sis! Whew, I thought I got it bad this morning, but you were on quite a roll." He smiled at Angelique. "I hope this means you're going to let him be part of the family." Marc laughed. "Mother's going to love this."

"Marc, don't be such a jerk. Be thankful we're now talking." Angelique said.

"Your Mother came and talked to me last week," Yves said to Angelique. "She asked for my forgiveness for her part in interfering with our relationship. She has accepted and taken responsibility for her actions. Your Mother, like me has paid a high price for the decision we made three years ago. Victoria has missed you and Vari."

Marc and Angelique's face both had looks of complete surprise when they heard this.

"I know that there is going to have to be a confrontation my Mother and me, but it isn't something I am going to initiate," Angelique said with a shake of her head. "It is for her to apologize to me, and then we'll see where we go from there. It has helped to be able to tell you what my feelings were, Yves. This is going to be some week ahead."

"Angel, are you coming back to the house with me?" Marc asked. "Yes, I'm coming with you."

Turning toward Yves, she said, "Come tomorrow at noon. Vari and I will be ready."

As they left the farm and headed home Marc asked. "How are you doing?

I'm glad you and Yves got a chance to talk, Sis." "Don't get too excited, Marc; its early days yet."

"Yes, I know, but I care about both of you, and I want you, especially, to be happy.

"We talked. That's a beginning. I have to be very careful, not only for my sake, but also Vari's. I know that Yves is hoping the outcome will be us getting back together, but it is really too soon to know if that's going to happen. In her heart Angelique had secretly hoped that Yves would come and they could be reunited, and now especially after that kiss, she knew that eventually they would.

"I can only hope to God that it does, Sis." Marc glanced over and smiled at Angelique.

"Me, too, Marc. Me, too." Angelique smiled back.

Entering the house when she got home, Angelique made her way back to the great room. She could hear Vari's laughter. Looking through the doorway, she found her mother on the floor playing dress-up with her daughter. On the floor beside them was an old, humpback travel trunk that held the family's collection of costumes and accessories. Cascading out of the trunk were multiple colored dresses, a bright pink boa, a top hat, some brightly colored beads, and numerous other odds and ends. The trunk was always available for playing dress-up or for use during one of the many family plays. Angelique wondered how many times she had played the same thing growing up as a child.

"Mommy, I am a princess and Gamma's a queen."

Victoria looked up at Angelique with tears in her eyes. "How did it go? I am so sorry for my interference and for the hurt it caused you. I enjoyed this time together with Vari. I hope I will get the chance to do it more."

"It went well. He's coming tomorrow to take me and Vari out for pizza. He's anxious to finally meet his daughter." Glancing down at Vari, she said quietly to her mother, "Thank you for the apology. I can't talk to you about that right now; we will talk later. As far as Vari goes, you can spend as much time as you want. I will be here for at least the next few months. Mémère has asked me to stay."

"Thank you. I will definitely make time each day to spend with her." Her mother stood up and smiled down at Vari. "Good night, my Princess. See you tomorrow." She nodded to Angelique, and then quickly left the room.

The following morning, Angelique sat down next to Vari and talked with her about Yves. "Vari, yesterday while you were napping, I went out and met with your daddy. We had a lot to talk about, including you. Vari, I know that I've told you a lot about your daddy, that he lives across the ocean and that's why we haven't seen him. He is here visiting and would you like to meet you. He would like to take us out for pizza."

Vari jumped off the bed and ran to her bureau; sitting on top was a 5x7 photo of Yves that Angelique had given her. Grabbing it, she bounced back across the room and looked questioningly at her mother.

"This is my daddy, right?"

"Yes." Angelique nodded.

"He wants to meet me!" Vari did a pirouette and then she did several leaps into the middle of the floor. For a little girl, really little more than a baby, she had mastered the moves of a much older dancer.

As Angelique watched, she marveled at the grace and dexterity of her very talented daughter.

"Vari, I guess this means that you want to meet him and have pizza?"

"Yes! Yippee, I love pizza!" Vari did her jump-up-and-down routine and danced all around the room.

For Yves, the day began with his awakening to the sound of rain pouring down on the roof above him. Though it was morning, the sky remained dark and only occasionally was it brightened from a bolt of lightning. As he pulled into the driveway, he gazed up at the old house with its warm lights pouring out of the windows, sending a soft glow upon the porch and walkway. He quickly exited his car and ran up to the porch. Victoria answered the door with a welcoming smile and motioned for Yves to come inside.

Soon he heard the sound of running feet. Looking up, he watched as his daughter spilled into the hallway and skidded to a halt. As he watched, he squatted down so he could be at her level. He could feel his heart racing and pounding inside his chest. The excitement was building as he gazed at his daughter for the first time. He was holding his breath as he tried to gain some composure but failed. His eyes filled with tears, and he realized he was shaking with fear and anxiety.

As Vari stopped, she backed up and hid behind her mother's leg. "Vari, this is your daddy."

Vari again peeked out and looked directly at Yves. This was his beautiful little girl with her curly hair and elfin face. She looked at him with big brown eyes that were exactly like the ones that stared back at him every morning in his mirror.

Yves waited, looking up at Angelique for assurance. Vari peeked around her mother's leg again and asked, "Are we getting pizza?"

Letting out a sigh of relief, he nodded as he said, "Yes, let's go get pizza!"

He watched as Vari danced around her mother in excitement. She invoked warmth inside him that was growing with each passing moment.

What started as an ember soon grew to be a roaring flame of love for this little girl that was a part of his and Angelique's love.

Angelique showed Yves how to secure Vari in the car seat. They safely buckled Vari in the back and drove off toward the restaurant. Vari chattered away, asking Yves lots of questions.

"Where do you live?" Vari asked.

"Right now in France," replied Yves. "Why?"

"I'm finishing a job."

"Do you like pizza? What kind?"

"Yes. I like pepperoni."

"Me, too! Are you really my daddy?"

"Yes." Yves chuckled.

"Mommy and I are living here now."

"I know."

They pulled up to the restaurant, and during the meal, the atmosphere continued on that note of laughter. Yves and Vari fell naturally into camaraderie with each other. Angelique hadn't noticed how much Vari was like Yves until they were together. Vari never stopped talking as they shared pizza and then a hot fudge sundae together. Angelique caught Yves several times just staring at their daughter. She was glad this day finally happened, and it felt good being together again with Yves.

"She's incredible; I can hardly believe she is ours. My heart is so filled with love it should burst from my chest." Yves smiled over at Angelique and then chuckled as Vari's face fell forward into the empty ice cream bowl.

"We have tired her out. Someone needs to go home to bed," Angelique said.

Yves lifted Vari into his arms and carried her out to his car. Placing her gently into her car seat, he buckled her in, and then settled into the driver's seat.

"I would like to see her again soon," said Yves. "I have appointments all day Monday and Tuesday with Marc and a breeder from New York. What time does Vari go to bed for the night?" he asked.

"She usually goes to bed at seven, but no later than eight." answered Angelique.

"Could I come and see her at 6:30 tomorrow? I would just like to play with her and get to know her a little more."

"That is the bath time, but if you want to come, then come. You might want to bring a change of clothes, though. She's as lively in the water as she is out of it."

Pulling up to the house for the second time that afternoon, Yves again felt like it was welcoming him.

"Yves, I …" "Angelique, I …"

Both spoke at the same time.

Yves said, "Angelique, thank you for letting me meet Vari. It's obvious that you have done a good job on your own raising her. I hope we can resolve all the issues we have between us. Seeing you and spending time with her only makes me want to regain the relationship we had before. Know that I love you. Thank you, for the chance to make things right for all of us."

"I'll admit I was nervous about this day. I always hoped that Vari could get to meet and know you. Let's take it a day at a time for now, but today went very well."

Getting out of the car, Angelique lifted the sleeping child into her arms. Yves disconnected the safety belt and pulled the car seat out of the car. He walked beside Angelique onto the porch. "You can leave the car seat right on the porch," she said, nodding as she opened the door. Turning to Yves, she smiled as she caught the look on his face. "We will see you tomorrow."

Gazing with a look of wonder at the sleeping child, he looked up at Angelique and smiled back. He leaned over and kissed Vari softly on the cheek and then Angelique quickly on the mouth. Turning, he walked down the steps to his car; he took one last look, waved, and then got into his car and drove away.

Watching the car go out of the driveway, she turned and entered the house. After putting Vari down for her nap, she made her way down to the sunroom and found Varvara, Jan, and Victoria.

"Hi, Mémère, Jan, Mother." Angelique said as she entered the room. Varvara looked up and smiled. "Things went well."

Angelique sat down in a chair with a sigh. "Yes, it's strange; In some ways it's as if we never were apart. Vari accepted him and they got along like two peas in a pod. There weren't any awkward moments."

Victoria was listening and it was her turn to sigh. "Oh, I'm relieved," she spoke softly. "I hoped that things would work themselves out."

Angelique turned to her mother. "We just got started," she snapped. Realizing she sounded harsh, she shook her head and looked at her mother and, apologizing, said, "I can't get into this with you right now. I have a pounding headache. It must be from the stress, and it's got the best of me. I think I'll go and lie down for a while."

The next day dragged by so slowly as Angelique waited for 6:30 to arrive. When he finally came, she caught her breath as she gazed at his strong physique encased in a tight—fitting black jeans and a blue T-shirt. Today his long black hair brushed the nape of his neck, and he had a black eye patch over his left eye. He reminded her of Johnny Depp in the movie "Pirates of the Caribbean." She gasped as she realized that just the sight of him stirred up a longing that created warmth throughout her body and had her face blushing. Her mood quickly changed as she realized that he carried in his hands a yellow duck with three baby ducks on its back. This made her smile. It was a cute bath toy and it showed his thoughtfulness.

"Hello, Angel."

"Hi. Vari is just slightly more excited than you are. She's asked every other minute for the last hour if it was time yet," she said as she guided him up the stairs and into Vari's bedroom. Upon entering, Vari jumped up and said, "Hi, Daddy."

Yves offered her the toy. After saying thank you, Vari ran off into the bathroom where Angelique was starting her bubble bath.

"Mommy, did you see my new ducks? It's a mommy and three babies! Can I take it into my bath with me?"

Yves stood watching from the doorway as Vari got undressed and jumped into the tub. Angelique motioned him into the room, and he joined her beside the tub. The next half-hour was filled with laughter and hilarity.

Yves was startled at how quickly the half-hour had passed. Looking up, he noticed standing in the doorway were Marc and Victoria, both of whom were holding their sides as they looked upon the scene with laughter.

For not only was Yves wet from head to toe, he had on top of his head a cloud of bubbles! He looked hilarious. Glancing in the bathroom mirror, he saw his reflection and had to laugh also.

Bundling up Vari in a large fluffy bath towel, Angelique carried her into the bedroom and quickly dressed her in pajamas. Victoria volunteered to mop up the bathroom while Marc guided Yves to his room so he could change out of his wet clothes. Upon returning, Yves overheard Vari ask. "Can Daddy read me a bedtime story, Mommy?"

Glancing at Yves, Angelique told Vari to go pick out a book. Vari returned with one of her favorites, and climbed into bed and settled amongst her pillows and stuffed animals. She reached for her mother's hand and held out her other for Yves to take. She began her prayers with a litany of "God bless Mommy, God bless Gamma and Gampa Tim, God bless Mémère, God bless my Uncle Marc, God bless Auntie Ann, God bless Gamma V. and God bless my new daddy, and good night to all my friends." She then gave the book to Yves to read.

In a quiet voice Yves read, "There was a farm filled with all kinds of animals."

Turning the page he continued with:

"Sarah and her dog Peanut were outside looking for an adventure. Suddenly, they came across a small ball of yellow fuzz. "I wonder what it is," questioned Sarah?"

"Peanut sniffed it with its nose and the ball of fuzz uncurled and let out a small quack."

"It is a baby duck," stated Sarah. "It must be lost from its mother." "Quack!" said the little duck."

At this Vari laughed, "It's like the ducks you brought me, Daddy."

Yves continued reading. Reaching the end of the story, he glanced down to see a sleeping Vari. Angelique smiled as she cautioned him to quietly leave the room. Once outside, they slowly walked together downstairs and joined the others in the great room. Yves turned slightly red as Victoria and Marc told the family that was gathered all about the bath scene they had just witnessed.

After several introductions were made, Victoria offered coffee and dessert in the dining room. As everyone made their way, Marc, Angelique, and Yves walked together. Their conversation was centered on Yves and Marc's plans for the next day. They had a meeting set up with several breeders who were interested in using the stud services of both Bellaire and Lynn Meadows Farm. Marc also was in negotiations for the sale of his own, one-year-old filly, he thought had good racing potential. Angelique noticed how animated and excited both Yves and Mark got when discussing their little herd of horses.

Angelique teasingly said to Marc, "I'm not sure you can handle letting one of your babies go. You've been like a mother hen with her chicks. I think you would have slept out in their stalls with them if their moms would have let you. You're going to have empty-nest syndrome if you sell them all."

This brought laughter from the group and a look of pride to Marc's face. He replied with laughter, "You're right-I would have. Don't worry, Sis, I should have a few new ones coming in early spring. I'll have plenty to do getting them trained and ready. Don't forget we have the shared interest in Midnight's daughter, Morning-Stars-Delight. She's running in her first race next month."

After telling her about their plans, Marc said he believed that they could be done by two o'clock.

Yves turned Angelique and asked. "Is there anything that we could do together tomorrow afternoon?"

Angelique thought for a moment. "Tomorrow is supposed to be a nice day. How about if we go to Misquamicut Beach? There is a playground there, and Vari loves the swings and slide, how about that?"

Any suggestion would've been good for Yves, but he quickly agreed to Angelique's idea. The following day found all three at the playground.

Vari's childish giggles could be heard echoing out of the playground as Yves pushed her on the swing.

"Higher! Daddy, higher!"

They played for an hour, and it was a tired Yves that walked Angelique and Vari back to the car.

"I didn't know playing with a child could be so exhausting," said Yves. Angelique laughed. "This is the easy part."

Yves shook his head. "Angelique, you have been with her for a while. I was really worried about just meeting Vari. Now I'm scared that I won't be good enough to be her dad."

She smiled at him and said, "There are two criterions for being a good dad."

"And they are?" asked Yves. "Love and time."

"I have the love part all set. No one, meeting Vari, can help falling in love with her. Time, I need to work on. I feel like I lost so much already."

As they drove back to the house, Angelique asked Yves what he was doing for Easter. Yves replied that he had made arrangements to go home and spend time seeing his family.

"I can't change my plans now. Mom hasn't been feeling well, and I need to see her. She and my dad are all excited about us talking things out. She has always been on your side. She told me I was a jerk for letting you go. They would like to meet you and see their grandchild." He paused, adding in a hopeful tone, "We can talk about that later."

Angelique cautioned Yves. "I can't say that I'm not still angry over your part in what happened back then. I can't tell you how or when I will be able to put it in the past. I can tell you that I want to and that I, too, want us back together. I can't give you back the last two and a half years, but I took videos of every important event in Vari's life, her birth, her two birthdays, when she started to crawl, her first step, to her trying to say her first word. They are all on a CD, and when I get back to the house I can give it to you. At least you can take the CD with you, and you and your family will be able to see Vari's growth up to now."

Yves was quite moved. He thanked Angelique for her thoughtfulness. When they arrived back at the house, he waited as Angelique went upstairs to get the CD. He didn't want to leave, but his flight to California was early the next morning. After picking up Vari, he twirled her around and gave her big kisses and hugs. He told her he would see her next Tuesday. Angelique came down the stairs and handed him the CD and walked outside on the porch with him. As soon as the door closed, Yves embraced Angelique and delivered a devastating kiss that left no questions about his feelings.

"I want you, but I accept that I will have to wait. Goodnight for now, my Angel. "Je t'aime." Yves stepped off the porch and returned to his car. With one final gaze at the house, he backed out of the driveway.

Angelique walked slowly up to her room after Yves left. She had a lot to think about. Stopping only to gaze into her daughter's bedroom, she found Victoria and Vari playing on the floor. "Is it all right if I go lie down for a while? Can you watch Vari?" Asked Angelique.

Victoria nodded. "I can take care of her, go lie down; I'll wake you in time for dinner."

Angelique fell upon her bed and quickly entered into a troubled sleep. She dreamt of that summer three years ago-remembering the day that she did her dressage routine for Yves, how her upcoming judging by Yves had kept her awake for a good part of the night. She woke up early, having had little sleep. The performance was on her mind during her morning dance routine and again as she pushed around her food at breakfast. She remembered how she had been listening to the chatter around the table, when suddenly the talking had stopped. She looked up with questioning eyes toward her great-great- uncle.

With his lilting French accent, he asked, "Angel, something is on your mind, no?"

Angelique smiled as she answered, "I am running through my routine for Yves this morning."

"Ah, the butterflies float in your stomach." He nodded.

There were nods of understanding and a few words of encouragement from those around the table.

Angelique pushed her chair away from the table and stood. She didn't need to pretend that she was eating anymore. With a sigh, she left the room and headed outside. The day was already warm as the sun shone brightly overhead. She was reviewing the routine again as she made her way toward the training ring. The soft nickering that greeted her brought her to look lovingly on the gray Percheron horse saddled and waiting for her. Midnight- Magic, born in the middle of the night four years before, he had been the love of her life ever since. Angelique had spent hours every day training him to perform in the ring. Scratching his head as he laid it on her shoulder, it was his way of showing affection. A stable boy was holding the horse and assisted Angelique by cupping his hand so she could step up into the saddle.

Entering the ring, she executed the first requirement of an extended walk, trot, and cantor. She turned and did the trot and cantor half pass (a movement where the horse crosses his front legs in each stride). She turned again and started the passage, the grand slow and precise suspended trot. Halfway across the ring, she guided Midnight-Magic to perform the piaffe, and then continued the passage to complete the turn. The pace picked up as she cantered her way through three tempi changes and then moved to the center ring to do her three pirouettes in a row. It was a difficult move to accomplish because you needed to keep your horse in the same place while turning a 360-degree circle. The routine continued with freestyle movements in double canter pirouettes, half pass in passage and a beautifully executed pirouette in piaffe. Like her dancing, she guided Midnight-Magic through the mandatory movements with grace and agility. She completed the routine by shutting-out the world about her. At that moment, it was just her and her horse. In tune and joined as one unit. Finishing the routine brought her back to the present. She noticed the family had gathered outside the ring and saw the look of amazement at the performance they had just seen. There were a few moments of silence and then a calliope of clapping, shouting, and whistles from the small group. She guided Midnight-Magic over to where Yves was clapping his hands slowly as he stood with everyone else.

He spoke as he opened the gate and let her pass. "I have studied many clips of your previous performances, and they don't compare to what I have witnessed today. It causes me to wonder about a few things. I have made many notes to discuss with you. We will talk later about a practice schedule." Angelique dismounted and handed off the reins to the stable boy. Softly patting Midnight-Magic's nose, she turned and was surrounded by her extended family as they all tried to talk at once. "Bravo!"

"Beautiful!"

"Your routine was amazing!" Her cousin Rachael commented.

"You remind me so much of your great-grandmother," Angelique's great- great-uncle stated as he hugged her to his side. "I knew you resembled her with your size and coloring, but today I see you have her magic way with a horse."

"Come, let's all go inside for a little refreshment," her Aunt Sasha said. "Yes, I would like that. I'll be there in a moment," replied Angelique.

She took a few deep breaths as she watched the family head toward the house and then quickly ran to the side of the barn and emptied all of her breakfast in the dirt. Yves had been watching from the doorway and approached her with a wet cloth.

"Do you always have this reaction after a performance?" he asked.

"Before, after, and once during a competition," she said through grated teeth. "The bigger the competition, the worse reactions I get. I can barely brave the small audience, let alone the big ones. We have tried lots of ways to cure my nervousness but have yet to find a way to stop them. I love to do dressage. I just hate the performance."

"Why, then, do you do it?" asked Yves.

She looked up into his face and replied, "My family expects it! How can I disappoint them when I have the ability? It's really complicated. A lot has to do with my mother and her expectations. If I fail them, the consequences aren't easy."

"Well, we will work on that as well as improve some of the elements. We start tomorrow, a half-hour after breakfast," he nodded and strolled away.

Angelique headed back to the house, chewing her lip in anticipation of the upcoming weeks. She was looking forward to learning all she could about training and breeding along with the work on her routine, but she wasn't so sure how she felt about spending so much time with Yves. The instant attraction made her nervous, and she was afraid of where it might lead. Her plans were to be in France for the summer, and either get the job in Paris or go home. She didn't believe in summer flings, and didn't want to get involved.

Angelique was woken from her dreams by her brother Marc. "Angel! Angel! Wake up. It's time for dinner."

Angelique made her way down to the family sitting at the table. She was quiet throughout dinner, thinking of the dreams that she had just had. After dinner, she settled down Vari for the night and then walked out onto the porch. This is where Marc found her.

"Are you okay, Angel?"

"I'm not sure, Marc. So much has happened in the last few days. There's so much going through my mind."

"Was seeing Yves such a bad thing?"

"No, actually seeing Yves was a good thing and seeing him with Vari, well…" Looking up at Marc, she smiled. "Okay, okay, being with Yves was wonderful, and watching him with Vari was too good to be true. I was just thinking he's going to be gone for a few days and I miss him already. How can that be true?"

"Angel, I think you've always missed him. You just were too stubborn to admit it. I've watched the both of you, both being miserable apart. I figure it's worth a try to get what you had back."

"I'm scared, Marc. I can't go through that hurt again." "I think it's worth the gamble, Sis, I really do."

"I am starting to believe that it is true. I really would love to have Yves back in my life. All this tension makes me tired. I think I'll go to bed now."

"Good night, Sis." "Good night, Marc."

Angelique walked slowly up to her room, stopping only to gaze one more time at her sleeping daughter. She adjusted the covers and continued to her bedroom. Going over the day as she undressed and got into bed, she thought she was not going to be able to sleep. But as soon as her head hit the pillows, she slept; her mind could not stop reflecting over the past.

The weeks were filled with exercise and practice. Yves was a hard task master, and every morning was spent going over and over the same parts of her routine until he was satisfied that she had it right. The first lesson began with instruction on making Midnight-Magic "through," having a horse perform to his full potential. Working with Yves, she learned how to make Midnight-Magic listen to the movement of her leg. Mastering this technique made for less request to do a movement. Her routine improved as she worked on this one element. Each day Yves would correct any minor thing he saw her do, including a constant reference to her seat. "No… No… You must sit back," was his constant command. It was a struggle for her to keep her weight in the back of the saddle. Even in her sleep she would hear his voice yelling, "Head up." There were daily strength exercises. They worked on subtle changes to her pirouettes to make Midnight-Magic come out more straight at the end. Angelique soon realized how good a trainer Yves was and began to respect his instruction. In the afternoon he would show her all his training techniques. And she absorbed all the information like a sponge.

During the first few weeks, sparks flew as both Yves and Angelique's strong personalities clashed constantly. For Angelique, Yves' brutal honesty and constant criticisms to get her routine pristine warred with the strong feeling of attraction for him. As those feelings increased, so did the tension between them. After about three weeks, Yves had Angelique re-enter the ring on Midnight-Magic to perform her routine again. He, too, had been suppressing the growing attraction between them. As he watched, he was amazed and moved by Angelique's grace and beauty. All he wanted right then was to take her off her horse and ravish her with kisses. He realized that she was near the end of her routine and he hadn't critiqued anything.

As she finished the last few movements, the knowledge that she had just completed a near-perfect routine made Angelique smile. She let out a loud whoop and then trotted over to where Yves was standing. She dismounted, marched right up to Yves and arrogantly got into his face. Being that close forced Yves to lose control, and he pulled her forward and kissed her with all his pent-up passion. What started out rough and passionate soon turned tender as Yves explored Angelique's mouth. When the kiss ended they pulled apart and each looked thoughtfully at each other.

"I can't say I'm sorry about that. I'm surprised it hasn't happened sooner," Yves said, a teasing grin spread across his face.

Angelique, touching her slightly swollen lips, replied "I don't know what to say. I agree that the tension between us has been building, but that was some first kiss." She smiled back at Yves.

They walked Midnight-Magic back to the barn and continued to talk. For the first time their conversation wasn't filled with tension, and surprisingly they found they had a lot in common.

The following summer months, Yves and Angelique spent all their free time exploring the historical sights, beaches, and the countryside. Angelique had heard about the famous boardwalk in Deauville called the Les Planches. It was the first place Yves and Angelique explored together. They walked along the wide and sandy beach, along the English Channel. Colorful umbrellas were scattered about, and at the edge of the sand were beach cabanas. They both laughed at the names that were on all the doors. Each had the name of a famous actor or producer. There was a Clint Eastwood, Yul Brenner, and Burt Lancaster, among others.

Another day, Yves brought Angelique to visit the American cemetery to put flowers on the grave of her great-uncle. On the same day, they went back to Bellaire to the family plot to place flowers on her great-great-grandfather's grave, including a dozen red roses that Angelique had promised from her great-great-grandmother, Varvara. They visited the Abbey du Mont Saint Michel, a 1,000-year-old gothic abbey built on an island. Exploring the coastline, they visited the seaport of Le Havre and Cherbourg and walked on Omaha Beach. One of Angelique's favorite places was the city of Rouen, with its cobblestone streets, medieval houses, and the beautiful stained glass window in the church of Joan of Arc. When there, she could imagine life and what it was like a hundred years ago. Normandy was a lot like the Hamptons or Newport in the U.S., she thought.

Some days they explored the countryside going down small roads looking at homes and the occasional beautiful vistas of the coast. They would find little out-of-the-way cafés or restaurants and order local delicacies. On several different evenings they went to the Bouvière de Deauville Casino. At Cote Fleurie, they bet on their choice of horses to win during the races. Yves wanted to take her to Honfleur so he could drive over the Pont de Normandy, a soaring long cables bridge connecting Honfleur to Le Harve. They also went to tour the Haras du Pin, the national museum of the royal stud. Started by King Louis XLX before the French Revolution, it had more than 2,000 acres and was used to raise horses for the military. Even in present day, the farm held over thirty stallions of ten different breeds. Spending so much time together, their relationship quickly grew from teacher-student, to friendship, and then developed into a deep love for one another.

Her dreams continued, remembering the first time they made love. Out for a ride in the country, they got caught in a sudden thunderstorm. Seeking shelter in a barn, they laughed as they shed their wet clothes and wrapped themselves in blankets. Sitting close to each other so as to draw in each other's warmth, Yves leaned in and gently kissed Angelique's lips. She moaned softly as the kiss deepened. Yves wasn't sure if the thunder he heard was the storm outside or the beating of his heart. Trailing kisses over her face and traveling down to her throat, his hands reached inside the blanket to feel the perfect mounds that fit exactly into the palms of his hands. His lips followed his hand, and Angelique arched her back as his mouth nipped and tugged on her breast.

Angelique started her own explorations, feeling the taut muscles along his back and shoulders. She trailed kisses over his face and let her hands work their way downward. It was Yves' turn to groan as she found and caressed his manhood. Gazing down at her beautiful body, Yves had to use extreme control not to just take her quickly. He wanted to slowly explore every inch of her. He wanted to pleasure her until she screamed for release. Following through on his thoughts, Angelique was panting his name and calling for him. Unable to wait any longer, he plunged into her and they quickly found a rhythm that brought them both to a climax. Yves fell down on top of Angelique and kissed her gently. He smiled down at her with love. Realizing the storm was passing, they quickly dressed in their damp clothes and started back. Yves chuckled as he looked over at Angelique. She had pieces of hay sticking out of her hair and clothing. She looked like a miniature scarecrow. He helped her brush away the worst of the hay, and then they continued home.

When Angelique wasn't on Midnight-Magic's back or busy being a tourist with Yves, she was working in the dance studio with her Aunt Sasha. If Angelique thought Yves was a hard task master, her Aunt Sasha was even tougher. Morning routine started out with stretches and exercises that pushed her already strong muscles to the limit. Then her dance routine was reviewed, each movement being tweaked to her aunt's satisfaction. They especially worked on a demanding and difficult section of pirouettés, fouettes, and a la seconde turns. There were mornings when Angelique worked on the same segment more than fifty times. The hard work did pay off, and she was confident that she was ready for her audition at the French School Of Ballet at the end of the summer.

The only time that Yves and Angelique fought was when they had discussions about their future. Yves struggled with the fact that Angelique came from money and he was from the working class. Though he was making a name for himself in the horse training world, it would be years before he made the kind of living to support Angelique in the custom she was used to. Angelique thought that money wasn't that important and that they could work together making a living, training and teaching dressage. She remembered one argument they had that got pretty heated.

"I have a degree in dressage training and all the experience of years of competition. You have all the talent," she said "We can create a great school and training center. I have money to invest in a farm or a riding school."

"Then I would be living off you. I won't do that!" Yves stated heatedly. "What if I wrote up a contract that loans you the money to buy the farm and you have to pay me back?"

"Why can't you trust me to earn enough money in the next year or so? Then I can match your investment, and we will be on even ground up."

"I don't want to wait for another year so. We can do it now."

The same argument came up on and off for the whole month of July and into August. Soon, it was time for Angelique to go to her ballet audition in Paris. She wasn't even sure why she was going. She learned so much over the past months that she was leaning toward training horses and teaching ballet instead of performing ballet. Her love for Yves overshadowed everything else, and she didn't want to leave him. He encouraged her to go.

"You need to know if they want you or not. Only then can you make a valid choice. If you don't try, you'll always wonder if you could have made it."

"I don't want to leave you! I could make a career of teaching dressage and ballet. I don't have to dance with the Ecole Françaises."

"I'm not going anywhere, and Paris isn't that far. You must go and see. I know part of this is your fear to perform, but I have seen you dance and its beauty that I see. Watching you takes me out of myself. You need to go."

"Okay, okay!" she said reluctantly. "I'll go."

At the end of August, Angelique drove down to Paris and registered into her hotel. She contacted the school and confirmed her audition the next day. The phone rang in the morning, and Angelique heard Yves' voice wishing her luck. She felt sick as she walked into the auditorium. She concentrated on her breathing, and as the music began, she lost herself to the dance. As she finished, there was an eerie silence. Then the panel of judges briefly talked with one another and told her they would be in touch with her.

Angelique said thank you and slowly walked out of the room. She was glad that was over with and knew she had danced well. With excitement, she walked back to her hotel room with a skip in her step. The phone was ringing when she entered the room. Thinking it was Yves, she grabbed the receiver and said hello.

"Hello, hello." Her mother's voice came over the line.

"Hello, Mother. It went very well," she said, knowing that was why her mother was calling. "They said they would let me know. I'm not sure if I'm going to take the offer if I do get it, though."

There was silence on the other end of the line, and then her mother's voice came back. "Why, Angelique, it is the chance of a lifetime! Is it this man you have become involved with?"

"Mother, wait …"

"Angelique, don't throw your life away on a man."

"Mother, I am not being influenced by Yves. He's the one who pushed me to go to the audition. If I get offered a position, I will decide if I am going to accept it or not. I will have a lot of thinking to do. I'll make my own decision, one that is best for me!"

"Angelique, I hope you choose to take this offer! I wish I could have had the opportunities that are being offered to you."

"I understand how you feel, and I will think carefully before I decide." She hung up the phone and waited all evening for Yves' call, which never came.

When Angelique returned to the estate from her audition, after numerous attempts to reach Yves, she found him to be preoccupied and distant. After a few days of not understanding what was happening, she confronted him in the barn.

"What is going on and why are you all of a sudden so distant? Have I missed something that I did or said that has made you angry with me? I don't understand what is going on. Talk to me!"

Yves looked sadly at Angelique and replied, "While you were away, I had time to think, and I realized that there are too many differences between us. You are wealthy and live in America. I am just a worker, and for now, I live here in France. You're so used to having money solve any of your problems; you don't seem to understand that I can't live off of that money. It will take me years to earn the kind of money that would make me even close to your equal. I can't see how I can ask or expect you to stay around and wait for that time to come. I also know that I can't live off of your money. The romance of the situation got the better of me, but I think we need to have time away from each other to see if our feelings are true."

Startled, Angelique at first couldn't speak. "What and how did you come up with that? Has my mother been talking to you? I bet she has. Yves, I know what I want out of life. This summer has shown me so much. I know I don't want to perform anymore and that teaching both ballet and dressage could bring me fulfillment. I love you! I know that for sure. Don't let anything come between us! If it's the money, I'll leave it in the bank. I won't use it. If I have to, I'll give it away. I'd rather be poor with you than rich and away from you. Please, please, don't do this! Don't give up what we have."

"This decision did not come from anyone but me. I want you to go to Paris and teach if that is what you want, but staying here is not the answer for you. I can't make that commitment at this time. I need time to build my career and make a name for myself."

Angelique stumbled out of the barn and ran into the house. Through tears, she told her uncle what had happened and ran up to her room. She started to pack what remained in her room. The next day, she confronted Yves once more to try to change his mind. When he wouldn't budge, she tearfully got in the car with her aunt, and headed back to Paris.

Arrangements had already been made for Midnight-Magic to go home to America. She wouldn't have time to train while teaching in Paris. She would miss him, but knew it was for the best.

When Angelique awoke the next morning, she was tense and upset. Her reflections had stirred up the feelings of anger toward her mother, and they again rose to the surface. It was unfortunate that right after breakfast, the first person she ran into was Victoria.

Victoria started the conversation by asking if Yves would be coming for Easter.

Angelique answered, "No, he already made plans to go visit his family, but he will be back on Tuesday."

"I have to say I'm sorry. At the time I thought I was doing what was best for you. I know now that my meddling caused you a lot of pain. I wish I could go back. I would do things differently if I had a chance."

Angelique listened to what her mother said, but just couldn't hold in the pent-up anger any longer.

"You know, Mother, I have been so angry at you for so long, and I have all these feelings twisted up inside me. Since I was a little girl, you have pushed me to be a ballerina. You should have trusted me three years ago and let me make my own decisions. Whether they were wrong or right didn't matter. It should have been my decision to make. Instead you chose to interfere. You were so sure you knew what was best. You never thought to talk to me about it. You planned out my life in your head and decided that's how it was going to be. Having me become a ballerina was always your focus. I was just a tool for you to use. I know all about why you couldn't follow your dream to become a ballerina. That car crash suddenly ended your promising career, but I always felt the pressure to be one for you. I just couldn't do it! Not for you and not for Yves. I couldn't take the pressure anymore. Did you ever once wonder why I always was getting sick? I hate to perform to an audience. I love ballet and teaching; it makes me fulfilled. I still don't understand why either of you thought I wasn't mature enough to know what was best for me. You couldn't get me to do what you wanted, so you turned to Yves and persuaded him to let me go so I could become what you wanted. You never listened to me! What I wanted or needed wasn't important-only your plans for me were. Your interference caused a lot of pain and heartache."

"I know that now, but you're right—I was incapable of hearing what you had to say back then. I assumed that I was right and bulldozed right through you. It has taken losing you and two years of therapy, but I finally can say I am a better person now. It's been two years and three months since I have had a drink, and I have made many changes to my life. I can accept and take responsibility for my actions and I am truly sorry for many things that happened when you were growing up. I only hope you can accept my sincere apology for my actions, especially my part in that disastrous situation between you and Yves." Victoria looked hopefully at her daughter.

"Going behind my back and getting Yves to believe that I needed space to find myself was the final straw. I know now that you put the thought in his head that he wasn't good enough for me. Why couldn't you have trusted me? Why didn't you leave me alone and just want me to be happy? Your constant interference in my life has caused us lots of problems before, but this was by far was the biggest blunder. It had unhappy repercussions for everyone. It just made me so angry with you. I want to get over it, but it is hard. I have all this built-up resentment toward you. I want to let it go; I really do."

Angelique thought back to some of her early childhood memories of her mother pushing her to do better, and always feeling she was not measuring- up to her mother's expectations.

Victoria interrupted her thoughts.

"Angel, there really isn't a good enough excuse for what I did. My therapist believes that when your father left me and took up with his secretary, plus the shock of the accident that killed them, all happened so suddenly I needed to be in control of the rest of my world. That meant I controlled yours, too. My abuse of drugs and the drinking didn't help the situation, either. I truly am sorry. Can you forgive me, and can we try to mend our relationship?"

Her mother's earnest pleas brought a softening to Angelique's heart.

"Ok, Mother, but just so you understand, there are going to be some ground rules. If we're going to get along, there will be no more interference of any kind."

"Yes, I agree."

"As far as Yves and I go, you will let me work it out for myself." "Yes."

"That goes for Vari, too. I have raised her on my own for two and a half years. I want no challenges to the way I am bringing her up."

"That one's easy to agree to. You are doing a phenomenal job raising her."

Angelique agreed that it was time to settle their differences. She reminded her mother again that she would not accept any interference in her life. Victoria agreed and said she had learned from her past mistakes and wouldn't repeat them. Angelique felt like a huge boulder had been lifted off her shoulders. She really did want her mother back in her life. She had missed her often, especially during the birth of Vari. She only hoped her mother would keep her word. There were happy tears running down each woman's face as they gathered each other into a warm embrace.

'There's so much I want to hear about the last years. Especially I would like to hear all about Vari. You may not realize it, but missing her first years was punishment enough for messing up your life. It wasn't just her; I missed you."

'Oh, Mom, I have missed you too! I have a video that I took of all Vari's firsts. Maybe you and I can watch it later along with Vari. She's probably seen it 100 times, but I think you'll enjoy watching it with her."

"That sounds wonderful. I think I'd enjoy that. On a totally different note, I think I need to tell you about someone."

"This is the mysterious man I keep hearing about," Angelique said laughing.

"Ah, the family grapevine has been talking."

"Yes, Marc has mentioned that you have a new man in your life." Victoria's face took on a glow at the mention of her new man. His name is Wayne, and I met him while I was at the hospital. No, he was not a patient; he's a doctor. I met him in the coffee shop. And I don't know it was like sparks flew. I love him and I hope you will come to love him, too. He's away at a conference this week and will be back for Mémère's birthday."

After the confrontation with her mother, Angelique needed to get some fresh air so she went for a walk along the beach. When she returned, she was surprised to find the entranceway engulfed in flowers. Victoria and Marc were laughing at a big stuffed white teddy bear holding a sign that said "Forgive Me?" There were at least a dozen different vases filled with flowers. A small white basket of mixed daisies had a card that said "Loyalty and Love." A pot of purple irises with a message: "Faith and your friendship mean so much to me." In a beautiful crystal vase were a dozen pink roses and again a message, "Thank you for Vari." Last, but not in any way the least, was a vase with two and a half dozen long-stemmed red roses. The card said, "One rose for each month we have been apart. "Je t'aime." Shocked, she looked up into her family's faces and then the situation struck her funny bone and she burst out laughing. "He's not going slowly or patiently, is he? Wow! Just look at all this! Smith's must be overjoyed at the business they're getting from us this week."

Laughing back at her, Marc shrugged and Victoria just smiled at her daughter. Vari, waking from her nap, saw the white bear and immediately ran over and tried to pick it up. The bear was so big that Vari toppled over it. She then decided it was more comfy to sit in its lap. Watching this caused more laughter from Victoria, Marc, and Angelique. They hadn't reached the door to the family room before the sound of laughter spilled out into the hallway and echoed off the walls. Inside, adults and children alike were busy coloring and decorating eggs.

Joining in on the fun, both Angelique and Mark sat down at the table and started decorating an egg. Vari joined a group of children at the children's table and claimed her own egg.

"I've got the champion egg right here!" someone said. "No, this looks like the champion."

"I hope mine is the winner this year."

"No. Mama's going to win it this year," Vari said from the small table where she worked.

Angelique smiled as she glanced over at her daughter. "That a girl," she thought.

Once again as she looked around the room, Angelique's heart swelled with love for the family she saw before her. She missed them more than she wanted to admit. Stubborn pride cost a lot.

Easter was always a special holiday for her family. Not only was Varvara's birthday around the same time, but there were also established traditions that had been passed down from generation to generation.

The coloring of eggs was one important ritual. There were more than four dozen hard-boiled eggs in the center of the table. All of them were waiting to be decorated in preparation for the egg fights on Easter morning.

At the end of the table, Great Aunt Elizabeth was coloring eggs with the dye made from boiled onion skins. These eggs were a dark reddish brown in color.

"Where is Auntie Karen?" asked Angelique to the people gathered around the table.

"She's in the kitchen making Choereg," said her cousin Sally.

Choereg! Angelique's mouth watered as she thought about the Armenian sweetbreads. It took hours to make them: first, making the batter and letting it rise. When the dough was ready, it was rolled out into thin strips. The strips were braided into three-inch rolls, brushed with a beaten egg, and sprinkled with sesame seeds. Then the rolls were set aside to let them rise. After about two hours, the rolls were placed on cookie sheets and placed in the oven to bake. After twelve or so minutes, you finally got a golden brown roll that was eaten at Easter breakfast. Angelique tried to make the rolls herself, but no one could make them as well as Auntie Karen could.

Angelique was awakened the next morning by a small body jumping on her stomach.

"Mommy, Mommy! It's Easter!"

Getting out of bed, Angelique quickly pushed her arms into the sleeves of her robe and was pulled downstairs by an excited Vari.

Easter morning was alive with the chatter of voices exclaiming over what was found in the individual Easter baskets laid out, on, and around the family room's fireplace. The adult baskets all had the standard chocolate bunny, Cadbury egg, jellybeans, foiled eggs, and yellow marshmallow Peeps, plus a personal trinket thoughtfully chosen just for the recipient. Marc found a money clip with his initials engraved on the front, and Angelique gasped as she lifted out a crystal ballerina hanging from a delicate chain. Then Angelique looked over to her daughter and started to laugh as she saw Vari doing pirouettes and hugging a big white stuffed bunny in her arms that was almost as big as she was.

Angelique turned toward the door as her cousin Noah came in carrying the largest pot of purple hyacinths she had ever seen. The card read: "These mean forgiveness. I will hope that you can."

She smiled to herself as she smelled the blooms. Marc just chuckled and, picking Vari up, went with the rest of the family as they gradually worked their way over to the dining table and picked their eggs out of the baskets in the center of the table. Children and adults alike held their eggs in their hands, ready to begin the egg fights. The rules to egg fighting were simple. You held the egg in your hand and let the other person hit the end of your egg with the end of his egg. If your end broke, you had to flip to the other end; if that broke, you were eliminated. As the fights began, sounds of groans, yays, and laughter filled the room as eggs were broken. The numbers quickly dwindled down until only five people were left. Victoria, Uncle Bermont, Marc, Angelique, and Rebecca were still holding unbroken eggs. Victoria and Uncle Bermont squared off. Victoria said, "Ouch!" as her egg dented in at the top. Switching it to the other end, she laughed as she dented both sides of Uncle Bermont's egg. Marc and Angelique fought next, and Marc was quickly eliminated. Victoria and Rebecca went at it next, and Rebecca came out the victor, but only had one side left intact. Angelique smiled at Rebecca, then, laughed when she noticed Vari jumping up and down with excitement in the corner of the room.

"I said she'd win!" shouted Vari at the top of her lungs.

"Becca, you can go first," said Angelique as she held out her egg.

Rebecca tapped her egg against Angelique's egg, and everyone looked to see as Angelique's egg revealed a dented top. Vari's face started to crumple as she saw her mother's egg was broken. Angelique shook her head in a silent message to not get upset. Rebecca held out her egg for Angelique and her light tap resulted in Rebecca's egg breaking. Rebecca let out a sigh as her egg was the last to go. Over this was the excited shriek coming from Vari.

"You won, Mommy! I told you, you would be the winner! This was fun!" Vari chatted away.

The whole family sat down to eat their Easter breakfast. Some peeled their eggs as others dug into the warm Choeregs. Everyone was talking and making plans for the day, when the doors opened and Varvara was wheeled in. Gracefully dressed in a light purple suit, she had pinned to the lapel the Faberge cross she owned since she was a child.

Vari, hopping and skipping, worked her way over to Varvara's chair. The old lady smiled as she watched the antics of the small child.

"Hi! Grand Mémère, are you going to church this morning?" asked Vari. "Yes, can I ride with you?"

"Sure. Mom, Grand Mémère is coming to church with us!" yelled Vari as she ran down the hall.

It seemed like someone had ordered an evacuation as the family streamed out of the house and climbed into their cars to head off to church. Angelique drove to Westerly and parked her car on Elm Street. She wheeled Varvara into the side entrance of the church. Christ Church, built of Westerly gray granite with red granite trim, was a beautiful Gothic-style building that had been built in 1891. The family all entered and filled up several rows, exchanging greetings with friends also home for the holiday. Across the aisle, her mother's friend Jean Mac Laughlin waved a welcome back. She was the secretary in the church office. The church sanctuary had pale pink plaster walls with brown trim with several stained glass windows along each side of the pews. There was a large round stained glass window above the pipe organ. Candles were lit all along the front of the church, and the scent of the vast array of white Easter lilies permeated the air. The service itself contained all of Angelique's favorite hymns and passages from the Bible. The music from the organ was stirring and the choir was truly magnificent. The sunlight was shining through the stained glass windows, entertaining Vari with prisms of light that flickered like butterflies along the floor and walls. Leaving the sanctuary after the service, there was an exchange of greetings with friends. Some people lingered to listen to the bells chime from the belfry of the church. Then the family all set out to return home.

Later that day, Varvara was sitting in the sunroom watching Angelique and Vari playing outside with her other grandchildren. She was glad that her plan, to get Vari and Angelique home, had worked. As she watched, someone must have called the children inside because in what seemed like seconds, the yard was emptied. Almost as fast, the sound of noisy chatter could be heard coming from the entrance hall. It was time for the annual jellybean hunt. Uncle Bermont and Victoria were handing out empty baskets and assigning teams. Small children were paired with teenagers in attempt to make the competition fair. Uncle Bermont's voice boomed out over all the other voices and yelled, "Ready, set, go!"

The hallway seemed to be gridlocked like a four p.m. exit off the freeway, and just as suddenly, as if given a green light, the children dispersed to go off into different rooms to search for jellybeans.

Children's laughter and squeals of delight could be heard as they found the jellybeans that were hidden on chairs, windowsills, and furniture throughout the house. Varvara remembered times in the past when she had found a stray jellybean months later in a forgotten hiding place. She watched as teams came and went from the sunroom. Each room on the ground floor had adults in them to supervise the search and to head off any conflict before it started. Soon it was obvious that most of the jellybeans had been found. All the teams made their way to the great room to count up their gathered jellybeans. The totals were close, but it was Uncle Bermont's grandchildren, the team of Megan and Amie, that came out on top. Varvara looked around the room and smiled to herself. With a nod of her head, she acknowledged her family and motioned for her nurse to take her out of the room.

"Blessed be," she said to one and all as she departed.

For the remainder of the afternoon and evening, family members were scattered throughout the house playing games, watching TV, or working on a 5,000-piece puzzle that had been started at Christmastime and hadn't yet been finished. Marc and Angelique were sitting among a few of the cousins discussing plans for the following Saturday, Varvara's 105th birthday party. It was going to be an all-day celebration. The great-grandchildren were going to serve Varvara breakfast in bed and then the family was going to dance their practice routine. Extended family and friends were to arrive at four and a grand dinner was planned. Everyone was getting dressed up.

"I will make sure the champagne is on ice," said Marc.

"I have ordered flowers from Smith's for all the tables and a corsage for Mémère," said Jennifer. She was one of the twin granddaughters of Aunt Elizabeth.

"I've arranged to have a table set up under the windows to put all her cards and gifts on," said Brian, another grandchild of Aunt Elizabeth.

"Well, it looks like we covered everything." This came from Jennifer's sister, Michelle.

"We'll talk during the week and meet early Saturday morning to help the little ones serve breakfast." commented Juliane, Aunt Karen's granddaughter. Angelique knew the upcoming week was going to be filled with a lot of preparations and that Saturday held some surprises for the family. Because of her discussions with Varvara when they met yesterday, she felt a little nervous about the upcoming event. Even she didn't know all the details.

Varvara's birthday party was surely going to be exciting, she thought.

Yves stood at the door holding a balloon in one hand and a box of chocolates in the other. An excited Vari jumped up and down to get her father's attention. To her, the number of days that her daddy had been gone seemed much longer. Picking her up, he swung her around and gave her a huge hug. He leaned over to Angelique and kissed her quickly. "Where are we off to today? What have you planned?" Vari and Angelique told him they were going to the Mashantucket Pequot Museum.

The museum was about a half-hour away, and Angelique gave Yves directions as they drove. Vari was a little chatterbox, informing Yves about the museum. Upon arrival, Yves walked toward the modern building. The front of the building was all windows and Angelique informed him it held 85,000 square feet of indoor exhibits.

"Wait 'til you see, Daddy. There are Indians and a huge elephant! Come, Daddy." Vari pulled on Yves' hand as they entered the tall glass building. The first thing Yves noticed was the pictures on the wall. He wanted to stop and look, but an excited Vari was pulling him along.

Angelique spoke to Vari. "I need to purchase tickets. Go show Daddy some of the pictures while I go get them."

Yves held Vari's hand as they explored the wall of Native Americans until Angelique returned. Yves then noticed the sound of water and the drop in temperature. Vari's voice told him they were entering the Ice Age Exhibit. "See Daddy, there is the elephant and the beaver!"

Yves and Angelique looked at the mastodon and beaver and then walked on to an exhibit on hunting caribou. It was lifelike and very impressive. Next was an exhibit on tools. Vari started to pull Yves' hand, wanting to get to the next part. Yves tried talking to Angelique, but an excited Vari kept him occupied. Angelique just laughed at his expression when his daughter pulled him away again. "Daddy, the village is next. You gotta see it!"

The Pequot Village was truly amazing, Yves thought. Lifelike, the village showed the natives doing daily chores such as cooking and weaving. The three of them walked through wigwams and listened to the sounds coming from the speakers that made it seem more real.

They walked through the rest of the exhibits and went to the farm on the outside. By the time they were finished, Yves was carrying a very sleepy Vari in his arms. After putting her in her car seat, she fell instantly asleep. Yves and Angelique took advantage of the quiet to discuss the future.

"I'm glad you and Vari get along so well. Not that I am surprised, you're very much alike."

"It's eerie sometimes, when she does something, and I see myself," laughed Yves.

"I know it happened so many times in the last three years. Made it difficult to try and forget you." Smiling as she said this, "Not that I could anyway."

"I'm hoping that we all will get along from now on. I want us to be a family," said Yves.

Angelique nodded, "I want that, too. I think that we have resolved most of our issues. I'm looking forward to the future. It's time to put the past behind us."

Arriving back at Seagull's Perch, Yves carried the still sleeping Vari up to her room and placed her in her bed.

Turning to Angelique he pulled her into his arms and gently kissed her lips. He pulled away for a moment to look down at Angelique's face and returned to kiss her lips and explore her mouth with his tongue. Kissing him back, she slid her arms up to caress his hair. Yves hands soon found their way to the soft mounds of Angelique's breast and teasingly nipped at them through her shirt. Angelique was doing some exploring of her own and soon felt the heat of Yves' manhood develop inside her hand. Their hearts beating heavily they soon needed to stop; Yves stepped back and dragging in a much needed breath said, "I think we need to find a better place to continue this."

Angelique glanced around to realize they were still in Vari's room. "Oh, boy I lost all thought there, yes we need to stop."

"I didn't say I wanted to stop," said Yves with a little frustration in his tone of voice.

"I didn't either, but this not the right time, and defiantly not the right place."

Recognizing the mood had changed. Yves went over and kissed Vari good night. Quietly he exited the room.

"I think I should go now," said Yves.

Angelique looked up and observed the struggle Yves was having getting his emotions under control. She saw the love in his eyes as he smiled down at her, and shrugged his shoulders.

"Ok, we'll see you tomorrow," stated Angelique.

They walked downstairs, and Yves startled Angelique with a quick kiss as he slipped out the door.

Getting into his car he exited the driveway, and drove a little too fast down the road. Recognizing that his mind wasn't on his driving, he pulled into the Watch Hill harbor's parking lot. Resting his head on the steering wheel, he began to think back to what happened three years ago.

He had just finished work and had the phone in his hand to call Angelique when it rang. He answered, expecting to hear Angelique's voice, and was startled to hear a stranger asking for him.

"Yves, this is Victoria, Angelique's mother. I'm calling you because I'm quite concerned about my daughter Angelique. I just got off the phone with her and she told me that she doesn't think she's going to take the ballet position even if it's offered to her. Now, I know you two have a budding summer romance, but I believe that after all the years of work Angelique has put into her ballet, she will regret it if she does not take this opportunity now."

Yves spoke up and said, "I agree with you."

Victoria interrupted, "Now, I'm not saying that there's anything wrong with your relationship. I just want you to give Angelique some time, to accept this opportunity, if it's offered to her.

He tried to speak again. "Yes, I agree with you. I encouraged Angelique to pursue her ballet career and that she should go to her audition. It was I who convinced her to go."

Victoria continued as if he hadn't spoken. "I know that you do not understand how much work has been invested in Angelique's education, but you must know that there is a vast difference in your financial situations. I know my daughter thinks that she can live without money, but that's because she never had to. I don't believe you can provide my daughter with the life she's accustomed to. Why, her little red sports car cost more than what you make in a year. Never mind the cost and upkeep of Midnight Magic." She threw every contrast she could at him and succeeded in making him feel inadequate and insecure. Her words were like bellows on a dying fire, fanning Yves' own thoughts about the vast difference between him and Angelique. By the time Victoria was finished, she had convinced Yves to break off the relationship and give Angelique a chance to dance in Paris.

After hanging up the phone, Yves played over in his head the many arguments he and Angelique had had over their differences. He knew she wanted to stay with him, and not take the opportunities that the Paris ballet school offered. He wasn't ready for a complete commitment he admitted. Shocked at this realization, Yves decided to go along with Angelique's mom and break off the relationship. He thought it would take him a year to save enough money to support a wife. He'd gain knowledge about training and Angelique would have the experience of working and dancing in Paris.

He had handled the whole situation wrong. Being honest and explaining how he was feeling to Angelique, jointly deciding to give their relationship a year's time away from each other would have left the door opened to communication. He would have known about Vari's existence much sooner. He'd grown up over the past few years and no one could influence his determination to marry Angelique and become a family with Vari. Heading home he vowed he would make it happen.

On Wednesday, they went to the Mystic Aquarium. Vari loved seeing the Beluga whales and the African penguins. They all enjoyed the sea lion show. Vari got to hold a bird in her hand and was quite awed by the experience. While Vari took a nap in her stroller, Yves and Angelique walked through the Titanic exhibit.

First a 25-foot replica of the ship's bow was on display. As they walked around it, Angelique remembered watching the movie Titanic and how amazing the bow looked in the scene with Rose standing at its railing. Now, the real Titanic's bow was encrusted with rust. The replica gave a haunting memory of the beautiful ship and the people who died there. Yves was very interested in the large reproduction of the Marconi radio room. They talked with each other about how the men who worked in that room must've felt during the crisis, knowing that the ship was sinking. They moved on, stopping to watch the film footage showing both the past and current expeditions. They walked past pictures that showed what had happened to the Titanic wreck since it was discovered. There was also a

14-foot replica of the ship spoilers and a display showing how deep the ship's wreckage is in comparison to the Empire State Building. All in all, Yves and Angelique found the exhibit quite interesting, and as they were exiting, Vari began to wake up from her nap. They decided to stop at Sandy's for lunch. Vari used her persuasive charms on Yves, and they all ended up back at Misquamicut's playground. After that, it was a tired group that returned to Seagulls Perch.

Thursday brought bright sunshine and unusually warm weather with temperatures in the low seventies. Angelique packed a picnic lunch and some sand toys and set off to go to Napatree Point with Yves and Vari. They soon were joined by Marc and their mother. Going over the dunes, the ocean breeze made it seem quite a lot colder. But they all had dressed warm and were ready for the wind that came off the ocean. Marc and Vari started building a sandcastle. Opening a chair, Victoria sat down and took out a book she was reading. Yves and Angelique spread out a blanket and then decided to walk along the beach.

"It's good to see your mother and you getting along again," Yves said. "You can tell she adores Vari. I hope she can accept the plans we are making. When can we tell them we are getting back together?" Yves looked hopeful as he glanced over at Angelique.

"We can tell Mom and Marc when we get back to the blanket, but I don't want to say anything to anyone else 'til after Mémère's party. It's her special day and I don't want to distract from it," Angelique responded.

Approaching the blanket, they noticed that Vari had fallen asleep. Sitting down, they told Marc and Victoria the news. Marc shook Yves' hand and gave Angelique a hug. Victoria smiled and said, "I'm so glad. I have been praying that this would happen."

"Are you going to get married?" asked Marc.

"We are not going to make any decisions 'til after Mémère's party," answered Angelique.

Yves answered at the same time, "As soon as I can convince her."

Laughing, Angelique asked Victoria, "Mom, do you think we could pull off a wedding in six weeks?"

Victoria's eyes filled with tears; this was the first time in years Angelique had called her mom. Between the two of us, she thought, "we can do anything once we set our minds to it."

After eating lunch and playing catch with Vari, the tired and sandy bunch made their way back to their car and then home.

Friday came and with it the usual last-minute adjustments that come with planning any large party. Everyone was kept busy checking to make sure nothing would go wrong. At the end of the day, Yves came to dinner. He spent time playing with Vari and helped give her a bath. He read her a story before settling her down for the night. Wanting to have some time alone with Angelique, he asked her to go for a drive. They started out toward Route 1 and ended up parking at the Misquamicut State Beach. Walking along the shore, just talking over how much they both had accomplished during the last two weeks. Angelique and Yves knew that they hadn't resolved everything. Both accepted that there were still issues to be resolved, but there was no question about their getting back together. Just as the sun was setting, Yves stopped Angelique and got down on one knee.

"Angelique, from the first time I saw you standing outside your uncle's barn, I have felt a strong connection with you. As I got to know you and discovered all your amazing qualities, that connection grew into a deep and abiding love. I know I've made many mistakes along the way, but nothing has diminished my respect and love for you. I can't imagine spending the rest of my life without you at my side. I pledge to you my undying love and hope that you will say yes…" Yves looked up to into Angelique's eyes, waiting upon her answer.

Angelique's eyes teared up as she gazed down at Yves' hopeful face. "Yes!"

At her words, Yves jumped up and gathered Angelique in his arms and began to swing her around in circles. After they stopped spinning, he let Angelique regain her footing. Holding her close, he ravished her mouth with his, leaving no question about his feelings. He pulled out a jewelry box from his pocket and opened it to reveal a sapphire and diamond ring. Placing it on Angelique's finger, he bent to kiss her hand and then his joy burst out in a jubilant "whoop!" that echoed down the beach. They continue to walk hand in hand, with Angelique occasionally lifting her hand to gaze at the sparkling ring. After finishing their walk they returned to the car.

Sitting sideways in the car, so she could brush off the sand from her feet Angelique couldn't stop the yawn from escaping and Yves teased her about it. They drove back to the house. Parking the car, Yves reached for Angelique and settled his lips over hers to give her a good night kiss. He was suddenly delving into her mouth with barely suppressed passion. The exchange of kisses just weren't enough, and he roughly pushed her top up to expose the fancy lace bra underneath. Trailing kisses over the lace brought a moan from Angelique and a gasp as Yves grazed her nipple with his teeth. Making out in a car wasn't something he had planned, and Yves let out a groan as he pulled away and returned the top back into place. With a grimace, he stated, "If we don't stop now, I can't control what might happen, and I want our reunion to be something special." Smiling down at Angelique, he said, "I will have to think about that." Helping her exit the car, he walked her to the door and after another kiss said good night. He whistled excitedly as he entered his car and left.

Angelique let herself into the house and quietly went up to her room. Glancing down at the ring on her finger she let out a suppressed squeal of delight. Victoria who had been sitting beside Vari's bed came to the doorway with a questioning look on her face. Angelique held up her hand to show off the ring. Mother and daughter hugged, sharing the excitement. Both thought to themselves, how glad they were that they had made up, and could share the moment. Angelique reminded Victoria that she wanted to keep it a secret until after the birthday party. Victoria agreed and gave Angelique another hug and a kiss on her cheek. "Good night." She whispered as she left the room. Angelique responded, "Good night." And she quickly crawled into bed.

Saturday morning came with a brilliant sunrise that colored the sky in gold, pink, and purple. It was one of those days with crystal—clear blue skies, a crisp spring breeze that made you question whether you needed to have a jacket. All the children had risen early in anticipation of serving breakfast to Mémère. Their chatter was filled with laughter and excitement. The doorbell kept ringing as deliveries of flowers, chocolates, and a large basket of fruit arrived for Varvara. Most of the family was busy decorating the rooms downstairs with streamers and balloons. Varvara was kept occupied and resting in her room. She planned a long nap in the afternoon so she could attend the evening's festivities. Marc was in charge of running errands, picking up chairs at the church, making a run to the liquor store, and doing a few odds and ends. Angelique, Michelle, and Jennifer kept watch over the little ones and found games to keep the teenagers occupied. Soon everything was done and the old house was itself looking like a wrapped present with all the decorations placed about. The family dispersed to their rooms to dress for the evening.

Angelique had chosen a simple black velvet dress that draped over her frame from thin straps at her shoulders. She placed tiny diamond studs in her ears and a cross on a thin silver chain around her throat. She added her silver bracelet that Marc had given her on her 16th birthday. Her gaze traveled to her jewelry box where her sapphire and diamond engagement ring sat twinkling back at her. She knew that she would have to wait one more day before she could slip it back on her finger where it belonged.

She then turned to Vari, who had been jumping up and down on the bed as if it were a trampoline. Angelique slipped the maroon velvet party dress over Vari's head and slipped on the black patent leather shoes. She gently smoothed the curls into place around Vari's little face. Glancing one more time in the mirror to do a final check on their appearance, Angelique held Vari's hand and left the room.

"Is my daddy coming Mommy?" asked Vari.

"Yes, yes, he is." Angelique replied with a nervous smile. She thought back to Saturday's meeting with Yves and all the events over the last week.

Even though there was still a lot to sort out, Angelique knew the door had been opened and it was only a matter of time before Yves, Vari, and she would be a complete family again. Angelique wanted a June wedding and it would be here before she knew it!

Vari started her usual bouncing up and down in excitement and raced ahead to suddenly stop, as there were many more people gathered in the main hall. Vari and Angelique both became aware of Yves, who was just walking in through the front door. He was dressed in a beautiful dark gray Armani suit with a teal shirt underneath. His striking good looks and well-muscled body had heads turning as Angelique made her way across the foyer. She reached Yves, drawing Vari up alongside her. Vari stepped out from behind her mother and smiled at Yves.

"Daddy, do you like my dress?" Vari did a perfect pirouette for her father. "Yes, you do look beautiful." Tears of joy and amazement filled his eyes as he looked at this small child who really was his. It was still overwhelming to him. Vari looked up at Yves and lifted up her arms, indicating she wanted to be picked up. Yves gathered her quickly, and again, tears welled up in his eyes as he looked over his daughter's head at Angelique. A feeling of completeness filled his heart and, as if a key had turned, he felt a part of him unlock and feelings he had closed off came pouring back. He experienced pure joy at having both Vari and Angelique back in his life. He was so happy that he was glowing just like a lighthouse on a foggy morning for the rest of the evening.

The party was in full swing and everyone was exchanging news with the other members of the family. Angelique was busy introducing Yves and Vari to several members of her extended family. She noticed a distinguished-looking gentleman standing near the fireplace that seemed to be watching her. A few minutes later her mother entered the room looking ravishing in a beaded red cocktail dress. She walked directly over to the mystery man and greeted him with a hug and kiss that was much more than a friendly greeting. Angelique had been wondering who he was.

Her mother turned and walked directly over toward her. "Angelique, I would like to introduce you to Dr. Wayne Devine," Victoria said with a smile.

"It's nice to meet you," replied Angelique.

"It's really nice to finally meet you. I've heard so much about you from your mother. I was so glad to hear that the two of you had finally made up."

With this comment, Angelique exchanged a questioning look with her mom.

"Oh, I guess the cat's out of the bag," Victoria said, laughing. "Wayne has been there for me almost from the beginning of our estrangement."

At that moment, Victoria was called away by her aunt Karen, leaving an awkward situation between Angelique and Wayne. She turned and started to introduce Wayne to Yves, but they were already shaking hands with familiarity. While all this was taking place, Vari had been pulling on Yves' pants leg.

"Daddy can you take me over to see Grams?" asked Vari. "I want to show her my dress."

Yves agreed. Angelique watched as the two walked away, leaving her alone with Wayne.

"I know that this is a little awkward, but your mother and I have a beautiful relationship which I indirectly have you to thank for," Wayne told her.

Angelique looked up with questioning eyes. "How could I possibly have anything to do with you and my mother when I have never met you?"

"The night Vari was born; your mother came to the hospital with your grandmother Jan and Mémère. She knew you wouldn't allow her to see you, but she still wanted to be there. She waited in the visitors' lounge until the nurse came out with the news that you had a healthy baby girl and everything was fine. She went to the chapel. I was passing by the chapel when I heard her crying. I entered to offer some assistance and found your mother asking God for help. I asked her to join me in the coffee shop; I guided her to a table and went for two coffees. As I sat down, she looked up at me. I found myself looking at the most beautiful woman I had ever seen with the saddest green eyes. I think I fell in love with your mother right then. I didn't hear the whole story then, but she later opened up to me and told me about her alcohol and substance abuse over the past 20 years, that she put her family through hell and had caused you to disown her. She took complete responsibility for her actions. We had a long talk, and I told her she had to fix herself before she could fix things with you. I guess I caught her at the right moment, because later talking with your grandmother, I learned the whole family had been trying to get her to seek help. I told her I knew of places that could help her and I gave her my business card. She called me the next day. Deciding to do something about it she signed herself in to the Drug and Alcohol Rehabilitation Center in North Kingston, Rhode Island."

Angelique looked up at Wayne. "It is strange but I feel as if I have known you for longer than a few minutes. I can understand my mother responding to your gentle kindness. I guess I don't know much about my mother's life over the last three years, but I am glad that there was someone was there for her. I regret now the three years we were apart. I can't thank you enough for helping her through her rehabilitation."

"Oh, I didn't do anything other than point her in the right direction. We talked several times the week you were in the hospital. There was just something about your mother that I knew I couldn't be her doctor. She evoked strong feeling from the moment I met her, and I knew even then that I wanted to have a relationship with her."

Angelique just smiled as Wayne said the last statement.

Wayne smiled back. "I have lots of stories that we can share, but I believe your mother wants time to fill in the spaces herself."

At that moment, Victoria, Yves, and Vari returned.

"It was nice meeting you, Wayne, and I hope we get to talk again soon," Angelique said.

"That would be my pleasure," replied Wayne.

"It's time for dinner," shouted Vari. "I'm hungry. Can we go and eat?" The adults smiled and everyone turned to go into dinner.

Dinner was eaten with enthusiasm and lots of laughter and noise. The family gathered in the entranceway to do a family portrait. There was laughter and some juggling to get the groups of the seven grandchildren and their extended families all together and gathered around Varvara in the center. The photographer had all the children fill the railings on the staircase and took a wonderful picture. Each family was then gathered and group pictures were taken. When finished, they gathered back in the family room where a large cake was wheeled into the room and everyone started to sing "Happy Birthday" to Varvara.

The room grew quiet as Varvara sat in front of the large cake.

"I don't have to make a wish when I blow out the candles. My wish came true when you all appeared today as I requested. My family gathered around me is my birthday wish." Taking a deep breath, Varvara blew out the candles. The cake was distributed and everyone watched as Varvara opened her gifts. She chuckled at the homemade cards made by all the young great-great- grandchildren. There were the usual oohs and aahs as each gift was revealed. Varvara opened up Angelique's gift and was moved by the thoughtfulness it showed. She lifted the delicate locket out of its box and opened the heart to reveal Vari's picture. Varvara turned and softly said, "Thank you."

Finished with the presents, the old woman looked at the family around her. Sitting in her wheelchair, she looked like royalty observing her court. She was dressed elegantly in a light aqua suit with her double string of pearls around her neck and her diamond and pearl earrings gracing her ears. These had been her wedding gift from her husband some ninety years ago. Her hair was styled and her face was impeccably made up. She had called them all together for her birthday; for she was certain it would be her last. She was now 105 and her health was starting to fail. It was heartwarming to see the five generations before her. She glanced at her son Bermont, the oldest at 86, who was her only living child. Varvara then looked lovingly over to two-and a half-year-old Vari, her namesake, the youngest in the group. Vari was so full of energy and inquisitiveness she flitted from place to place like a butterfly in a garden.

"Thank you all for coming home this Easter," Varvara said. "I'm hoping that spending time this week with each other has brought you all closer. I know for some of you it was difficult to do. My health has been failing over the past year, and I recognize that though we all would like to, we can't live forever.

"Many of you have been urging me to tell my life story and get it written down. I have decided to do just that. For the next several weeks, there will be a young woman documenting me telling the story. Her name is Stephanie White. I'm sure most of you have seen her taking pictures here tonight. I wanted Angelique to bring Vari home because I wanted to be seen telling the story to all my great-great-grandchildren. Along with the videotaping, I arranged for the family portrait that was taken tonight. Over the next few days, she will be taking pictures of each family and individual pictures of everyone. There will also be a stenographer taking down my words."

The murmur of voices grew, as the family heard and digested the news. Some looked surprised and others just showed acknowledgement with a nod of their head. Victoria looked over at her daughter and smiled, letting her know how thankful she was that there was an end to the bitterness between them. Angelique sat holding Vari and was grateful that she was home. Some came over and told her how happy they were that she was back. Her thoughts were interrupted by her Uncle Bermont, who came over and said, "I am glad that the story is finally going to be told. This is good for the family, no?" He smiled at Vari and drifted off to speak to his mother.

The group dispersed, going off in different directions. Before leaving, Varvara spoke to the group as a whole. "Any or all of you are invited to watch or participate in the filming. We will be starting on Monday. I have set aside time from eleven a.m. to one p.m. Monday through Friday for the next three weeks."

There were voices of acceptance from the family.

"Okay. Mémère I will have Vari and me here on time," Angelique said. "Why don't you rest now? It has been a long day."

Maverick, Varvara's companion for the last fourteen years, guided the chair out of the room and wheeled the grand lady away toward her room. "Blessed be," Varvara said to one and all as she departed.

Angelique watched with love and, then glancing at Yves and then down at her daughter, she wondered what the future days would bring.

The day after Varvara's birthday party, Victoria, Angelique, Jan, and Varvara sat in the sun porch enjoying the morning sunshine and a much- needed cup of coffee. The room was a restful sanctuary in complete contrast to the previous evening's boisterous celebration. Varvara looked from Victoria to Angelique and asked, "So, when's the wedding?"

Both women gave startled looks back.

Victoria laughed and replied with a question, "How did you know?"

At the same time, Angelique, glowing with excitement said, "It's in six weeks, the second Saturday in June. How did you know?"

Varvara smiled back and said, "Angelique, my dear, you have been walking on air for over a week, but the clincher was seeing you and Yves last night dancing. Bought back memories of Jean and I when we were young. I also had a small discussion with Yves last night. He told me to ask you this morning. As far as your mother, I've watched her and Wayne fall in love with each other."

Angelique turned towards her mother and asked, "Mom, Are you and Wayne getting married?"

Victoria smiled down at Angelique and replied, "We eloped in February on Valentine's Day. I haven't had a chance to tell you yet."

"Oh." Angelique, surprised, was caught off guard at the news, but quickly responded, "Actually, I'm glad because I really liked him. I watched you together last night, and I have never seen you glow with happiness the way you did when he was around." Turning toward Varvara, Angelique continued, "Mémère`, thank you so much for insisting I come home. Being stubborn, even though I had my reasons, cost too much; we all have a lot to catch up on."

The conversation continued with Angelique telling Varvara about her dreams and ideas for the wedding. As the women were discussing ideas, the room began to fill up with other members of the family. Uncle Bermont, guiding Aunt Sasha to her chair, smiled at the circle of woman.

"Wedding? Angelique and Yves! Oh, my!" Tears filled Aunt Sasha's eyes as they came to rest on Angelique. "Magnifique, finally! Mon infant, my prayers have been answered, non."

Uncle Bermont lifted Angelique into a loving hug. Whispering words of love and congratulations.

Coming in behind Uncle Bermont was Angelique's grandfather Tim. "What's this I hear about somebody getting married? I don't think you're old enough to get married, Angelique. Yes. You're still my little girl." He then chuckled. Gathering her into his arms, he kissed her and gave her his blessing.

Smiling up into his eyes, she asked, "Would you walk me down the aisle? You're the closest thing I have to a dad."

Twirling her around in a circle, he replied, "Yes, my Angel, with honor."

The news spread as each member entered the room, and then Yves walked in carrying a smiling Vari. The room filled with sounds of cheering and clapping.

Vari, wanting in on the excitement, announced, "Mommy, Daddy says we're getting married." Laughing, Angelique said, "Yes, we are."

For the rest of the day, discussions and planning took place as ideas and suggestions were offered. Plans for a trip to Providence to look at dresses in the next coming weeks were made. By the end of the day, Yves and Angelique lifted a sleeping Vari and began to leave the room. Angelique turned and reminded everyone that tomorrow the taping of Varvara's documentary would start.

When Angelique entered the sunroom with Vari the next day, she found it was being set up with a camera and tripod. She carefully made her way over to the beautiful redhead working at the camera.

"Hi, Stephanie, it's been a long time since we've seen each other." Angelique said.

"Angel, how are you?" asked Stephanie as she hugged Angelique. "It's good to be home. This is my daughter, Vari."

"Hello." said Stephanie.

"Mémère will be down shortly. Are you going to be doing all of the taping?"

"Yes." Stephanie answered, "I am. I am just finishing attaching the mike to the camera and then I'll be ready. I thought we would film all of the children listening to Varvara talk first. I will use these for photo cutaway shots that I can edit in the finished video later. That should take only a few minutes, and then we will proceed to videotape Varvara. She'll state her name and age and begin telling her story at her birth. I'm really excited to be doing this. I've met with your grandmother, and we have mapped out a series of events we are going to cover, an outline, if you will. I understand we will have to be flexible on times due to Varvara's age, and health but I hope to be finished in about three weeks. I have been told that some of the relatives have to leave to go home by then. Besides videotaping, I'll be taking portrait pictures of everyone individually as well as family groups. My stenographer should be here shortly and then we can begin."

"Wow! I'm impressed. When I last saw you, you were just assisting your dad." Angelique remarked.

"Dad's still part of the business, but I do most of the work now. Especially, videotaping, I'm looking forward to doing this video."

Angelique greeted a few of her cousins as they came into the room, and then Varvara, accompanied by a young woman, entered the room behind them. Angelique's heart warmed as she smiled at the elegant lady in front of her.

"Mémère, you look wonderful! You look like royalty sitting in that chair." Varvara chuckled. "I just might be, child, I might just be." Looking over to Stephanie, she stated she was ready to begin.

"Okay. As I just told your great-granddaughter, I want to take a few photos of the grandchildren listening to you," Stephanie said to Varvara. "It will only take two or three minutes and then we'll begin. I want you to sit and talk to your grandchildren naturally, just as if you were telling them a story." Stephanie snapped photos of each child and a few of Varvara, and in just a short time, the necessary shots were done and they were ready to begin. Stephanie acknowledged the young woman who sat herself in the far corner of the room and took out a small tape recorder and laptop. She was introduced as Louise Cantrell.

Varvara had Vari sitting in front of her on a small chair. The rest of the grandchildren were seated in chairs and on the rug before her. Her voice, with only a slight quiver, began:

"My name is Varvara Haroutunian Le Blanc, and I am 105 years old. I have around me many of my great- and great-great grandchildren.

I guess the best way to start my story is at the beginning. I don't know much about my ancestors. My grandfather was a horse breeder from Armenia. He traveled to Russia in the late 1800s and sold his horses to Czar Alexander III. My mother wanted to be a ballerina and got accepted to the Russian School of Ballet. She attended the school from the time she was ten until she was eighteen or nineteen. She traveled with the Royal Ballet to Petrograd to perform for the royal family. She met my father while visiting there and soon began a love affair. I was born in St. Petersburg in April a year later. I had a very happy childhood. One of the first memories I have is of a group of people dancing and laughing in my mother's living room. Dancing was our life. I was probably doing pliés even before I could walk. Mama's house was always filled with music. My mother's friends were some of the most famous Russian performers of that time. Some of the people I called Auntie or Uncle were performers from the Mariinsky Theater. You could often find Anna Pavlova, Tamara Karsavine, Mathilda Kschessinska, Olga Preobrajenska, and Agrippine Vaganova sitting at our kitchen table. These famous people taught me ballet from infancy until I turned ten and began formal instruction at the Imperial School of Ballet. From our living room, music could be heard from singers Valentina Kusa, Mariya Stavina, Dimitri Buchtoyyarov, and Maria Kuznelsova-Benoit. My favorite visitor was the tenor Valdimir Kastorsky. To this day I can remember his beautiful voice singing me lullabies.

"My father's name is still a mystery to me. My mother would never tell me who he was, though others implied he was part of the royal Romanov family. I only have a few memories of him. I remember seeing a large dark-haired man in our kitchen. He had a deep laugh that bounced off the walls and echoed down the hallways. We once went to Peterhof Palace and I played in the gardens. There is a garden there with lots of stepping stones. I was hopping from stone to stone when I discovered that if you stepped on the right stone, a shower of water squirted up and over a bench. I found out later that this was a joke that Peter the Great had made. It entertained me for quite some time as my parents talked with each other. The last time I saw my father I was twelve or thirteen. It was late at night and I was awoken by a loud argument going on in my mother's kitchen. I listened to my parents fighting over the political atmosphere in Russia and what my father believed would happen. He wanted her to go to Paris with him and be safe. She refused to go. He slammed out of our apartment, and I ran to my window and watched as he quickly marched down the street. I never saw him after that.

"We stayed in Russia, and my father's fears eventually came true. I had started attending the Imperial Ballet School at the age of ten. Then when the revolution of 1917 started, our lives got pretty difficult. Over the next several years, we struggled to survive. The wars had taken their toll on the city.

There was little food, a lack of coal for heating and lots of sickness. My mama caught a chill and was coughing a lot. After one extremely bad bout, her handkerchief was splattered with blood. I had to leave school to take care of her. Over the next year, her health gradually worsened, and she became very weak. I knew that she was very ill. I didn't know it, but she had a plan to get me out of Russia. When she told me of her plans, she wouldn't listen to any of my pleas or pay attention to my tears. With determination, she set into action plans for me to move to France to go live with my uncle. Through her connections with people in the ballet, she arranged for me to travel with a small group of dancers going to Paris to perform with the Russian Russes.

"It was a somber group that gathered in my mother's kitchen on the day I was to leave. Outside there was a bitter wind blowing that rattled the windows and sent an eerie moaning down the hallway. The sound echoed the feelings I held in my heart. I was tearfully saying goodbye to my mama. I knew that it would be the last time I saw her. I stared at her face, trying to memorize every feature so I could carry it with me.

"Earlier that day, my mama had sat me down and had given me her treasure box. A good-sized wooden trunk, it held all my mother's important papers and her valuables. She took out her birth certificate and then mine. Then she removed a small black Bible. There was an envelope with family photos. My mother talked in a quiet voice, telling the importance of each item. I remember that she had to stop several times because of her dreadful coughing. She continued taking out items from the box. There was a matched set of pale translucent amber hair combs, a gift from my father to her. Their design resembled a stylized plume of feathers and they were mirror images of each other. Then she gently lifted out the Faberge egg; it wasn't very big, but it was a depiction of Noah's Ark with the egg being part of the boat and animals circling around the ark. All the animal eyes were different jewels. The giraffe had emeralds, the elephant had sapphire, the lion had yellow topaz, the zebra had diamonds, and the hippo had rubies. The egg opened and inside was a diamond- encrusted cross. The cross was approximately three and one half by two and one half inches and was in the 'Edwardian' style. It sparkled with square cut diamonds angled in bangle settings at the end of each arm.

The interior of the cross flaunted a leaf design swathed with pave set, round, clear diamonds at the center. The same kind of diamonds lined the borders of the pendant, infusing extra sparkle into the cross. Varvara showed the children the diamonds a she talked. I was told that this was given to my mother by my father in honor of my birth in 1905.

My mother really loved the story of Noah and told it to me often. She would also include that it was special because the real Noah's Ark was in Armenia on Mount Arrat.

"A porcelain figurine wrapped in a velvet piece of cloth was unwrapped to reveal a ballerina; it was marked with a raised pink triangle that included the company name, the Duxer Porzellanmanufaktur. The company is better known as Royal Dux. The figurine had a bodice made of lapis, which was encrusted with a row of diamonds across the top, and the skirt was edged in gold, as were the point shoes and crown atop her head. In the crown were tiny diamonds. This also was a gift given by my father to her. She next revealed a brush, comb, and mirror set that were all sterling silver. There were also a few small pins in the shape of butterflies. Also in the box was an 'Edwardian' style sapphire and diamond dinner ring. The ring was made of platinum and featured a sapphire in the center with tiny diamonds clustered around it. There were thirty-two round-cut diamonds and thirty-six buff- top sapphires that fanned out to form a delicate flower.

Angelique remembered playing with the items in the trunk and admiring the beautiful ring.

Near the bottom of the trunk there were some linen doilies and a tablecloth. Finally, she withdrew a small wrapped object. Unfolding layers of tissue paper, she lifted out a delicately made lace christening gown. 'Your godmother, Mathilda Kschesinska, had this made especially for you. She lives in Paris now. Try to see her while you are there.' She also gave me a purse of money to take with me. We carefully repacked the trunk and put it on top of my traveling trunk.

"My mother gave me her black seal coat and hat. 'I have sewn some jewels in the lining of your coat just in case,' my mother said. 'There is also a bank account in your name in Paris. Your uncle is expecting you, and he will take care of you. Go with the ballet troupe and be safe. Be strong and proud of who you are.'

"Suddenly there was a loud knocking at our door, and the time had come for me to leave. Clinging to my mother, I didn't want to go. As tears coursed down my face, I was pulled away from her. I was forced to leave the only home I had ever known. As I was pulled down the steps and entered the street, I looked up one last time; I saw my mother standing in the window waving goodbye.

"The wind was blowing bits of ice and snow into our faces as we headed toward the train station. I watched as my trunks were loaded on board and then gave the attendant my ticket. As I entered the train car, I was greeted by other members of the ballet troupe. I sat down in my seat and sobbed my heart out. No one could comfort me, though a few tried. Too soon I heard the train whistle blow, and I quickly looked out the window and watched as the city and the only home I knew disappeared from sight. The young girls of the ballet encouraged me to join in their conversations and games. It helped to pass the time. The train traveled slowly through the countryside, and after twelve long hours, we arrived in Moscow at the Byelorussian Baltic station. We had only an hour before the next leg of the journey would start. I quickly bought a drink and some pastry, and on the way back toward the train, an old woman stopped me. I thought at first she was begging for money, but strangely she grabbed my hand and told me my fortune.

"Young lady, you will have a long eventful life. It will split in two. One will be in the old world and one in the new. Most things will come in threes. Yes, in threes. Heed my words; they are your destiny. You will cross oceans and you will see the world change.' She let go of my hand and I turned to look at the train, when I turned back, she was gone. I thought about her words as I boarded the train to Berlin. What did my life would come in three's mean? How can I live in two worlds? The lady was really strange and her words didn't make any sense."

"We traveled by day and night for twenty-three long and boring hours. I couldn't sleep well with the constant clack of the train wheels on the track and the calliope of snores and constant chatter from the other passengers that surrounded me. Each mile that we traveled took me farther away from home and my mother. I often fell asleep, exhausted from crying. During the daylight hours, I watched the country outside my train's window. I found the variety of scenery from snow-capped mountains, deep green valleys, and dark, dense forest quite breathtaking. It was a tired, disheveled group that departed the train when we arrived in Berlin in the early morning hours. I am sure the others felt as I did and were not looking forward to getting on a train again to head southwest toward Paris. Finally, we headed out on our final leg of our journey, and after eight hours, the train pulled in to Paris in the early evening. My somber mood echoed the wet, stormy weather that greeted us as we dragged ourselves out of the train car onto the platform. We were quickly ushered into a taxi bus, and I watched as my trunks were loaded on a truck. I was so tired I could barely keep my eyes open as we drove away from the train station. I eagerly looked out my window and saw the crowded streets of Paris. I watched as we passed shop windows with colorful advertisements and vendors that lined both sides of the street. People of all shapes and sizes were going off in different directions. Cars and trucks and farmers' carts seemed to move effortlessly amongst the crowd. As I traveled through the city, the echoes of horns honking and shouts of items for sale came to my ears. I was so tired that my eyes began to close, but before they did, I caught a glimpse of the Eiffel Tower. We were taken to our rooms near the Theater Mogador. After my trunks were brought in, I had a fast bath and changed into a clean nightgown. Dropping into bed, I slept for fifteen hours. I awoke to sunshine on my face and birds singing outside my window. Just like the fresh spring air brought out the beginning of a new day, my awakening started my new life in France. It was 1922 and I was seventeen. I spent the next several weeks exploring the sights with the other girls. We ate at outdoor cafés and walked around the Arc de Triomphe, and we visited the Eiffel Tower. I also looked up several of Mama's friends and visited with them. I attended the premiere of the ballet 'Renaud' by Igor Stravinsky. I had sent a message to my Uncle Harry and was waiting for him to come get me.

"Then one morning, he finally came. My uncle was a big man, over six feet tall and well-muscled, and he had dark black hair and bushy eyebrows. He had a large prominent nose, full lips, and soft warm brown eyes. But it was his hands that drew your attention. They were so large, yet they weren't rough when he touched my cheek in greeting. Though you couldn't say he was handsome, the total package was very striking. When he came for me, I was extremely nervous, but when he smiled, he looked so much like my mama, tears quickly filled my eyes. Enveloped in his strong arms, I received the first of many crushing hugs from him. He made me do a pirouette.

"'You have grown into a beautiful young lady. And you have the look of your mother, I think, no? How do you like Paris? Have you seen any of the sights? Missing your mama and home, I bet.' Uncle Harry spoke non-stop. 'Varvara, you have choices to make. Do you want to stay in Paris, or would you like to come home with me to Normandy? I have a modest home on the Bellaire estate, and I work as a trainer and breeder for Monsieur Le Blanc. He has assured me that you are welcome for as long as you like. I am afraid to hope that you will decide to come with me. You are the last of my family, except for your mother. I miss her and know that she is unwell. I tried to get her to come years ago, but now it is too late. Seeing you, has brought back so many memories of her.' Uncle Harry finished speaking with a sigh.

"'Mama wanted me to be with you, and that's what I want too,' I replied. '"Good. Good, we will leave in a few days' time,' said my uncle.

"Over the next few days we went shopping, making sure I had the proper attire for living on a farm. I went to the bank and withdrew the money that was there. A good set of walking boots and long pants were the main purchases. I was excited about the pants because Mama would never let me wear them.

"And soon I found myself traveling with my uncle, leaving Paris and heading north to Normandy. The beautiful rolling hills with their lush green carpet spread out before my eyes. There were farms with horses, sheep, and cows grazing in paddocks. This scenery brought me a sense of peace. As we drove, he told me about Bellaire and the people I would meet. Monsieur Le Blanc, the owner, was a widower with two children. My uncle thought they were a little older than I. He started to continue talking but he stopped. He looked over at me and chuckled because I was yawning. Uncle Harry said, 'You are tired,' and even though I tried to deny it, I soon was asleep. The next thing I knew, I was being awakened because we had arrived at Bellaire." Varvara stopped talking and looked around at the listening children, some of whom had fallen asleep. She smiled at the group and gave her usual

"Blessed be" and was wheeled away by her nurse.

"That's all for today," said Stephanie. She smiled at the group before her. She loved her job and this story had really captured her interest. She turned to Varvara as she was leaving and asked, "Could you please bring the box tomorrow? I would like to video you showing all the contents to your grandchildren."

Varvara nodded her head and then asked her nurse to take her upstairs.

Stephanie was taking the camera off its tripod and talking with her stenographer when Marc entered the room and announced it was lunchtime. Angelique turned and asked Stephanie and Louise to stay. They both shook their heads and said they had another appointment.

"Okay. Stephanie you know my brother, but Louise, let me introduce you to my brother. Louise, Marc."

"Hi." Marc said to both girls.

"Nice to see you again, Red," He smiled as he said this.

"You haven't changed, still teasing," Stephanie, laughed. She told Louise that Marc was in her class in high school and they were on the track team together.

"I'm instructed to tell you, you are welcome to lunch any time after a filming," said Marc. "Do you need help to bring down the equipment?"

"I'm okay. It all fits in one bag, but thanks for the offer," said Stephanie. Angelique picked up Vari and with Marc, walked the two girls to the door.

Angelique thanked them, and said that they would see them tomorrow. Angelique told Marc about what was done during the filming as they turned to walk down the hallway and go to lunch.

Angelique and Vari entered the sunroom the next morning and found several other cousins standing around and looking like they didn't know where to put themselves. On the floor near the coffee table was the chest that usually was beside Varvara's bed. Vari instantly ran over to the trunk and tried to open it. Angelique cautioned her to wait for Mémère and Stephanie. As if her words had called them, both appeared in the doorway. Stephanie quickly checked her equipment and, glancing over to Vari, winked and smiled.

"I'll be ready in a minute. Would you all find somewhere to sit either in the chairs or on the carpet in front of Varvara?" Stephanie asked.

Angelique leaned down and gave Varvara a kiss. Varvara pulled up close to Vari and began taking things out of the chest. She showed the group of grandchildren the birth certificates and the family Bible, pointing out to them their grandparents' and parent's name along with their own recorded in the family tree that was in the front cover. She gently lifted out the christening gown and told how it was made by her mother's friend and that every child had been baptized in it.

"Even me?" asked Vari. "Yes, you too."

Varvara continued. She placed on the table all the items that she had talked about in yesterday's filming. The children gathered around the items and asked Varvara about them. Kayla, Emily, Elizabeth's great-granddaughter along with Vari were fascinated with the Faberge egg that depicted Noah's Ark. Vari pointed to the different animals and said their names. Juliane, Karen's granddaughter was holding the porcelain ballerina. Brian, Matthew, and Noah, Maryann's three boys, were pretending to comb and brush their hair, but soon were entertaining each other by making funny faces into the mirror. Varvara lifted hair combs out and showed Michelle and Jennifer, Elizabeth's two daughters, how to arrange them in their hair. Angelique, Rebecca, Rachael and Bermont's great-grand daughter Amie, were looking at the other items especially the sapphire and diamond ring. Amie's sister, Megan was holding up the Christening gown and examining the delicate lace. Stephanie continued filming. She was careful to capture the range of feelings that traveled across Varvara's face as she spread out the artifacts of her life. Soon the chest was empty. Everyone in the room looked at all the items spread out before them. Varvara had been talking for more than an hour and suddenly seemed to run out of steam. Stephanie and Angelique exchanged a look. The two nodded in understanding and the taping stopped for the day.

Each day started out the same way, with Varvara telling her story to various members of the family. "Where was I?" became the question that she asked every day. Varvara would then begin the next segment of her life story.

"When we arrived in Normandy, the beauty of the landscape with its roaming hills and vast green valley gave me a sense of coming home. As we approached Bellaire, my uncle expressed his hope that I could be happy with him.

"The entrance to the estate had stone pillars, which supported black cast-iron horses. The horses held an arched sign saying 'Bellaire.' Driving up the driveway, there were large paddocks on each side, their plush green grass spread out like a blanket and framed in white fencing. A few horses could be seen grazing in the distance. At the end of the main driveway sat an enormous house in the classic Normandy style. It had white siding with brown straps running parallel up the sides, large mullion windows, and a double door entranceway. Beautiful flower gardens adorned each side of the doorway. The best feature of the home was its chocolate brown thatched roof. The driveway veered to the left, and as we went past the house, the rest of the property spread out before us. Over to the right were two large buildings; the first was the main training center. There were stalls, a large indoor arena, a dressing center, a training ring, a grooming area, and a large tack room. Off of this building were seven large paddocks, many of which had several horses grazing in them. Set a little farther back was the second large building, which was another stable with fifteen stalls, and it had an area for equipment, storage, and hay. A short distance from the barns, nestled under a grove of trees, sat four small cottages. They also had the Normandy thatched roofs, and I thought they looked like mushroom houses for fairies. The largest of these was soon to become my home. Behind all of the buildings, the land stretched out for as far as I could see with more green pastures and then woods. I was to learn later that the farm had 75 acres. As we parked the car and started toward the house, a large gray horse and rider came trotting right up to us. As he approached us, he reined in his horse and dismounted.

"A very handsome man with blond curly hair bowed toward me and said, 'Bonjour. Welcome to Bellaire!'

"'Varvara, this is Jean Le Blanc, the son of the family.' '"Bonjour."

"'The man's eyes were a beautiful sea green, and they twinkled with laughter as he gave me a little half bow and walked past me toward the barn. He was your great-great-great grandfather. But I haven't got to that part of the story yet," Varvara said chuckling.

"My eyes gazed after him, but Uncle Harry called for me to come and I turned and entered the cottage. The cottage had a large homey kitchen; along one wall was a row of cabinets and countertop, which had a sink that was under a window. Another wall held an ice box and cook stove. Along another wall was a table covered in a brightly patterned tablecloth surrounded by four chairs, and curled up under the table was a white and black fluffy cat. Noticing the cat caused me to jump back. I was nervous because I had never been around pets before. In the corner a fire was burning in a potbelly stove. A brightly patterned rug adorned the floor on which sat a large rocking chair and a sleeping big dog. The dog opened his eyes only for a moment to check who was entering. If the cat made me nervous, the dog outright scared me, and I gave him a wide girth as I was led through a door way into the living room. This room also had a sense of warmth to it. Along one wall was a fireplace with shelves overflowing with books and knick-knacks on each side. An overstuffed couch and chairs in a blue and white plaid along with a few end tables were arranged around the fireplace. On the opposite side of the room, windows let in warm sunlight. Off of the living room were two bedrooms and a bath. Coming out of one was a tall, lean woman with a smile on her face. She was big bosomed and had beautiful white-silver wavy hair. Her kind voice said, 'Inch bes ses!' (Hello and welcome).

"My uncle then introduced me to my Aunt Genevieve. And again I was enveloped in a warm and loving hug. She would soon become a second mother to me. I was given the large bedroom on the left. As I entered, I was amazed at its lovely interior. The walls were finished with white stucco, and the floor was made of large wooden planks. Along one wall was a large bed with a brass frame headboard. The bed itself was covered with a beautiful handmade quilt in multiple squares in different patterns of violets. A pale green rug was on the floor. Next to the bed was a small table under a window that had white curtains drawn back with ties made of the same material as the quilt. A bureau was along another wall, and this had a large vase filled with flowers on top of it. My eyes filled with tears as I felt the room's welcome. I turned as a large young man of about thirteen or fourteen brought my trunks in and placed them in the room.

"Aunt Gen, as I soon learned to call her, introduced me to her son Markart.

And so began my stay in Normandy.

"It took a while to settle in, but the little cottage became a safe haven for me. It wrapped me like a blanket with its loving warmth. My uncle constructed an exercise bar and placed it in the dressing area of the first barn. I did my morning routine there every day. I learned that my uncle had married Genevieve and adopted her son when he found they had survived the Armenian genocide of 1915. He had been looking for his wife and three children, only to find Genevieve and Markart were the only two survivors from his village. His wife and children, along with the rest of his family, were gone. Genevieve had been married to his wife's brother, so he brought her to France and married her. During the telling of her story, my new aunt looked down at me with a smile on her face and soft, sad brown eyes. She made sure I knew she welcomed me. I always felt loved and cherished by her and she always treated me as her own.

"Two weeks after my arrival at Bellaire, a telegram came with the news that Mama had passed away in her sleep. It was a devastating blow, even though I knew it was happening. I still wasn't prepared when my uncle came and told me, 'everyone is gone but you, Markart, Auntie Gen and I,' he told me. 'We are the only ones left.' I felt so lost and alone. My uncle and aunt lavished me with affection and understanding as I tried to handle my grief.

I struggled with my grief for several weeks and the only time I felt at peace was doing the ballet routine that Mama had taught me.

We had a memorial service for Mama that was attended by most of the staff and family on the estate. Even Monsieur Le Blanc and his children,

Madeline and Jean, came and gave their condolences. Uncle Harry told me that they had lost their mother years before in a riding accident.

Markart was a typical teenager who teased and taunted me. He knew of my insecurities around animals, especially the house cat and dog. It seemed that he and the cat were in partnership as to who could startle me the most. Markart got a great amount of pleasure when the cat would suddenly appear underneath the table and swat at my legs. I would jump a mile high in fright and his laughter could be heard throughout the house as he rolled on the floor in enjoyment. Auntie Gen would scold him, but sooner or later he would find something else to annoy or scare me. Often I would find a frog or spider left in a box on my bed and Markart peeking in to see what my reaction would be. Even though he was full of mischief, I grew to love him and he me.

"Auntie Gen wanted me to know how to cook and began teaching me her favorite recipes, many of which were traditional Armenian dishes. We spent many happy moments in her sunny kitchen choosing different recipes to cook. Over the next several months I learned to cook Lahmajoon (meat pie), shish kebab, rice pilaf, a spinach and egg dish called Havgitov Spanagh, and stuffed vegetables. These were all tasty, but her desserts were absolutely mouthwatering. She showed me how to make Choerag (a sweet bread roll), Baklava and kadayif, both sticky sweet desserts, and also what would become my favorites, devil dogs and rice pudding. While we were cooking, she would tell me stories about her early life in Armenia and the people I never knew, including my grandparents. Her cooking drew almost everyone to our door at one time or another. Later when I began having dance classes, she would bring a plate of goodies over to share with my students, and often there was something tempting waiting to be shared when I returned from dance class and we sat down for our afternoon tea.

"Sometimes on Sundays we would travel to an Armenian church for services. It was a common practice after church for families to picnic together in a park. My uncle encouraged both Markart and I to practice our Armenian with others so we wouldn't lose it. We would often listen to the elders tell tales of the old country. Most of the time a group of young men would bring out some musical instruments like the dumbeg (a kind of drum) or oud (it looked like a mandolin) and a clarinet. They would start to play, and then people of all ages would join their little fingers together and start to dance in a line, weaving to form a circle. It was truly an amazing thing to watch, and when I made a few friends, I joined them in the dancing. The picnics were always fun.

"One morning while I was running through my morning exercise, I was interrupted by Monsieur Le Blanc, the owner of the Bellaire estate. He explained that he had observed me dancing and was interested in me teaching his daughter how to do ballet. I agreed and soon I was asked to include several girls that were friends of Madeline's. I showed the girls how ballet could improve not only their posture but could help them with balance, too. The class was always filled with laughter, and soon the girls and I became friends. I was beginning to feel at home, but I kept getting a feeling that I was being watched. I would look around but didn't see anyone there. It remained a mystery for several weeks, but I soon found out who my watcher was.

"One night I had trouble sleeping. I finally gave up trying to sleep and got up. I thought if I could do my ballet routine, I would relax enough to be able to sleep. Entering the barn, I witnessed Jean Le Blanc attempting to do an exercise routine at the barre. I tried to stifle my laughter as I watched him, but it soon bubbled out of me like a shaken bottle of soda. Jean looked over at me as his face turned a beet red with embarrassment. He angrily strutted over to me and ordered. 'You will not tell anyone what you saw this morning!'

"Why, are you too manly to admit that ballet could help you?' I challenged. "No, I just don't want to be among the girls and their silly laughter.'

"Why didn't you ask me for lessons? I could give them to you at a different time,' I offered.

"I didn't want to be embarrassed.'

"Jean, Could you teach me how to ride a horse?' "Certainly. Maybe we trade lesson for lesson, yes?' "Oh, yes, that would work!'

"And so we began to spend time together. We spent an hour or two most days exchanging knowledge. He patiently started to teach me not only about how to ride but also how to care for a horse. I was surprised at all the equipment that went into the upkeep of just one horse. He gave me a gentle mare named Delight to learn on. Jean showed me how to brush her down and clean her hooves. The brushing part I liked to do, but the cleaning of the hooves was stinky. We laughed together as I struggled with getting the bridle up on Delight's head. I constantly had one ear in front or was holding the bridle upside down. It took a while, but I finally accomplished it. Putting the blanket and saddle on and getting the girth tight was the cause of many strangled mutterings, but eventually we did get to ride. Roaming the countryside on horseback was a delight, but in the beginning it also came with a few aching muscles. Our days were filled with laughter, and I was constantly teasing him about his gracefulness. He was always tripping over something or bumping into a door jam. He never watched where he was going. Over the course of several weeks, his tenderness toward me, and the way he carefully instructed me on how to ride, helped me to come to terms with the loss of my mama. I showed him how to do exercises to help him with posture, and we developed a routine that I would later use to teach other equestrians. Jean would sometimes come in after I was done teaching and ask if I would dance just for him. There was never at any time a conscious decision to have a relationship with each other. I believe we both thought the other was out of reach. After all, he was the wealthy landowner's son and also so much older than I. I also was the poor refugee from Russia. Nothing prepared us for the storm of feeling that developed between us. It was as if we woke up one morning and we were in love. We kept the relationship between the two of us for a little while, but soon people began to notice how often we were together.

"This brought us some difficult moments, as family members on both sides were upset with us. My uncle cornered Jean and had a serious and heated discussion over our age difference. He expressed his concern over the issues he could foresee in the future if we continued our relationship. Mostly he showed his love and concern for me and made sure that Jean was going to be honorable.

"Madeline was a little less subtle in her objections. She accosted Jean and blasted him with questions. She also brought up our ages and told him he should find someone his own age. Everyone seemed to be concerned that he was nineteen years older than me. She expressed how worried for me she was and admonished her brother for spoiling the friendship she had developed with me. Though we tried to calm everyone's fears, no amount of interference or negativity affected us. We continued our courtship for several months and then decided to go ahead and get married.

Once the decision was made, our family came around and, probably with reservations, supported our relationship. We had Jean's sister Madeline and my cousin Markart as our attendants. It was just Uncle Harry, Auntie Gen, and Monsieur Le Blanc that watched from the pews. I was married to him for thirty-seven years. I loved him and have missed him every day since he has been gone.

"Our life together was filled with laughter and companionship. We expanded the dance lessons offered at the school. I soon was busy teaching several classes each day. The classes grew in size. I offered a class to students of Jeans that needed help with stature and balance, but there was one class that was just girls wanting to learn ballet. I liked and enjoyed teaching the first class, but I loved watching the girls learn and develop their talent in my ballet class. I still took lessons from Jean, and I eventually learned how to ride a horse quite well. Jean tried to teach me dressage, but I never mastered the art. For Jean, horses were his first love. Training, breeding, and dressage occupied all of his time. He may have been clumsy when walking, but when astride Mystique, Jean was the epitome of gracefulness. His stallion Mystique was a large black Percheron over 18 hands. He had lots of character and was full of mischief. Jean said Mystique was jealous of me. When Jean and I were walking together, Mystique would nudge his head between us just like a child. I always carried treats for the horses in my pockets-anything from carrots and sugar cubes to candy canes. I had found out that for some reason, horses love peppermint. Mystique would nip at me if I got too close to him, trying to get to all the treats. Jean just watched all the antics and laughed, saying we were both jealous lovers. I enjoyed going out for a ride with Jean in the afternoon, and we sometimes packed a light supper and had a picnic.

"Each day brought us closer together as we shared the workings of the farm. Jean was anxiously waiting for his prize mare Starlight to give birth. He woke me early one morning and brought me with him to watch the birth. I stood outside the stall, watching as the mare's sides quivered with each contraction. Jean knelt at her head and whispered calming words to her. Uncle Harry was watching at the other end. After what seemed like hours, a wet spindly leg appeared, and shortly I recognized the small nose appearing along with another hoof. I was shocked as Starlight rose to her feet and stood panting with her foal half in and half out of her. Jean and

Turning Point

Uncle Harry chuckled and assured me that this was normal. After a short while, she lay down again, and after a few more contractions and a little help from Uncle Harry, the filly was born. A soft welcoming neigh from its mother welcomed the newborn into our world. The little one lay in the hay as Uncle Harry cleaned away the afterbirth. Starlight rose to her feet and nuzzled the foal. Its attempts at standing had me laughing, as her legs didn't quite support her, and she tumbled over. On her second attempt, the legs splayed out in different directions, making her fall again. On her third attempt, she stood and remained standing. She was a real beauty-all black except for four white stockings and a little white star like her mother's on her forehead. Jean informed me that she was going to be named Ballerina. I was touched, and tears again filled my eyes as I thanked him for his thoughtfulness and love. Starlight softly cleaned and guided the newborn toward her teat for its first meal. I have witnessed a good amount of births since then, and each one still fills me with awe.

"One day I was entering the barn to meet Jean, and I barely got out a greeting before I felt dizzy and fainted. Jean panicked and rushed me back to the house. He insisted on calling for a doctor, and after examining me, the doctor confirmed what I already expected. I was going to have a baby. Jean and I were both excited to find out about the baby. Jean treated me as if I were a fragile egg. It was fun in the beginning to have all his attention, but I soon needed to show him I was made of sturdy stock. What fun I had decorating and planning for that first baby. Madeline and Auntie Gen showered me with handmade sweaters and layettes.

"We shared a happy life together living on the estate and teaching. We went to Paris that year to see 'The Train Blew,' the newest performance by the ballet company. We went backstage to meet my old friend, Vaslav Nijinsky. We were invited to a party and we met some of Mama's friends while there. You would have thought we were amongst a group of cackling hens from the noise a few Russian women made at the news I was having a child. The elegant Mathilda Kschesinska wiped tears from her eyes and said she would be there for me because her old friend was not. While sitting and exchanging news, I noticed a man sketching across the room. When I was getting ready to leave, he handed me a colored sketch. I was amazed at the detail he had completed in just a short time. The picture looked very much like me and was signed Picasso. I learned that he designed the background for the ballet and the program posters." Varvara smiled. "I kept that picture, not many people can say they have a portrait signed by Picasso. When I was amongst the ballet community, I felt treasured and cared for by all.

"In June I gave birth to a baby girl and named her Irene. She had big green eyes and tufts of hair that stuck out at all angles. To me and Jean, she was beautiful. She was such a happy baby. I spent my days taking care of her and teaching my classes. We had set up a little cart for her to play in while I taught. Auntie Gen was always there to cuddle and shower Irene with love. If she even started to fuss, someone was picking her up and comforting her. Even as a baby, she seemed to love the music and dance of the ballet.

"The next year brought us a boy, who we named Aurele after Jean's father. He was a fat, round, happy baby. Jean was planning to buy him his first pony before he was even weaned. Then, we were surprised three years later with the birth of our third child- a boy we named Bermont. He, too, was a happy baby, and we were delighted in our good fortune to be blessed with all three.

"Having children and watching them grow to become young adults filled me with a great sense of contentment that I had never felt before. Jean and I tried to teach them all we knew about ballet and dressage. I remember one late morning I had just finished teaching a class and went in search of the children, who were supposed to be with Aunty Gen. I found her sleeping peacefully in a chair on the porch with the children nowhere to be seen. Continuing my search, I heard Jean's voice coming from the main barn. As I walked into the barn, I glanced in the tack room and there were all three children sitting on a bale of hay and being taught about the tack that hung on the wall. Their little faces were all fixed on Jean as if he was telling them a story, and they all turned toward me as I entered. With joyous shouts, they welcomed me and I joined them and listened as Jean continued to talk about the equipment. It wouldn't be the last time I would find Jean had taken the children to teach them about the horses."

Varvara paused and then looked up at Bermont, who was standing in the corner of the room, and both nodded to each other in acknowledgement of a shared memory.

Stephanie was quick to swing the camera in time to catch the exchange and then returned to Varvara as she then continued with her story.

"As the years passed, each child developed their own talents and chose the direction their lives would take, and we were very proud of all of them."

"The timer went off signaling it was time to stop, and Stephanie called a halt to the filming for that day. After Varvara left, the group discussed the day's taping and where the Picasso print was located. A small group of grandchildren walked into the study to look at the Picasso print hanging on the wall.

"Look how beautiful Mémère was," said Brian.

His brother, Matthew, said. "Wow. I can't believe I didn't recognize this before now!"

"How much is a Picasso print worth," Asked, Michelle?

"Hey, Angelique, you look an awful lot like Varvara in this sketch. It could be you if I didn't know better," said Jennifer.

"I can't wait for tomorrow. Listening to Mémère tell her story is better than going to any movie. It's like a giant history lesson. I was so intent on what she was saying I almost forgot to breathe. The time went by so quickly, and I didn't want her to stop," said Angelique. The group wondered what would be revealed by Varvara's story telling on the morrow.

The decedents' of Varvara gathered around as Varvara continued to tell her story the next day.

"The years went quickly by, bringing us life challenges. We were saddened by the loss of Jean's dad. Madeline, who lived in England, had gotten married to a businessman she had met while working in Paris. They both came to the quiet private ceremony we held, and we buried him beside his wife up on the hill. Aunt Geneviève complained of chest pains and we rushed her to the hospital, but she had a massive coronary along the way and we suffered another loss. There was nothing Uncle Harry or I could do but comfort each other. It wasn't much later that Markart informed Uncle Harry that he was going to go to the United States to live. As Uncle Harry was getting too old to take care of himself, we had him move up to the main house.

"As the years passed, the children developed their own personalities and interests. There were the usual mishaps and childhood illnesses. You can't live around horses without getting a few cuts, bruises, and sometimes a broken bone. For the most part, our days were filled with lessons. Everyone did the morning dance routine, with the boys doing the expected moaning and groaning as they got older. Aurele stopped doing the routine when he began to seriously train for dressage competition. In ballet, you stretch your leg muscles, and in dressage, you need tight muscles to give the signals silently to your horse. It is very rare that someone does both.

"Irene loved the ballet. You could always find her dancing. She very rarely walked but rather floated into a room. She quickly became an accomplished dancer. When she was thirteen, I started sending her to Paris to study with the Paris Ballet several weeks a year. I had maintained contact with my friends within the ballet community, and they took Irene under their wings. She started to train to dance on pointe and shortly began performing solos. The Paris community had turned her into a polished and sophisticated young woman. Every fall she would return to show us some new routine and grace us with a performance on pointe.

"Now, Aurele was another story. From birth he was a mischievous, adventure-seeking character. He rarely thought before he did something, and this was constantly getting him into trouble with Jean. One morning I heard yelling coming from the barn.

"'Christ de Christ de Christ'!" echoed out of the barn, letting me know Jean was very upset. It was the only time you heard him swear. When I entered, I found Jean white as a ghost and dressing down a seven-year-old Aurele. Aurele had tried to mimic his father and ride Mystique. I think the scare took ten years off Jean's life, but it didn't faze Aurele. Jean was always wondering where this wild child came from. I just shook my head at most of his antics and loved his exuberance. Aurele and his dad shared their love of horses and dressage. Once on the back of his stallion Pharaoh, it was hard to see where the horse stopped and Aurele started; it was as if they were one. Once Aurele started competition, it was rare he came home without top ribbons. He was an attractive young man full of vitality and handsome good looks that attracted people to him and made him well-liked among his peers.

"Bermont was the baby. He tried to follow his brother, but he did not have the same nature as Aurele. Where Aurele was outgoing and boisterous, Bermont had a quiet nature and was very studious. There was rarely a time you saw him without a book. He didn't have any interest in ballet like Irene, and though he rode well, he didn't enjoy dressage competition. He could do a perfect routine in practice, but would be stiff and tense during the judging. Jean and I at first were worried about him, but we soon found out that his talents lay in the breeding area of the farm. Bermont spent any free time at Haras National du Pin, the royal stud farm in Deauville, located north of Bellaire. He learned from the experts their knowledge of breeding different horses to get the desired trait. It became known that he had the natural talent, a gift, of matching the right stallion to mare to produce whatever trait you were looking for in its offspring. He would pour over the bloodlines of each horse and instinctively choose the right match. He worked with Uncle Harry, showing him charts and figures that I never could follow or understand. His desk was always covered with charts and diagrams. He often tried to show me his way of cross referencing different traits like strength or speed, but I had difficulty following it all. I might not have understood his theories, but his breeding technique was producing excellent results on the racetrack and at Bellaire. Jean was happy with the two foals born out of Mystique and Morning Star, especially Tempest. Jean and Aurele began training Tempest to do dressage. Aurele couldn't stop talking about getting a chance to ride him. He was a beauty from birth with a magnificent head and long neck. He was totally black except for a white star on his forehead. Out in the pasture, Tempest would prance around and then stop and pose like he was saying, 'Hey, look at me. I'm beautiful.' Even as a teenager, Bermont was sought out by breeders asking him for his advice and knowledge. To this day, his advice is sought out by some of the most famous breeders of the world."

Varvara stopped and looked at the people who were standing about the room. Every day members of the family would show up and quietly listen to her tell her story. She smiled at Angelique. "You are very much like your Uncle Bermont when it comes to competition. I had heard all about your stomach trouble when you tried to compete. Ah, again you are surprised by what I know," she said, noticing Angelique's surprised expression. "Nothing much gets past me."

Varvara smiled down at Vari. "You, you are like your great-great-uncle Aurele, always moving and shaking things up." She chuckled and then addressed the gathering. "I am tired, so I will leave you all. 'Til tomorrow, blessed be."

Marc and Angelique helped straighten up the room. Gathering up Vari, Angelique checked with Stephanie and Louise on whether they were staying for lunch.

As they all walked down to the great room, a lively discussion was exchanged about all the details that they hadn't heard before that day and how everyone couldn't wait to hear more of her story tomorrow. Stephanie admitted she had found it hard to stop filming because the story was so interesting. They discussed what had already been filmed and how well it was going. Vari was getting cranky so Angelique got up to take her to bed. She was going out later with Yves, but he was coming early to get a chance to play with Vari and Angelique wanted her rested.

After putting the child down for a nap, she and her mother spent the next few hours going over wedding plans. There were so many things to get done. Stephanie's dad was doing the photography. They made appointments to meet with the wedding coordinator at Ocean House and with the florist. They also discussed the wedding party and when to get dresses. Angelique was surprised at how well her mother and she got along. After commenting on this, Victoria laughed and replied, "I finally have grown up. I'm grateful that we can share this time together."

Yves arrived and there was an hour of riotous noise and running around by not only Vari and Yves, but also joining in on the play were Marc, Stephanie, and Victoria. Angelique watched from the sidelines and thought to herself how interesting it was that Marc always seemed to be around when Stephanie was in the house.

Angelique slipped upstairs to change her clothes and returned downstairs to hear Vari complaining. Though Vari whined that she wanted to go with them, Yves told her this was Mommy and Daddy's time and he'd come back to play with her again soon. Angelique asked where he was taking her, but he said it was a surprise.

Getting into the car, they traveled to Route 2. Heading north, the towers of Foxwoods Casino soon came into view. At night the neon teal lights shined everywhere you looked. Yves turned into the driveway and handed his keys to the valet to park the car. They walked hand in hand and as they entered the casino. They looked at the fish in the large fish tank and walked past the fountain. Sounds of the slot machines could be heard, along with an occasional shout as someone won at the tables. Angelique admired different items as they walked through the mall, which was made to look like a street. Before they knew it, they arrived and entered Paragon. Angelique had never been inside the restaurant and was excited to be eating there. Yves told them he had made reservations, and they were escorted to a private table in a corner. Angelique looked around at the décor of the restaurant. It was tastefully decorated with cream tablecloths, orange and brown chairs, and gold carpeting. As they sat down, Angelique noticed that a bottle of champagne was chilling in a wine bucket. Holding out a chair for Angelique the waiter offered menus for them to look at. Angelique tried not to gasp at the prices on the card. She had not touched any of her inheritance for the last three years and lived on what she earned. Yves laughed at her, saying again it was a special night.

When the waiter returned, Angelique ordered the lobster chowder and the wood grilled lobster dinner and Yves chose the satay, the heirloom tomato salad, and the Australian sirloin.

"It was so hard to say no to Vari tonight. She puts on that sad sack face and crocodile tears, and my heart just melts," Yves told Angelique.

Laughing Angelique replied, "You'll learn. Vari is a smart kid and knows how to use those tears to her advantage. I have learned not to let them sway me."

"I am so awed by the way you have raised her so far. I'm glad that I get the benefit of your experience so I won't make so many mistakes. I want to be a good father," said Yves.

"Don't worry so much. Like I told you before, just love her. The rest comes naturally. You do your best to decide what is good for Vari, and if you find you have made a wrong choice, you make changes. I know I'm simplifying, but I believe you have all that you need to be a great dad." Angelique smiled back at Yves.

"Okay. I will take you advice," replied Yves. Then changing topics, he asked, "Can you really pull off the wedding in such a short time?"

"Mother and I got a great start this afternoon. We have appointments with Ocean House and the florist next week. We talked about dress hunting and the wedding party. You know another good thing that has come out of my coming home is that the relationship between my mother and me is better. She has changed and I really like her. That sounds so strange, but it's a good thing. I know that Mémére and Gamma are relieved that we have patched things up, Angelique said.

"I know that Marc is glad. He and your grandfather were talking to me about how great it was that the tension was gone from the family. Also, how good that the wedding will be a celebration of the family being together again." Yves paused. "We really haven't discussed what we are going to do about living arrangements after the wedding. I'm still under contract with your uncle until the end of this year. That means I will still have to be in France for much of that time. Do you mind coming to France?" Yves asked.

Chuckling again, Angelique replied, "I think I could suffer through six months. Vari already has a passport. I was thinking about going to France, anyway."

Surprised, Yves asked, "Were you going to come to see me?"

"I always intended for you to meet Vari, and I was saving enough money so I could return to France."

"That's good to know. After the six months is up, Marc and I are planning to have a breeding, training center in Rhode Island and work along with your cousins at Bellaire in France."

"I've heard some of your conversations over that the last few weeks, and I assumed that was what you were planning."

As they ate their dinner, they continued to talk about where they were going to live and what they wanted for the future. It was surprising that their views were still very much the same as they were three years before.

Yves started to talk about the mistake he made when he broke off their relationship so she would go to Paris, his belief that her mother was right and she was too young to make a commitment to him, and how much it hurt to tell Angelique to leave. They talked about Yves' accident. How learning that in his attempt to save a child from harm he had injured himself so badly he might not walk again. He had been scared and all his insecurities had come back. He told Angelique that was why he refused to see her. I was depressed for months and then things changed and I started improving. It took a lot of therapy, but going through that experience made him realize the mistake he made in letting her go. How sad he was when Angelique refused to answer his calls, when he finally did recover. Yves told her the story of when Marc first met him at Bellaire and that Marc had punched him.

Yves and Angelique talked for hours, but in the end the past was laid to rest. The food was delicious and they finished the dinner off with coffee and dessert.

After leaving the restaurant, they headed down to the casino and played the tables and slots for an hour. Angelique expressed how late it was getting and thought that it was time to head home. Yves chuckled and informed her that the night had just begun. He escorted her to an elevator and then into the executive suite.

"What about Vari?"

"It is all taken care of. Your mother is going to watch her tonight, and we'll be home in the morning to have breakfast with her. Relax."

She started to ask about clothes and then saw the boxes on the bed. She loved presents and excitedly began examining the boxes. She lifted the cover off of one box and found it held an emerald cashmere sweater with gray wool slacks. She opened the next box to expose a delicate rose-colored negligee and wrap. In another box held flimsy bits of lace that were a matched set of lingerie. Angelique's eyes were shimmering with tears as she opened box after box. Yves had thought of everything. Uncovering another box, she found it held her favorite perfume. Yves sat down beside her and gave her the final box, which was obviously from the jewelers. Gently opening the lid revealed a sapphire teardrop necklace and matching earrings inside.

Overwhelmed with his generosity, Angelique turned and kissed Yves. The kiss, though simple, ignited a fire inside Yves and unleashed his need to make love to her. His kisses devoured her face, and his tongue played war on her mouth. His hand caressed her body as he held her in his arms. Soon the barrier of clothes became too much, and each helped the other strip until their bodies were displayed naked before each other. Yves began to explore her, noticing the subtle changes that childbirth had brought to Angelique's body. He trailed kisses down the middle of her chest and teased each nipple with his teeth 'til they were taut with excitement. He delved into her navel and then continued on traveling downward until his mouth was exploring the mound between her legs. Moaning in pleasure, Angelique dug her hands into Yves' hair, not sure whether she wanted him to continue or stop. Crying out, she climaxed. Yves rose above her and plunged deep inside her. They soon created a frenzied rhythm that had both plunging over the top.

Yves gazed down into Angelique's flushed face and smiled. He stood and walked into the bathroom to fill the Jacuzzi. Lifting Angelique up, he gently placed her in the warm, swirling water. He lit the candles surrounding the tub, filled two glasses with a sparkling white wine, handed one to Angelique and then slid down beside her.

Relaxing in the water, Yves began another exploration of Angelique's mouth. Not to be outdone, Angelique started her own exploration of Yves' body. She found the scar on his temple and the large one lacing down his side from his waist to thigh. She marveled at how quickly he was recovering from their lovemaking. As her hands surrounded him, his manhood grew. It was Yves' turn to groan as her hands brought him pleasure. Not being able to contain his passion, he lifted her wet body and made it only as far as the rug before he entered her again, finding satisfaction in her greediness for him. They made their way to the bed and crawled under the covers. Yves tickled and teased Angelique. He enjoyed hearing her bubbling laughter. His hands began to pleasure her where his mouth had been earlier, and they made love again for the third time. Exhausted, they fell asleep in each other's arms.

Angelique awoke disorientated. There was a moment when she forgot the past evening's events. Smiling to herself, she lifted Yves' arm and started to slip out of the bed, only to be dragged back to receive a loving kiss from a disheveled Yves.

"Je t'aime, my Angel."

"I love you, too." Angelique laughed. She climbed out of bed and went to take a shower. Angelique marveled at how everything Yves had bought for her fit so well. Entering the bedroom she thanked him again for his thoughtfulness. Yves quickly got dressed himself, and as they were walking toward the exit said, "Thank you for a lovely evening."

"I had an incredible time with you last night," Angelique told Yves.

Yves smiled down at Angelique and groaning, reminded her that the wedding was still weeks away.

"We'll just have to use our imaginations to come up with ways to repeat this," Angelique responded.

With that said, Yves just laughed out loud, causing people to look at them. What they saw were two people very much in love. Hand in hand their eyes only for each other they walked out to their car.

At home, they found an impatient daughter waiting for them. "Are you going to eat breakfast with me?" Vari asked.

Unable to hold in his joy, he laughed and lifted up Vari. Twirling her around in a circle, he carried her toward the dining room, answering her questions with light banter.

"Mommy, you're smiling," Vari said. "That's because Mommy is happy."

Angelique smiled again at Yves as they all sat down to breakfast. Afterwards, they were still both laughing and smiling as they walked into the sunroom to find Varvara waiting for them.

"Well, the lovers return." Varvara chuckled as her words brought an embarrassed cough from Yves and caused Angelique to blush. "You know, you two remind me so much of how it was between my Jean and me. It is good to see you together. Love should not be wasted. Now, where were we?"

It had been decided by the family that the younger children wouldn't understand and might be frighten by the war stories; so only the teenagers and adults were listening as Varvara began again to tell her story.

"Our peaceful lives were soon to be interrupted by the constant rumors and stories coming from other parts of the continent. Jean was worried; he believed another major war was coming. Jean soon began going into the village to talk and gather any news about what was happening. Each evening we gathered around the radio listening to the BBC. With heavy hearts we'd hear of the countries that fell under Hitler's rule. It was as if some dark cloud had gathered around us preparing us for a coming storm. There seemed to be no one who could stop Hitler. We waited with dreaded anticipation for his arrival in France. There were also the frightening rumors of concentration camps. We went on our usual visit to Paris, but found the atmosphere quite different. The French people were worried about Hitler entering France. The streets were crowded, filled with refugees that told horror stories about mass murders and of gas chambers. We didn't enjoy our visit that year and returned to Bellaire very disheartened.

"Because of all we had heard in Paris about Hitler's treatment of the Jews, Jean and I made arrangements for our Jewish friends to leave Europe. Irene's best friend Anna and her sister left along with a few members of the ballet company. Some people, including Anna's parents, refused to leave France. They were rounded up by the Germans and were sent to Auschwitz in the summer of 1940.

"In the beginning of 1940, Hitler's army was advancing on France, and in May their invasion began. They were rounding up all the men and sending them to Germany to work in their factories. There wasn't any choice given. Jean left and went to England with Charles De Gaulle; he was the General leading what was left of the French army. Madeline offered her home to Jean. She was so frightened of Hitler and his army that she couldn't wait for him to stay. She wanted the children and me to come also, but I was afraid of all the bombing in London and felt we were safer on the farm. We tearfully watched Jean depart. Every night we would listen to the BBC on the radio. Soon after Jean left we heard De Gaulle give his famous speech encouraging all French people to resist the German Army.

"For the next four years, I struggled to keep the children and the farm going. There were constant food shortages and we all got used to not having sugar and drinking chicory coffee. We grew our own vegetables but often found them stolen or confiscated. There was little or no soap to be had, and we learned to make it out of fats and caustic soda. A curfew was imposed and no one was allowed out at night.

"In late 1942, many French men refused to be conscripted into the work force of German factories and farms. These men took to hiding and the French resistance was formed. 'The Marquis,' which the resistance was generally known, received weapons such as submachine guns, US M1 carbines, ammunitions, and plastic explosives from the British RAF. These were parachute-dropped or brought in by solo landings. The Marquis started sabotaging the Germans in any way they could. Blowing up train depots and ammunitions supplies and derailing trains were reported to be happening all over France.

"In the beginning, I didn't know that my children were working with the resistance. I shouldn't have been surprised given Aurele's adventuresome nature. He had been sneaking out of the house, and I caught him returning one morning. I tried to convince him that what he was doing was too dangerous, but at seventeen, he was determined to do anything to end the German's occupation. I was even more shocked when I discovered that Irene was doing her own part to help the resistance. She was drawing detailed maps of the area's gun placements and passing them on to the Marquis to forward to England. Irene and I had our first major argument over her involvement. I couldn't give a reason other than wanting her safe, and she ended the argument with words I'll never forget: 'Mom, how can you expect us to sit back and do nothing? We were raised on stories about what happened to your family in Armenia, and Hitler is doing the same thing to the Jews.' I had no answer to give her. Though I was afraid for them, I was also extremely proud of their patriotism and courage.

"In May there was an increase of bombings by the RAF. An invasion by the Allied forces was expected, and on June 11, we heard the planes flying over us as the first indication that it had begun. The ground seemed to shake as the German guns fired out to sea. That morning would put into action events that would change my life forever. Both Irene and Aurele were out of the house, and I kept watch for them. Irene came home extremely agitated and completely disheveled. She was dirty and white as a ghost. I had to calm her down before I could understand what she was saying.

'Mom, I need bandages and food right away. I have two American soldiers and an Englishman in the barn. One has a broken ankle, but the other American is in a bad way. He has a gunshot wound in his shoulder and another went right through his calf. Has Aurele come back yet? He was retrieving another soldier who was caught in a tree by his parachute. He sent me back with the first three we rescued.' As she talked, Irene was gathering up the supplies she needed. She turned to go back to the barn, telling me that the Allied forces were battling the Germans all over Normandy and would soon be in control. 'I'm going to take care of them, until that happens, in the barn. Aurele is going to bring back others as well.'

"But later that evening, Aurele still had not returned. I walked down to the barn and found Irene tending the wounded, and to my surprise Bermont, who I had thought was in his room, talking to a group of soldiers. All had been caught behind enemy lines and were being brought to the farm by members of the Marquis. Irene informed me that the Marquis were out looking for Aurele. She asked if I could watch over the wounded so she could go look for him herself. 'I know all our hiding places and maybe he is in one of them,' she said. I didn't want her to go but agreed in the end. She returned later with the news that she had found him. She needed the truck because he was wounded and so was the soldier he had tried to rescue. I went with her this time and we carefully placed both the soldier and Aurele in the back of the truck. I climbed in and held his head as Irene gunned the truck and sped toward home.

"Aurele talked about what had happened to him as we journeyed to the farm. 'Mom, they were just shooting them in the trees. They weren't taking any prisoners. I found one dead from a broken neck, and then as I was cutting down this soldier, I began to hear guns firing. I started for home with him and we were seen by some Germans. They started shooting at us, and we both ran into the woods along the back field. We both realized that each other had been wounded. He was bleeding from a head wound and I have several." Aurele was struggling to breathe and I cautioned him to stop talking. We arrived at the house and brought the two men inside. While we were gone, Bermont had informed Uncle Harry of the events and he had just returned with the doctor.

"The doctor examined Aurele's wounds and came to me with tears in his eyes. He had been his doctor since his birth. I didn't want to hear what he was going to say. 'There is nothing I can do, and he wants to talk to you. There isn't much time.'

"I entered the room and my heart broke at the sight before me. Aurele was paler than parchment. Irene and Bermont sat at his side with tears rolling down both their faces. Aurele opened his eyes and looked at me with sadness.

"Je suis désole maman.' (I'm sorry, Mom.)

'Non, non ne vous inquiétez pas has entre en paix. Jet'aime." (No, no, hush, don't worry about it. I love you.)

The room was quiet as tears were rolling down Varvara's face along with everyone else in the room who had been listening. Varvara said that no one should outlive their children.

Stephanie, wiping tears from her eyes, announced that the filming was done for the day. She spoke to Varvara, thanking her for her story. "Let me know if you are up to doing a session again tomorrow."

Just then, Vari ran into the room. Seeing all the sad faces and not understanding what was going on, she walked over to Varvara and patted her hand.

"Mémère, don't be sad. I love you, this much." She spread her arms out wide and did a pirouette. This caused Varvara to chuckle and also lightened the mood in the room.

The next day the filming was cancelled, as Varvara was exhausted from telling her tale the day before. Her nurse expressed concern because her vitals were not stable. It was decided she spend the next few days resting. No one was surprised and all made different plans for the day. Angelique decided to visit the farm with Vari. They found Yves, Marc, and her cousin Joshua looking over the horses. They all went to lunch together. They were entering Sandy's, a restaurant in town, and who did they see exiting her car but Stephanie. Marc was quick to invite her to join them. The shared meal was filled with laughter, mostly because Vari was putting on a performance for her dad and Stephanie, but there was a camaraderie shared by all. They all couldn't stop discussing Varvara's story, the interesting people she knew and the last sad tale of losing her son. Yves looked at Vari, and though he had only known her a few weeks, he couldn't imagine the cost of losing her. He glanced over at Angelique, and her eyes mirrored his thoughts.

Marc, Yves, and Joshua were going away that weekend to scout out a stallion. They weren't sure if he was worth looking at for breeding purposes, but they all thought he might be an interesting prospect for dressage training.

Angelique had her own plans with Victoria that involved shopping for her wedding dress. Angelique and Victoria set off for Providence to Wishing Well Bridal. Angelique had looked online and had picked out twelve gowns that she thought were potentials. Victoria had secretly picked out two others that she liked. It was a beautiful spring morning with clear blue skies and bright sunshine. They even saw a group of robins by the roadside.

It felt good to be together again with her mother, but Angelique had a few misgivings about picking out a wedding gown with her. Their budding new relationship seemed to be going well, but Victoria's history of controlling interference was hard to forget. Victoria was just happy to have her daughter include her again in her life.

They entered the shop and the bridal consultant, Pam, met them, guiding them to a fitting room where the gowns were waiting. Slipping out of her clothes, Angelique selected the first gown by designer Alfred Angelo. Over the next hour, she tried on dress after dress and had shortened the selection down to four. She had tried on the two that Victoria had chosen, and surprisingly one of the two was among her favorites. They decided to go out and eat lunch and then come back. Victoria, with concern and worry, asked Angelique if she was angry about the extra dresses she had added.

"No, I really like the Maggi Sottero. I think my choice is between that and the Sophia Tolle. I want to try both of those on again, and I think I could decide which one it will be."

After eating lunch, they returned to the shop, and much to Victoria's delight, the choice was her Maggie Sottero gown. Angelique had already decided to wear flowers in her hair instead of a veil, and they decided that the next time they came back for the first fitting; they would bring Jan, Varvara, and Vari with them to pick out gowns. Tired, they set out for home.

Sunday came and was spent quietly resting and playing with Vari. Varvara was still worn out and kept to her room. Yves, Marc, and Joshua returned in time for supper, and they entertained everyone with their stories about the horse they had just seen.

"I swear this horse was nothing like what we were expecting," said Marc. "The blood lines and information suggested he would be a good prospect,"

Yves said in his defense.

"I know, but he certainly wasn't anything I'd want in my barn," Marc replied, laughing.

"He was ugly and bowlegged," Joshua said. "You should have seen Yves and Marc's expressions when they first saw this horse."

The camaraderie and conversation continued with the cousins all discussing the future plans for a joint effort in breeding and training horses on both sides of the Atlantic.

Marc smiling at Yves and Angelique said, "I'm so glad you two are together now. It's going to be fun working as a team."

"I feel extremely lucky to have Angel." Yves replied. Then changing the subject said, "We need to name the stables here, Bellaire is already established in France."

Joshua, making funny faces at the three cousins, said, "I don't know about you three, but I'm looking forward to making this the best breeding and training center on both sides of the Atlantic."

Angelique listened to all that was being discussed and then said, "I'm new to this, but what do you think about the name Majestic Breeding and Training Center."

Marc, Yves, and Joshua agreed that it was a good name. Yves reached over and hugged Angelique reassuring her that she was a welcome part of the team. That prompted Joshua to start teasing them about the upcoming wedding. Angelique responded that they had to finish the filming of Varvara's life story before the wedding and on that note she reminded them that the filming was starting again in the morning.

Monday morning found most of the older grandchildren seated and waiting for Varvara to come and start her story again. It had been decided not to have the little ones come, because of the subject matter Varvara would be talking about. After she entered, she began to talk again as if she hadn't stopped.

"With the loss of Aurele, I was inconsolable. I wandered around the house all day just going through the motions but not really engaging in the life of the farm. Even the sounds of guns going off in the distance could not bring me around. Uncle Harry tried to hold it all together, but at his age it was too difficult. He came to me and spoke about Jean's need of me to keep the farm going in his absence and that I still had two children who needed me. I tried from then on to keep my sorrow inside.

The soldiers who had been with us were soon taken to the hospitals that had been set up after the area had been secured- all accept the airman that had been saved by Aurele. He had a concussion, and his wound had become infected. The doctors didn't feel it was safe to move him. Irene volunteered to nurse him. The first couple of days, he lay in the bed with no sign of his coming to. Irene barely left his side. She told me, 'My brother lost his life saving him and I'll not let him die. I won't let Aurele's death be for nothing!' There were some signs that he was improving when he started tossing about in his sleep. Most of what he said was not understandable, but a few words like: 'Mom,' 'Richard,' 'too close,' and 'the trees' were.

"On a routine visit, the doctor examined the patient and told Irene that she was doing a good job and not to worry. I entered the room the next morning, surprised to find the soldier awake and Irene feeding him some broth with a spoon. We found out that his name was Leslie Clayton. He was from a small town in Rhode Island called Watch Hill. He told how his plane had been shot down and of his parachute coming down amongst the trees. He said he was so thankful to Aurele for rescuing him. It was then that Leslie asked after Aurele and was saddened at hearing the news of his death. He told Irene he had a brother in the Army and that he was worried about him. His brother Richard was part of the landing forces on the Normandy beaches. Irene volunteered to try to locate him. She sadly had to inform him that he was listed among the casualties of the first day's fighting. Richard had died on Omaha Beach. It gave them one more thing that they had in common. For the next several weeks, the two sat, talked, and laughed with each other. Leslie was pronounced fit enough to be moved and was taken to the 42 Field Hospital set up in Montebourg. Irene still visited with him every day. In my grief over losing Aurele, I didn't realize that D-Day was going to take more than one child away from my home.

"About this time there were two surprises, both happy events amongst the horrors of war that still surrounded us. The first was the arrival of Jean. He was exhausted but unharmed. I was returning to the house from the barn when I looked up and there stood my Jean. He opened his arms and I ran into them, bursting into tears. There is nothing like the safety of being in your lover's arms. I treasured each moment I spent with Jean over the next few days. While Jean was home, we spent our days talking and catching up on what each had been doing while we were apart from each other and our nights wrapped in each other's arms. We had a long discussion about our children, and Jean expressed the pride he had for all they had done. On a beautiful sunny day, we walked together to the family plot and cried over Aurele's grave. Jean spent time with Irene and Bermont, expressing his love and pride in them. Too soon, the time came when he informed me he had to return to his troops. He was proud that the Free French army was assisting in the fight to get Hitler out of France. He said he wanted the war over.

"Two days later, another surprise was on our doorstep. This one was in the shape of a tall, black curly-haired U.S. Army ranger. The change in appearance since I last saw him had me barely recognizing my cousin Markart. Uncle Harry did though; he rushed forward and pulled him into a bone-crushing hug. He was with the 2nd Ranger Battalion and had survived the assault on Pointe du Hoc. He only had two days leave and spent most of that time talking to Uncle Harry. He showed off pictures of his wife and son. His stay with us passed too quickly. Before he left, I gave him all the information I had about Jean's whereabouts in case he came anywhere near him. His visit made Uncle Harry in better spirits than I had seen him in, in a long time.

"As the war continued, we listened to the radio to hear the news of the day. There were reports of major battles going on in the north. The Northern armies, mostly Canadian and British forces, pushed through Belgium and the Netherlands, and by September, they had reached the German border. In the south, the combined forces of the French and U.S. armies invaded the south of France and started pressing north and east. I believed that Jean was fighting with this group. During the month of August, the French resistance staged a major uprising, and after six days they liberated Paris. During the rest of August into September, the armies slowly advanced toward Germany's border. During the winter we heard that there were heavy casualties from several battles. We hadn't received any communication from any of our men, and that worried all of us at the farm. Irene had been exchanging letters with Leslie, but she hadn't received any for a week.

"Christmas came and went, and soon winter turned into early spring. We still gathered around the radio every evening listening intently for any information about the fighting and for when the war would end. The fighting continued in Italy, Hungary, and Germany. In March Germany launched its last offensive but lost. Hungary was liberated. In April the Russians reached Berlin. The U.S. president, Roosevelt, died on April 12. Mussolini, the Italian dictator, was captured and hanged by the Italian partisans on April 28. News of Hitler's suicide was reported on April 30. May 7 the German surrender was signed, and on May 8 church bells rang out and people gathered to cheer and celebrate the end of the war. For us at the farm, we still waited to hear how our men had faired, but were relieved to be at peace.

"Uncle Harry was the first to hear anything. A Red Cross worker called to inform him that Markart, though wounded, was recovering in a hospital in Paris. Next, Irene received a call from Leslie informing her that he was safe and unharmed. He was heading for Le Havre, as this was the last stop before shipping out for home. They had already discussed getting married in their letters, and he told her that he still wanted to do that before he went home. My Jean came home last and was not in good health. At age fifty-nine, his once strong body was frail and he had a terrible rattle in his chest. It would be months before he would completely recover.

Turning Point

"As Leslie was scheduled to ship out, he and Irene came and told us that they planned to marry. Jean started to protest. I don't think he wanted her going over to America, but I shook my head. I had more time to accept their love for each other and knew that just like me and Jean years before, no amount of opposition was going to stop them. We arranged a small wedding in the chapel in Falaise. Leslie went home, and it would take five months before Irene would join him in the U.S. Markart left us soon after that. I'm not sure who had the saddest face Uncle Harry or Irene.

"In the months after the end of the war, life on the farm became settled as we made adjustments to having Jean home. Even though we weren't at war anymore, the shortages and difficulties didn't disappear overnight. We slowly took on our individual roles and life began to get back to normal. We all missed Aurele, and he was constantly on our minds as the days went by.

"Bermont, who was now nineteen, began training and searching for new horses to breed. With Jean, there were not many young people interested in dressage training, so the classes weren't being offered. There were a few who wanted private lessons, and this occupied some of Jean's time. He was still tired and weak, and the lightened work load was actually a blessing. I would sometimes find him sitting near Aurele's grave having a conversation. I was very worried about him as he turned sixty that October.

"As for me, the last months of 1945 were very busy. I spent most of my time shopping and packing with Irene. I treasured the time we spent together, as I knew very soon there would be an ocean between us. She was going to be living in the home of the Claytons and didn't need to have much in the way of home goods. I did give her some linen and crystal that had belonged to Jean's mother. We purchased gifts for Leslie's sister and mother. Leslie had called and we knew that they were still having trouble with shortages in the U.S. We found each a pair of nylons and some French perfume. We also bought each a brightly printed silk shirtwaist dress. We went to Cannes and visited the haute couture houses. We bought a few outfits for Irene. Two were by Dior in his 'New Style.' The first had a gray jacket with a large lapel that fell from soft shoulders to a synched-in waist that was held together by double buttons. It had little scooped pockets and was matched with a trim pencil skirt. We added a light pink blouse with a Peter Pan collar. The next suit had three pieces to it. The blouse's style was very military looking. It was pale green with two sets of large double buttons. The jacket, made in navy blue, carried the same military style but had no lapel; instead it had cream piping running along the edges. It also had the two sets of double buttons but was tailored narrow to the waist. The skirt was a beautiful cream color and was full and fell just below the knee. We bought another skirt in the same style in navy so Irene could mix and match. We added a few shirtwaist dresses in lighter fabric and print. I also bought a few shirtwaist dresses for myself and a black suit much like Irene's.

We returned home and Irene repacked her trunk. As she was doing this, I entered and placed my christening dress on top. 'I think you might need this, before I see you again.' Surprised, she asked how I knew that she was expecting. 'Mothers always know,' I told her. So for the final week of her stay, we bought baby things, including a delicately woven layette set. The time had finally come, and Irene was on her way to her new home in America.

"There was a part of me that was longing to go to America and be with her, especially now with the baby coming, but I knew it wasn't possible and Jean and Bermont needed me in France. After the war, I had resumed the dance classes, and the ballet school occupied all my time. With Irene gone, I put all my energy into it. It was hard to start over with small classes, but I slowly built the business back into shape. Dancing again gave me the solace I needed to carry on.

"The year 1946 brought with it the news of Irene's first child, a little girl they named Jan Leslie. I received in the mail a package with pictures of a chunky baby, sitting between her two very proud parents, Irene and Leslie.

"In late summer, Uncle Harry came in from the barn one afternoon, hung up his coat in the closet, sat down for his afternoon nap and passed quietly in his sleep. My heart struggled over his loss. It seemed that in just a few years, I had lost through death or moving half the family I loved. I contacted Markart and he came with his family for the funeral. His wife Doris was a cute girl; she looked like a pixie with her short hair and four-foot-eleven frame. Their children were beautiful. The oldest, at four, was the spitting image of his father, and the baby was as cute as a button blowing raspberries and cooing at everyone. After the funeral, they stayed for three weeks exploring France. With promises to write and keep in touch, the time came for them to go home. Again, it was hard to say goodbye.

"There were two special things that stood out in the year 1947. Both were gifts from Jean. The first was for our 25th wedding anniversary. Jean surprised me with a trip to Venice. We arrived at the Marco Polo Airport and were taken by water taxi to our hotel. Jean had booked a room at the historical Hotel Palazzo Abadessa. I was like a child at Christmas looking at the presents under the tree. I was bubbling with laughter and joy as we drove through the canals and docked outside the hotel. I marveled at the exquisite atrium with its marble floor, wooden ceiling, and magnificent staircase that led us to the first floor. Everywhere you looked there were amazing antiques. Ornate Venetian mirrors and Murango glass lamps graced the walls that were papered with damask silk wallpaper. The floors were engraved wood, and when you looked up, the ceilings were amazingly decorated with stucco and frescos from the 1500s. Our room continued the luxurious detail with walls decorated in pale green. There were three floor-to-ceiling windows covered with sheer white curtains. The furniture again was all antiques from the 1700s. I just loved the little gold dressing table in the corner of the room. There was an immense bed in the center of the room with tables on either side. A large armoire was across from the bed. A small table held a beautiful bouquet of flowers. The elegance of the room gave the distinct impression of stepping back in time.

"The week was filled with sightseeing and shopping. Every morning we ate a leisurely breakfast in the private garden in the back of the hotel. Small tables for two were spread around multicolored scented flower beds. Marble statues and benches were scattered around to make a peaceful area to relax or read a book. We toured St. Mark's Basilica, a beautiful multi-domed church right on the Adriatic Sea. Roaming through the halls of the Doge's Palace, we were impressed by all the gold trim on the walls and ceilings that framed amazing murals. The Gothic architecture and the lace cement artwork made the exterior of the building look like a wedding cake. We spent a lot of our afternoons just walking the main canal, stopping at little shops, and admiring the buildings and walking across the Ponte di Rialto and the Ponte dei Sospiri (Bridge of Sighs). On our last evening in Venice, Jean reserved a gondola and we were guided through the canals with our gondolier singing love songs. It was so romantic. We topped the evening off with a candlelight dinner at The Grande Canal. Jean gave me a beautiful butterfly broach encrusted with diamonds and pearls. We returned to our hotel, Jean and I talked well into the night until we drifted off to sleep.

"Heading home the next day, Jean hinted there was a surprise waiting for me when I returned home. The surprise came in a little white package and weighed no more than five pounds. My first hint at what it might be was the yipping sound coming from inside the box. I had been admiring the Maltese breed for some time, and inside the box was a beautiful white ball of fur with the most expressive eyes staring out of its tiny face. I lifted it gently and was rewarded with a lap of its tongue across my cheek. I named her Belle, and she would be my constant companion for the next thirteen years.

"In late summer, the family and I traveled to Paris to see 'L'enfant et Les Sortilèges.' We again visited my old friends. While having tea in Mathilda Kschesinskaya's drawing room, Bermont met a girl named Sasha Rutkevitch. She was studying ballet under Olga Preobrajenska, my mother's old friend.

Of Lithuanian decent, she and her parents had fled to Paris to escape Hitler's army during the war. She was tall and willowy with silver blonde hair and deep blue eyes. Bermont was instantly enchanted. Over the next couple of months, weekly trips to Paris became a pattern. Jean complained that Bermont was barely ever home. We weren't surprised when he came to us at Christmas and told us of his plans to get married. Sasha wanted a church wedding, and the date was set for August 27.

"In January, Irene and Leslie called to tell us about the birth of their second child, another girl they named Elizabeth. Informed of the wedding at the end of summer, they told us that they would be coming to visit then and were looking forward to spending time with everyone.

"Shortly after hearing from Irene, Jean was contacted by our old friend, Jean Saint-Fort Pollard, asking him for help. He needed some work done on his routine for the upcoming Olympics being held in England. We were extremely excited because he would be riding Sous les Ceps, a horse that Bermont had bred. It was confusing in the beginning having two Jeans working together until someone came up with the idea to call Jean Pollard, Jack. They worked for several weeks and then it was time for the Olympics. There were many friends participating in equestrian events, and we made plans to make the crossing over to England to watch them compete. We called on Jean's sister Madeline and her husband Keith, whom we had seen at the wedding the year before and arranged to stay with them for two weeks. We were like typical tourists, sightseeing Big Ben and Buckingham Castle and watching the changing of the guard. We were delighted when the competition started and Andre Jousseaume won silver for France on Haragonn. The French team took the gold medal in dressage. Both Jean and Bermont acted like proud parents when the medal was placed around Jean Saint-Fort Pollard's neck. We were excited when Bernard Chevallier won gold on Aiglonne. Bermont had been involved in the breeding of this horse also. His friend Jean Francois won gold in jumping. We all went out for a celebratory dinner at Sweetings on Queen Victoria Street in the heart of London. All evening the men were discussing horses. The women made plans to go shopping the next day. I was excited to go to Harrods. I still remember I purchased two outfits and a darling little purse in red leather. Too soon, it was time to return home and we left promising that we would return again. With the success of the Olympics, Bermont was sought out by several breeders. Some of them were from European countries, along with some from the U.S.

"After we returned to France, the wedding was just a few weeks away. I was counting the days, and they seemed to fly by so quickly that it surprised me how soon the wedding was upon us.

"Irene and family arrived a week early and I got a chance to see my grandbabies for the first time. I spent hours in their company, enjoying the antics of two-year-old Jan. Elizabeth was still just an infant, but she was always making faces and smiling. She absolutely loved her grandfather, and when she heard his voice, her large green eyes would light up and she would immediately gurgle and laugh.

"The wedding was a major event and took a lot of planning. We were hoping that it wouldn't rain, and getting up early, we were excited to see clear sunny skies. The family all got into cars and headed for Falaise. Arriving at the church, the family all took their seats in the front. The altar was decorated with baskets of flowers. There were lighted candles along the front, and the smell of roses permeated the air. The church was filled with family and friends.

"As the organ began to play, I started to walk down the aisle on Jean's arm. I had purchased a silver-gray dress that draped softly over my shoulders and was held together by a beautiful wide belt embroidered in sequins. Following me down the aisle was Sasha's mother. She had chosen a classic silk suit in a beautiful shade of periwinkle blue. The bridesmaids were all dressed in pastel blue chiffon and had small white flowers in their hair. They all carried bouquets of white and pink roses.

"The congregation rose in anticipation and turned to watch Sasha, elegantly attired in a cream silk taffeta wedding gown, walk slowly down the aisle. The dress had a low-cut sweetheart neckline with an inset of beaded French lace. The waist-hugging top was a contrast to the very full double pleated skirt. Stiff backing and two layers of netting were underneath the dress to make it full. The long fitted sleeves had six covered buttons. The back of the dress had a scooped- out neckline, also inserted with the same French lace as the front. It was fastened with 28 covered buttons. A light veil covered Sasha's blonde hair, which she had braided and circled around her head like a crown.

"I sat in the pew, wiping tears away from my eyes, as I watched my baby, get married. Holding Jean's hand, I thought about Aurele for a moment, but then gathered myself together to enjoy the day.

"After the ceremony, we returned to Bellaire, where the main barn had been decorated and turned into a reception area. We had hired caterers to handle the dinner, and I was relieved when the meal was served and everyone was eating and enjoying themselves. It was nice that everyone got a chance to talk and catch up with each other over dinner. We also had hired a live band and the floor was soon filled with people dancing. The dancing went on for hours, and the room echoed with music and laughter. Everyone was enjoying themselves, and the reception was a success. Soon the guests started to depart and the family made their way back to the house and their beds. In our bedroom, Jean and I talked about the events of the day and what the future might hold for our children. It still felt good to lay in the comfort of Jean's arms and fall asleep. Over the next few days, everyone departed for their homes. We saw Sasha and Bermont leave for their honeymoon. Then Irene and Leslie left with the girls. We were making plans to go visit them sometime in the next year. Jean and I enjoyed the peace and quiet that resumed at the farm."

The room remained quiet, even though Varvara had stopped talking. It was as if everyone was waiting for her to begin again, but also the story had captured their interest and they were impatient to hear more. Even Stephanie had gotten caught up in the story and had taped over her two-hour limit. Varvara was very tired and departed for a much needed nap.

Angelique sat talking with Stephanie and Victoria about the wedding of Uncle Bermont and Aunt Sasha, which led into a discussion of her upcoming wedding. There were only a few weeks left and so much needed to be done. Plans were made to return to the dress shop on Saturday with Jan, Varvara, and Vari to get their dresses. Victoria had found a dress online and ordered it through the dress shop. It had arrived and was waiting at the shop for her to try on. Angelique had asked Stephanie to be one of her bridesmaids, even though they hadn't seen each other long time, they had renewed their friendship. Angelique also knew Marc had special feelings for her. Yves sister Nicole was the other bridesmaid, and Angelique's friend Ann was the maid of honor. Stephanie also talked about the pictures for the wedding. She jotted down a list of people and groups that Angelique wanted. Stephanie reassured herself and Angelique that everything was all set.

Each day continued to reveal the history of Varvara and the growing family.

"The year 1950 brought two new grandchildren into the family. Bermont and Sasha had a baby boy in late February, and they decided to name him Jean. No one was more excited than my Jean at the sight of that chubby little baby. Irene and Leslie had their third child, another girl, and named her Karen.

"Because of the success of the Olympics the year before, interest in dressage drew new students to the farm. At age 75, Jean began to show signs of being tired, and he soon couldn't keep up with all the classes. Bermont was slowly taking over the reins of running the farm and hired a trainer to help run the school. Sasha was teaching most of the classes at the ballet school. How Jean and I spent our days changed. There were quiet rides in the country and time spent playing with our grandson, whom we called LJ, short for little Jean.

"In 1951 we traveled for the first time to the U.S. to visit Irene and Leslie. We spent an entire month visiting and enjoying the grandchildren. Jan at four and Elizabeth at two were beautiful little girls. They were full of energy and kept us busy chasing after them. We enjoyed holding the six-month-old Karen, who was quite a charmer and always seemed to have a smile on her face. I really liked the large house on the beach and enjoyed watching the surf from the sunroom's window. I soon fell in love with a quiet patch of beach and spent many moments sitting in a chair watching sailboats in the distance and listening to the calming cadence of the waves crashing on the beach. I even enjoyed the raucous screams of the seagulls. There were many mornings that Jean came searching for me, only to find me enjoying my morning cup of coffee in quiet solitude.

"We traveled to New York and were impressed by its vast landscape of tall buildings. We toured the American Ballet Theater, and I had a lovely visit with some of my old friends from the Marjinsky Theater. It was heartwarming that a lot of my classmates were living in New York and were still performing or teaching. Alicia Markova and Mia Slavenska, along with Sonia Wajerkouska and Natalia Balachnecheva, went out to dinner with me.

Jean had decided to rest in our room and declined our invitation to go out with us. I was sorry to see the evening end; it had been filled with much laughter as we talked about our youth. Saying goodbye brought a moment of sadness but couldn't erase my feelings of enjoyment that I had experienced all evening.

"I returned to my hotel room and related the evening's events to Jean. We settled in for a comfortable night's rest and returned to Watch Hill and the children the next day. The remainder of the vacation was spent visiting the local area haunts including the Watch Hill Lighthouse and taking the girls to the Flying Horse Carousel. Jean laughed at the grandchildren all astride the beautiful wooden horses, saying how they all were great riders even Elizabeth at age two. We built sandcastles on the beach and were entertained by a ballet performance that had us laughing at the antics of Jan and Elizabeth as they tried to outdo each other in pirouettes.

"Leslie took us to see his new airplane at the Westerly Airport. He was so proud of the C170A, a four-seater with metal wings, single struts and a dorsal fin tail. It cruised 115 to 120 miles an hour and could stay in the air for up to four hours. Leslie took us for a flight over the area, including Block Island. Take-off made me a little nervous, but when we were in the air, I really enjoyed the experience. Jean loved it. Leslie was an experienced pilot and handled the plane well. There is quite a big difference from flying in a commercial airplane to a front seat in the cockpit of a small airplane. The views were amazing, especially over the ocean. It was quite a thrill being so high up with such an immense view spread out before you. On our return, Leslie brought the plane in for an effortless landing. Jean and I were quite impressed with it all. Leslie explained how he was starting a shuttle service to the islands and had hopes of building up a good business.

"On our final evening, we went to dinner at the Olympia Tea Room Restaurant with Irene and Leslie. It had been a wonderful experience and the time went by too quickly. The next morning after hugging the children, we wiped tears from our eyes and made promises to return. We said our goodbyes and left to return home.

"Arriving from the U.S., life at Bellaire developed into a pattern of activities that would remain in place for several years. I would rise early and go through my morning routine, then return to have a leisurely breakfast with Jean. When the weather permitted, we would go out riding on the trails, and sometimes Bermont would join us. During the next few years, Leslie and Irene had two more children-one in 1952 they named Peter and in 1954 another boy named Richard, after Leslie's brother. Sasha and Bermont had another child in 1954, also another boy they named Leo. That made seven grandchildren in all.

"Bermont's boys were riding ponies almost as soon as they could sit up. When LJ turned five, Jean decided to start teaching him dressage. Though Sasha and I were concerned about him still being a baby, Jean and Bermont weren't worried and assured us he would be safe. Dressage horses and riders learn a variety of movements based on those once used for war: movements designed to protect the rider while allowing him to fight with a sword; movements to evade the enemy, to circle, back and stop; and the most famous and ballet-like moves called 'airs above ground.' Beginners started out with the simplest of movements, and at each level, different components were added to make the routine in the ring more complex. Jean chose a gentle mare for LJ. Walking slowly around the ring at an even pace was the first movement taught. I was watching him train one afternoon and noticed that his face, which was normally always smiling, was scrunched up in a frown of concentration. He was determined to follow his grandpa's directions and do everything right. Each day the routine was worked on, and different elements were added. He worked extremely hard until he mastered each one.

"Through all the training, Jean seemed to gain strength and energy. It was as if the training of LJ had given Jean a dose of the fountain of youth. His green eyes twinkled with excitement whenever we discussed LJ.

"Over the next several years, they trained and designed a routine for competition. Going to small competitions, LJ started the intro level with just walking and a trot around the ring. Working his way through the four tests of the training level, LJ had to walk, trot, and canter. The training level adds 20 meter circles in the trot and canter, halt, free walk, medium walk, change rein across the diagonal in the trot, trot rising and sitting, and serpentines on the centerline in the trot. We held small competitions at the farm every year, and this would be the first time a family member participated since Aurele had competed in 1942. Jean was so excited and

LJ nervous that the house was bursting with barely contained energy and emotion.

"The day dawned bright and sunny, and the farm began to fill with contestants and their families. With any equestrian event, there are many people behind the performers in the ring. Trainers, farriers, mane braiders or plaiters, and also vets were among the people milling about a horse getting ready to compete. When you get to the upper levels, many riders come to competitions with their own entourage of people. I worked my way through the crowd and spoke to LJ. He told me he was nervous and didn't want to disappoint his grandpa. I patted his shoulder and said, 'Nothing you do would disappoint him; just give it your best.' As I left the barn, I glanced over and smiled as I watched Jean with a new pep in his step greeting old friends and watching over the judging table. He had checked everything twice to make sure the competition would run smoothly as planned.

"Sasha, Bermont, and I all gathered to watch LJ work the whole routine out in the ring. We also greeted several acquaintances as we made our way to our seats. LJ held himself well as he entered the ring dressed in the riding attire of black short jacket, beige jodhpurs, black riding boots, white shirt, white stock and beige gloves. He gave the nod that his routine was starting. Beginning at a walking trot, LJ executed a circle of the whole ring. He continued to perform each element with determination and grace. He was such a little man atop a large horse. I couldn't help but look back to when we were training Aurele all those years ago and realized that the circle of life continues. I had always enjoyed the beginner levels and I was a typical grandmother, sitting on the edge of my seat with nervous anticipation. I realized I was biting my lips and holding my breath as I watched him complete his routine. He placed fifth in a group of twelve riders, and for a beginner, that was pretty good. It would be the last time he placed any lower than third. In the coming years, he and his brother would participate in competitions not only in France but most of Europe and eventually the United States.

"In the winter of 1957, Jean came down with a terrible cough that soon developed into pneumonia. For several weeks, it was touch and go as to whether he was going to make it. He recovered slowly, but the illness stripped him of all his energy. He struggled to get back on his feet and impatiently waited for competitions to start.

"Jean wanted to take LJ to the National Dressage Competitions held every year in Pompadour, France. We decided to make it a family vacation and invited Leslie, Irene, and the five grandchildren to join us on the French Riviera. We spent a week in a rented villa overlooking the water that was just a short walk away. We had hired an au pair for the week to help with the children, and she had them busy enjoying play at the beach, and hikes into the hills, as well as planning an evening's entertainment to be performed at the end of the week. The children enjoyed discovering each other's interests and common bonds. The men spent the week mostly talking about horses; they dabbled in a round of golf and established a cribbage tournament. The children were also excited about the large TV in the family room as they didn't have one at home. The evenings were filled with everyone participating in games of one sort or another. Irene, Sasha, and I relaxed either on the beach watching the children, especially the baby Richard or on the covered patio. We particularly liked the patio during the evenings when the lights of the village twinkled up at us, and the moon laid a glimmering path across the water leading us to dream we could follow it anywhere. It was a natural gathering place for sharing a glass of wine and adult conversations.

"Jean and Bermont talked with Leslie about LJ's future competitions and the plans to work him up to international levels. Leslie suggested that LJ come to the U.S. to participate in some competitions that were held there.

"The days flew by as we enjoyed being a family together, and soon it was time to go to Pompador. LJ was surprisingly calm for a nine-year-old. The family was sitting in the stands with me as I nervously waited for his turn to begin. I wanted him to do well and he didn't disappoint me. He won his first blue ribbon. I'm not sure who was flying higher-Jean or LJ. I know Sasha and Bermont were beaming with pride. We were still celebrating as we drove home to Bellaire. When we arrived, it was late and we all were exhausted. We quickly dispersed to our rooms. Jean and I enjoyed a companionable time together and talked quietly about the week's events. He expressed his nightly, 'La bonne nuit. Je vous aime V,' and we went to sleep.

"I awoke the next morning and got ready to go down for my morning routine. As was my habit to do, I went to kiss Jean good morning and I found him cold and lifeless. My anguished cries brought Bermont and Sasha rushing into our bedroom. I held Jean in my arms, rocking his lifeless body and crying. We had been together for 35 years, and he was only 73. Leslie and Irene soon entered with the children attempting to follow, but they were quickly sent downstairs. Irene and Bermont guided me out of the room.

"The following day, arrangements were made for a military funeral. My children handled everything, for I was incapable; I was lost and desolate in my grief. The morning of the funeral dawned gloomy with the skies filled with dark and dense clouds from which a heavy downpour was falling. I remember thinking that the sky was crying for Jean, too. The funeral passed with me in a daze. Dressed in a black crepe double-breasted suit and black hat, I was guided to the front pew of the church. I sat between Irene and Bermont. The grandchildren were all around me. All I can remember is feeling numb. The church was filled with family and friends. Jean's sister Madeline and her husband sat behind me. After the service, as we left the church, the sun broke through the clouds, scattering rays of sunshine. Jean and I had often talked about the sun's rays being the fingers of God, and seeing the sight before me brought me a sense of comfort. It was as if Jean was sending me a personal message. We drove to Bellaire, and entering the driveway, I noticed Jean's horse was tied up out front with a black wreath around his neck. We buried Jean beside Aurele in the family plot. I then stood in the parlor and greeted the guests as they paid their respects. Some of Jean's old Army buddies came. I know that that would have pleased him. My friends in the ballet community came up from Paris, and a large group from the horse set came.

"The children and grandchildren gathered around me during the following week. Leslie had to return home, but Irene and the children stayed on. Flowers and letters of condolence poured in from people around the world. Karen was extremely impressed by a personal note from Charles de Gaulle expressing his sympathy and his own sense of loss. I wandered around the rooms of the farm lost in my sorrow. I couldn't seem to find the motivation to move on with my life. Not even the daily routine of ballet could comfort me this time. I slowly slipped into a depression that had me sitting in my bedroom just staring out the window to the hill where Jean and Aurele lay. Even Belle couldn't comfort me, though she sat in my lap constantly. There was an immense vital part of me missing, and I couldn't seem to be resilient enough to pull myself together. I barely remember Irene and the children saying goodbye and leaving to go back to the States."

Softly crying, Varvara stopped talking and Stephanie shut off the camera. Most of the adults in the room were remembering their own grief at Jean's passing, and hugs and comments were exchanged. LJ shared a story about some of the early days when Jean began training him. He soon had the group laughing and the mood changed. Everyone began telling their own tales about the good times they shared with Jean. Even Varvara sat smiling and putting her own two cents in.

Taping was finished for the week, and Angelique and Victoria welcomed the break. Varvara was getting tired so easily, and they both worried about her health. She admitted to them that the doctors had told her that her heart was wearing out. But, not many people live to see the age of 105, she had said.

It was a happy group that set out for Providence on Saturday morning. There had been a rainstorm during the night, and light fog hung in the air as the woman met outside of Seagull's Perch waiting for the limo. A large white limousine pulled into the driveway, its tires crunching across the stones. It took a short time to install Vari's car seat and securely buckle her in. The driver and Jan helped Varvara get comfortable while the rest of the group settled into their seats. Excited voices discussing the upcoming trip and the style of dresses they all liked. The talking was interrupted by Vari's voice. "I'm going to get a beautiful dress for my mommy and daddy's wedding. We're going to be a family." Everyone exchanged smiles as Angelique agreed.

Pulling up to the curb, the limo driver opened doors for the girls, and then unfolded Varvara's wheel chair and assisted her out. Jan made sure she was comfortable and the group all gathered to go into Wishing Well Bridal. Upon entering, they were greeted by Pam.

"Hello and welcome." Turning to Angelique, she asked, "How many girls are in your party? Do you know the style or color of dress that you like?"

"I'm leaning toward strapless and pastel colors, possibly yellow or aqua for the girls. I'd like to see something in lilac or rose for my grandmother and great-grandmother."

"Let's start with the girls first. I have chosen several styles that fit your criteria. Let's see where this takes us."

The girls were guided into a changing area and began showing dresses to Angelique, Victoria, Jan, Varvara, and a very excited Vari.

Stephanie and Ann came out in two dresses. Ann was dressed in a pink chiffon floor-length gown. The only thing that Angelique liked was the off-the-shoulder draping that looked very Grecian in style. Stephanie modeled a knee-length chiffon dress with a gathered strapless bodice. The overskirt draped to the side and formed a fanciful pleat. Satin ruching accented the umpire waist. It was in a pale teal, and as Stephanie turned, it fanned out as if being blown by a gentle breeze.

Angelique looked at the two dresses, "What do you think?" she asked. "This dress isn't very flattering on me and I like the one Stephanie has on much better," Ann said. "I usually like both those colors, but the pink dress just washes me out. It is not flattering at all."

Stephanie looked at Angelique and smiled. "I agree. I don't care for the style of her dress. I love this one. It's so flattering. I feel like a princess."

Jan, Victoria, and Varvara were whispering amongst themselves. They agreed that Stephanie's dress was better. The girls were led back to the dressing room to try on more dresses. Ann came back in a yellow and white petal dress. There were layers of chiffon petals over a white slip topped by a princess-shaped bodice. Though pretty, it made Ann, who was quite slim, look chunky. Stephanie had on a light tangerine strapless evening dress that was so striking in its simplicity. After trying on a few more styles, it was decided to go back to the teal dress, but to see it in different colors. Stephanie and Ann came out in the dress in two colors: yellow and a surprising apricot. Ann, dressed in the apricot dress, looked amazing and expressed her desire to wear that shade. There was some discussion over the teal or yellow, but in the end it was decided that the yellow worked best. Ann, who was well-endowed, wondered about the dress staying up. Pam said all the dresses came with straps that could be attached and brought over the matching apricot straps. After they were on the dress, everyone agreed that this was the style they liked best.

Angelique asked Pam for the style number, as Yves' sister was waiting to get the dress in California.

Attention was then turned to what Vari was going to wear. An attendant with her, Vari entered the dressing room. The attendant brought three dresses she thought would match the girls' dresses. The first, a white dress with a wide satin ribbon in multi pastel shades, was slipped over Vari's head. She danced out to the waiting group and did a perfect pirouette.

"How did you like this one?"

Almost in unison, a solid "no" was voiced.

The second dress, a solid white miniature wedding dress, was vetoed also. "I think I want to be the only one in white," Angelique remarked.

Vari headed back to try on another dress. "Mommy, mommy, wait'til you see!" Vari's voice carried out before her. She bounded into the room and did a twirl in front of the group. This time Vari was dressed in a simple sundress with little capped sleeves and the dress was the same color apricot of Ann's dress. As Vari skipped around the room the oohs and ahhs could be heard. There was no need to try on any more dresses.

Tears filled several eyes as they gazed upon the little girl standing in front of them. Varvara spoke to Angelique and said, "This is the one. "She looks like a fairy." Everyone agreed this was the obvious choice for the wedding.

Next, it was Varvara's turn to try on her dress. Victoria, Jan, and Varvara had already asked the attendant for dresses that they had seen online. Looking over the selection of dresses, Angelique chose a wine colored dress with embroidered lace jacket. Varvara laughed and told her that it was her favorite. The dress fit perfectly and was packed away to be taken home at the end of the day. Jan was the last to choose a dress and tried on two that were among the several shown to her. The first was a strapless navy blue form fitting tea- length dress with a sequined trim at the top and a light scattering of sequins spread out on the skirt. While Jan was looking at her reflection in the mirror, the women in the room shook their heads in unison as Angelique spoke up.

"Grams, it's not special enough for you. Will you try on the other one?"

Jan returned again from the fitting roam. Dressed in a strapless chiffon mock wrap A-line dress with scalloped sweetheart neckline, hand-beaded lace Empire bodice, side draped skirt with beaded accent, cascading ruffle and sweep train. In a beautiful royal blue it accented Jan's shape and coloring to a t. The room for a few seconds was quiet then everyone seemed to voice their approval.

"It's gorgeous on you." "Beautiful."

"It compliments everyone else."

"I think that this is the one," Victoria commented. "Mom I have never seen you look so amazing."

"Grams, I agree this dress is amazing and just what I wanted for you. You look incredible and Grampa Tim is going to be knocked off his feet," stated Angelique. "Now everyone is finished except mom and me. Looking at Vari, she asked Ann and Stephanie to take Vari over to Slater Park to ride the Looff Carousel while she and Victoria had their fittings.

Jan and Varvara were staying at the bridal shop to see Victoria and Angelique's gowns. Victoria went first and came out a drop waist emerald green gown. Simple and elegant it had light beading along the high neckline but when she turned around the dress scooped low showing off her elegant shoulders and back. It also fit perfectly except an adjustment to the hem. Victoria glanced hesitantly at Angelique for her approval. With tears in her eyes she nodded.

"It's perfect mom. I can't wait to see Wayne's face when he sees the back," laughed Angelique. Since meeting Wayne at Mémère's birthday party, and finding out her mother was married to him. Angelique had accepted the new relationship after seeing the way her mother softened at just the sight of Wayne. Love certainly was in the air.

Finally, it was Angelique's turn and the white gown was dropped over her head. There was an audible silence from the group of women waiting in the outer room.

"You're breathtaking, it's even more striking seeing it on you for the second time." Victoria's words were trembling as she gazed at her daughter.

"Absolutely beautiful," said Jan as she asked Angelique to turn around. "Your grandfather is going to have a hard time to keep from crying when he sees you in this," she said as she wiped tears from her own eyes.

Looking over to Varvara she was startled to see her smiling through a tear streaked face. "We're all going to need a make-up repair after this," she chuckled. Then addressing Angelique she commented, "You are going to live up to your name on your wedding day, child. You look like an angel. Yves is going to be blown away."

After changing back into her clothes she joined the three women and then exited the shop. Angelique again thought how lucky she was to have her family back in her life. The limo was waiting for the woman and quickly brought them to the park.

They could hear Vari's laughter even before they saw her. She was sitting on a handsomely carved white horse and laughing up at Ann and Stephanie who were acting afraid of the lion, giraffe, and camel. Angelique loved carousels and joined the girls for a ride. She admired the great craftsmanship of the horse she was sitting on. Over a hundred years old The Looff Carousel was built in 1895 and installed in Slater Park in 1910. It is the second oldest antique wooden carousel in Rhode Island. It was hard convincing Vari to get off her horse. Only the promise of going to eat at the Cheesecake Factory made her come, though she kept her pout of displeasure most of the ride over to the Providence Place Mall. It was a happy group that entered the Cheesecake Factory, and the celebratory atmosphere continued through- out lunch. Everyone was full and satisfied, and they all returned to the limousine to head back home. Within minutes of getting on the highway, Vari was sound sleep. Angelique was thinking that it had been a wonderful and exhausting day.

On Monday the taping resumed, and again a small group gathered to hear Varvara tell her story.

"The early 60's brought so many changes to the world and our lives. Adjusting to life without Jean was difficult, but I soon began to find interest in LJ's competitions and the lives of all my grandchildren in France and the U.S. Irene and I still kept contact with each other through weekly phone calls. Often I would talk with the children, learning news about what was happening in their lives. With my dog on my lap, I would listen to Jan complaining about her parents being too strict, that they wouldn't let her wear the mini-skirt that was in fashion, she consulted me as to whether she should she keep her hair long or cut it short. Thirteen year old Elizabeth was interested in horses and competing. She would talk about her routine and what she was working on in the ring. Karen was my serious grandchild. Our conversations ranged from talk about the current politics to her plans to become a nurse so she could help people. Pete at nine was into the ballet, and we talked about who I knew and the current dancers he wanted to see, especially Rudolph Nureyev. Little Richard was interested in Disney and GI Joe's. Jean continued to have a passion for dressage and was usually in the ring when he wasn't in school. Leo was into sports. He played rugby and basketball and followed racing. The children also talked with each other, exchanging information on the latest singers and bands. The girls were all in love with Ricky Nelson, Elvis, Bobby Darin, and then some band called The Beatles.

"In the summer of 1961, I traveled to Paris for my annual visit to the ballet. I was feeling more myself and was excited that I would be seeing the new Russian dancer Rudolph Nureyev. I had made plans to see an evening performance of Sleeping Beauty. I had heard many good things about Nureyev from some of my friends, but nothing prepared me for the experience or emotions that his powerful and creative movements stirred in me. He was so different; his form of dancing made him a feature of the ballet instead of just a support for the ballerina. His dancing would change how ballet would be danced from then on. I had not experienced a more moving dance routine and I was very impressed. As I made my way backstage, I picked up several pictures, which I had Nureyev sign. Peter would be thrilled to have them, and I planned to go to the States in the next year.

"At the end of '62 I decided to visit the U.S. again and bring LJ and Leo with me. We made arrangements, and in February, the three of us went, along with my new dog Ballerina. Belle had passed away at the end of the year. We boarded a plane for England to make a connecting flight to New York. LJ and Leo were excited about their first visit to the United States. When we landed in London, we were surprised at the amount of security at Heathrow Airport. Some band was flying out, and there were hundreds of girls screaming behind barriers. We boarded our plane to discover that the band The Beatles were on our flight. LJ and Leo knew who they were and went to get autographs for themselves and especially for their cousins. LJ expressed how lucky they were to get the autographs and how envious his cousins were going to be. Leo said the girls were going to faint when they found out that they had actually talked to John, Paul and George and some guy named Ringo. I was impressed that they were going to be on the Ed Sullivan Show. We sometimes watched that on Sunday evenings.

"The crowd that greeted us in New York was in the thousands. I was worried about the boys' safety. We were rushed through the screaming crowd and safely escorted into the terminal, where we found Leslie waiting for us. After gathering up our luggage, we left for Rhode Island with the boys regaling Leslie about their flight with The Beatles. When we arrived in Watch Hill, the car had barely stopped when the boys were jumping out and running up to the girls that were standing out on the front porch. At the boys' telling of their news, there was a loud eruption of screaming. This brought Irene rushing outside, where she found Leslie, the boys and I laughing at the antics the girls were displaying over The Beatles. Hushing the girls, she guided us all inside."

"After greetings were exchanged, we sat down to a lovely tea that Irene had prepared for us. I looked around, amazed at my grandchildren. I wondered where the babies went to as I gazed upon the girls, who were now all teenagers sitting at the table. Peter, at eleven was very quiet, and didn't say much to anyone except to pass something. Richard, all grown up at seven, was a mischievous and comical character who chattered non-stop until his father admonished him with a 'Hush!' This brought out a silly smirk that stopped me from breathing for a second, as I went back forty years before to when Aurele would have made that same face. I looked over at Irene, and she smiled and nodded in total understanding. Looking over to LJ and Leo, who could barely keep their eyes open; it was obvious that jet-lag had set in. We made our way to our rooms for a much needed rest.

"Morning exercise found me in the company of Irene, her girls, and Peter. As we went through the routine, I watched Peter and found myself very impressed with his agility and talent that already showed for a boy of eleven. I gave him the signed photos of Nureyev, and we talked about him for a while. I told Peter that I thought he was very good for his age. Though he was blushing, it was apparent that he was proud of the well-deserved praise. I reminded myself to speak to Irene about him later."

"When we joined the rest of the children at the breakfast table, they were all chattering away, making plans for the rest of the day. LJ and Elizabeth had made arrangements previously for LJ to go to her riding school and do some demonstrations for some of the teams that were preparing for the coming year's competitions. She was glowing with excitement to show off her handsome cousin from France. Leslie was going to take them over to the stables after breakfast. Jan, at seventeen was busy with her friends, and was leaving to go shopping with them. Leo, Peter, and Karen all wanted to go to the movies, and Leslie volunteered to come back and take them after he dropped off LJ and Elizabeth. The only one left was Richard, who was pouting until Irene told him that his best friend was coming over to spend the day. I also said he could take Ballerina for a walk later, and he jumped at the chance to spend some time with her.

"With all the children settled with their individual plans, Irene and I were free to enjoy the day together. Relaxing companionably in the sunroom with a cup of tea and Ballerina snuggled on my lap, we talked about Bellaire and Bermont and Sasha. After catching up Irene with all the news from France, I brought up the subject of Peter. I told her I thought he had incredible potential that needed to be developed, adding that he should be attending a private school that specialized in dance and ballet. I also mentioned that he wouldn't run into as much prejudice in a dance school, where gays weren't ridiculed but accepted as normal. At first Irene was startled by my comments. Not so much that I thought he was talented but that I recognized his sexual preference. She agreed that he had already had issues with some of his classmates. We talked about different schools he could go to, as she wanted him to stay in the United States until he was older. I said I would start to lay some ground work so he could eventually come and study in France."

"We talked about all the other children and plans for college for all of them. Jan was graduating from high school in June and wanted to go away to a girls' college in Massachusetts called Anna Maria. Elizabeth wanted equestrian studies but also wanted to become a veterinarian. She had plans to attend Johnson & Wales University in Providence, Rhode Island. Irene was concerned with Karen because she wanted to enter the military and become a nurse. This brought a chuckle from me because Karen was almost a carbon copy of Irene at the same age, and I had had the same concerns about her."

"We discussed the political atmosphere with Kennedy in the White House and the Vietnam conflict. Both she and Leslie believed that the advisors being sent over there would only escalate the situation into a war. I agreed with her and discussed how France couldn't control the Vietcong in the '50s and I didn't think that much had changed since then. Irene still had her passion for politics and was actively involved with the Democratic Party. She had campaigned for President Kennedy and was just getting involved with the peace movement and a civil rights group led by Martin Luther King. She told me about his 'I Have a Dream Speech' and how it had impressed her. We continued to talk about peaceful demonstrations, and I expressed my worry over her becoming too involved. We discussed my life without Jean and the loneliness I felt each day missing him.

"Richard and his friend then came in and we all had lunch together. I settled back in the sunroom and quickly fell asleep in the warmth of the sunshine pouring into the room through the glass windows. The children started returning late in the afternoon, each relating their day's activities.

"The next day we all got up early to catch the train for New York City. We had a whole day mapped out with shopping in the morning for the girls and a museum trip for Leslie and the boys. We were having lunch at the Hard Rock Café and heading to the theater to catch the matinee. Over lunch, the boys shared their adventures and we showed off our bargains from our shopping spree. When we arrived at the ballet theater, we were treated like movie stars by the theater employees and were escorted to a private box seat. By this time, Peter was so excited his feet barely touched the floor. If he'd had been a balloon, he would have floated away. Soon the lights dimmed and Sleeping Beauty was danced. Peter sat at the edge of his seat, watching everything that was happening on stage. It was a wonderful performance. We made our way backstage to meet some of my old friends. I got quite a thrill showing off my grandchildren. Sadly, the day was over way too soon, and we needed to return to the train station to catch the train home. Nine tired tourists boarded the train and almost immediately everyone but Irene, Peter, and I were asleep. We sat in quiet conversation as the wheels click-clacked over the tracks. Peter, still excited about seeing the ballet, asked about the differences I saw in comparing Paris ballet to New York's. I told him about how moved I was by Nureyev's dancing and said I would try to get him to see him dance if I could.

"Wednesday brought sleet and a snowstorm from off the ocean. The wind blew tiny bits of ice against the windows, and a wet, white snow poured from the sky. Sitting in the safety of the sunroom, I watched, fascinated, as the enormous waves crashed over the beach. The storm seemed filled with anger as it whipped the crest of each wave against the rock wall. Even Ballerina seemed to sense the tension in the air as the storm developed over us. While she snuggled in my lap, she would occasionally let out a soft whine and lick my face. Irene came over with a pot of tea and we talked about a variety of different things. In the afternoon, it was decided that everyone was going to participate in a Hand and Foot competition. We divided into teams of two and chose who we were going to play against. Karen teamed up with Richard/Irene (Richard needed help), and they were playing against LJ and Elizabeth. Jan and Claude were playing against Peter and me. The game, a family tradition, was played with five decks of cards-a kind of canasta that you played in four sets, with each set getting more difficult to play. The cards had different values: jokers were wild cards, and were worth fifty points, the number two, also a wild card, was twenty points, and the ace fifteen. Threes were dead cards and needed to be discarded. If caught with a red three when the other team went out it cost you a negative five hundred points. Four through nine had a five-point value and the ten, jack, queen and king were all worth ten. What made the game interesting was you were allowed to talk to your partner. Each person was dealt two decks of thirteen cards. Each player chose which deck to start with-that was called his hand-and the other deck was set aside, and that was the player's foot. Each hand you needed to have a certain number of points to open; fifty for the first hand, seventy five for the second, ninety for the third, and one hundred twenty for the last hand. Each hand could go on for twenty to thirty minutes, and a game could last for two hours. There were plenty of snacks laid out, and as we played, there were sounds of moans and cheers of conquest heard from players at each table. It was a great way to spend an afternoon when the weather kept you locked inside your home."

"The storm raged outside and continued through the night and into the next morning. The children spent most of Thursday morning working on a talent show they were planning for us that evening. There were going to be joint performances of ballet and singing. Peter was doing a solo. The three girls were singing a song, 'Where the Boys Are.' Karen was going to recite two of her poems, and the boys had formed an impromptu band and were going to be The Beatles. In the evening after dinner, we all gathered in the family room to watch the show. It was an enjoyable evening filled with laughter. I was again impressed with Peter, and I told him so after the end of the show.

"As all vacations seem to end too soon, the time came much too quickly for us to pack and head home. The boys expressed how much they enjoyed their trip and gave me appreciative hugs and words of thanks.

"The world seemed to be spinning on fast forward as the multitude of events carved out the identity of a new generation. Our lives moved on, and in November we were sad to hear from Irene that President Kennedy had been shot and killed in Texas. She was upset and I tried to comfort her, but it was difficult with an ocean separating us. The year 1964 passed quietly. Irene and Leslie's worries were coming true, and the war in Vietnam escalated. Irene started actively participating in the war protests. In November, forty thousand people circled the White House in a peaceful demonstration against the war. Irene, Jan, Elizabeth, and Karen all were there and took part. Each week when we would talk on the phone, Irene kept me posted of everything that was happening in the U.S. In France, Sasha and Bermont carried out the running of the dressage and ballet schools. LJ continued to work his way through his levels and, with his brother following in his footsteps, we were often traveling to different competitions.

"It was during one of these competitions that I ran into an acquaintance named Michael Trudeau. Michael was a charmer. His attractive good looks and genuine elegance made many a head turn. At age 65, he still had dark brown hair that was accented with silver white wings spread out over each ear. Deep-set eyes and a long patrician nose stood out in his handsome face. He had full lips and a slight cleft in his chin. People often commented that he resembled Cary Grant. I found out that his granddaughter Jacqueline was actually competing against Leo. We began talking about our grandchildren and then about our lives. A widower, he had lost his wife to a stroke two years before and was still struggling to accept her death. We found we had a lot of things in common and, much to my surprise, he asked me out to dinner. Being 60 years old, I wasn't looking for a relationship. I wasn't sure I wanted one, either. I questioned Sasha for advice and her thoughts were that you had to live your own life and do what was going to make you happy. She said that I didn't die when Jean did. That she hoped there were a lot of years ahead. Sasha advised that I live them to the fullest. Bermont's attitude was at first disapproving; he didn't like thinking someone was going to take his father's place, but I assured him that that wasn't possible. I expressed my feelings of loneliness and lack of companionship, and after we had talked for a while, he said he understood and took his objections away. Irene surprised me the most by saying that for a person who was as happy as I was with her father, it was only natural I would want to be involved in another relationship, that life was for living and her dad would have encouraged me to get on with my life. So I agreed to go out to dinner with Michael at the end of the week.

"During the week and as the evening drew near, I began to rethink my decision. There were so many questions running through my head. What was I going to wear, a dress or a pantsuit? I spent a whole day going through my closet dumping clothes on the bed as I rejected them as too dressy or not dressy enough. I finally pulled out a cashmere dress that I had bought in Paris and had never worn. With that decision made, I began to worry over what I was going to talk about: And what if he wants to kiss me? Do I let him? By Thursday afternoon, I was ready to call him up and cancel, but Sasha and Bermont convinced me not to. I was a bundle of nerves and felt frightened and foolish for the feelings I was having."

"Friday morning I went to the hairdresser and had my hair cut in a classy short bob that fell in soft waves that framed my face. I then went and had a manicure and pedicure that had my nails looking good in a soft shade of pink. The afternoon was spent soaking in the hot tub and completing my toiletries. The evening finally came, and my nerves were still causing me to feel as if someone was doing the rumba inside my stomach. I was pacing the floor and biting my lip when I heard the doorbell ring, announcing Michael's arrival. I did a last check in the mirror. The simple, soft, sea foam green cashmere dress that I had chosen to wear was flattering and showed off my trim figure. I put on my three-inch black heels, grabbed my little clutch purse, and headed downstairs. Michael looked very handsome in a dark double-breasted suit. Bermont came over gave me a kiss and wished me to have a good time. Michael helped me on with my coat and we headed to his car. When we went outside, I actually giggled like a schoolgirl when I saw the car parked in front of me. It was a bright red 1964 Jaguar Roadster. I loved cars and this one was a powerful six-cylinder, manual transmission, four-speed, two-door beauty. It could go up to speeds of 150 mph. Michael held my door for me as I slid into the plush black leather seats. I think I surprised Michael with my knowledge of cars, and the conversation flowed easily as we drove to the restaurant.

"We went to a lovely restaurant located in Caen called The Lion d'Or (The Golden Lion). You entered through an iron archway to an enclosed patio that had hanging plants filled with flowers decorating the outside walls. Inside the restaurant, the décor was light with beige walls and dark wood beamed ceilings. The accent lamps on the wall had red shades. The tables were covered in light gold tablecloths with black chaser plates and stemware of red crystal. There were roses in the center of the table and small candles. Over in a corner was a comfortable lounge with black leather couches and white chairs arranged around a fireplace that had a red hood. We sat down at a corner table, and our waiter came over with a towel over his arm and informed us of the evening's specials. Looking at the menu, I decided to have the marinated baby artichokes, pissaladieve, zucchini, blossom beignet, radish with tapenade, vegetable 'forci' and brandade nicoise as an appetizer. Michael chose the winter cassolette, green and white asparagus, Jerusalem artichoke salsify, and black truffle. My main meal choice was a citrus-crusted duck groton of asparagus, fennel and carrots, and rosemary polenta. His choice was salmon braised endives a l'orange endive salad with blood orange garlic croquette and aged balsamic. We enjoyed a lovely white wine with the meal and we both had a Manjara chocolate mousse with Corsica signature coffee. During all of dinner, the conversation just flowed from one topic to another. I found Michael interesting with a wealth of knowledge about many subjects. After dinner we moved from our table to the lounge and sat before the fire conversing while enjoying a snifter of Remy Martin XO Congac."

The evening drive home was spent in companionable silence. I worried over whether he would kiss me and if I had bad breath. He escorted me to the door and thanked me for a wonderful evening. Giving me a kiss on both cheeks, he said he wished to see me again. I thanked him in return and agreed that I, too, would like to go out again. Entering the house, I closed the door and let out a soft sigh. The evening had gone well, but it still left me slightly on edge in regards to where things might lead.

"The next day while sitting at breakfast, a dozen white roses were delivered to me. The note said a simple 'Thank you.' Sasha asked how the dinner went. I told her all about the restaurant and said that the evening went well. Michael called with plans to go see a movie. I had wanted to see Dr. Zhavago because I was interested in seeing how Russia was depicted and to compare it to how I had experienced it when I was a child. I loved the movie and was teary-eyed as we left the theater. We talked a lot on the way home and discussed my life and compared the differences I had seen in the movie.

"For the next few weeks, I didn't hear from Michael. I wondered what his silence meant, and I soon learned that his children were displeased that he was spending time with a woman. His granddaughter explained to Leo that her mother and aunt were having issues with their father dating and they needed to work it out. I was disappointed that Michael hadn't called to tell me this himself, and surprised, it made me recognize how attracted to Michael I really was.

"I heard from Irene that there was going to be another addition to our family. Jan had gotten married to Timothy St. Paul in a small ceremony in Christ Church. Elizabeth was her attendant along with Timothy's brother

Robert. Timothy was a Marine and was being sent to Vietnam. Both Irene and Jan had difficulty dealing with his deployment because they were so against the war. Timothy and Jan came to Bellaire before going to Paris for their honeymoon. I liked Timothy immediately. His attentiveness toward Jan showed how much he cared for her. Timothy and I had a conversation about Jan on the evening before they left for Paris. He confided how worried he was about Jan if anything happened to him while he was in Vietnam. He was proud to be a Marine and to be serving his country, but agreed with Jan about the war. He had to do his duty and asked if I would try to watch over Jan for him. He was a remarkable young man, and I told him I would check on Jan while he was away.

"In the beginning of 1966, Michael re-entered my life. Though his daughters weren't happy about him moving forward with his life, they accepted his decision to do so. We saw each other often during the next several months, and we discovered we liked being in each other's company. I walked around with a permanent smile on my face.

"We watched our grandchildren compete against each other in the ring and often took them out to dinner afterwards. I heard from Irene the current news of the U.S. with its protest and peace marches. She also informed me that by the end of the year, I would be a great-grandmother. In December, Jan had a baby girl and named her Victoria. Varvara turned to Vari and told her that was her 'gamma'."

Angelique smiled at Vari and Victoria, thinking how the many generations were there in the room listening to Varvara.

The filming stopped there for the day and the family dispersed for lunch. Varvara's story continued the next day with the years 1967 and '68. "Elizabeth married Dr. Harrison Green in June of 1967. Martin Luther King was leading protest marches in Chicago. Thousands of young men and women were sent to Vietnam. In 1968, both Martin Luther King Jr. and Robert Kennedy were assassinated. The world was beginning to protest the Vietnam War, and the Berlin Wall was built. Near the end of 1968, Elizabeth had a baby boy she named Nicholas.

"Life in France hadn't changed much for any of Bermont and Sasha's family. The boys were older and each had a girlfriend, but they maintained much the same life that I had lived with Jean and my children. They also found their days filled with dancing or riding instruction. During this time, Michael and I spent a lot of time together discovering each other and developing a deep affection for one another. I found him not only attractive, but his vast knowledge on so many different subjects kept our conversations lively and interesting. Just listening to him talk brought out my admiration and interest. He would make me laugh with his comic faces and terrible jokes. We were beginning to become more than just companions, and our feelings were leading us to a deeper relationship.

"In February of 1969, Michael asked me to go on vacation with him. We decided to take a cruise around the Mediterranean Sea. This would change our relationship from companions enjoying each other's company to lovers. I was excited and nervous at the same time. Even though I knew I was quite fit for an old lady, I wasn't sure how I felt about letting Michael see me in the buff. To prepare for the trip, Sasha and I went shopping. We bought long sundresses and a few capris with colorful tops. I purchased a couple of large pairs of sunglasses in several colors. I tried on several bathing suits and finally chose a dark teal one-piece with a matching lacy cover-up. We shopped for beautiful lacy underwear with matching bras. I bought a comfortable pair of shoes for sightseeing and a beautiful pair of white and black sandals with a wedged three-inch heel. We went to Dior's to look for an evening gown and found a gold silk concoction that had a halter top held up by a beaded collar. The skirt floated out from a narrow waistband. I was pleased that it flattered my body and that it was backless. I found a pair of beaded gold sandals and a little purse to match that completed the outfit. I also purchased a black and white pantsuit and found a wide brimmed hat with black silk roses and feathers accenting the brim. I thought I was ready, but when the day came to board the ship, a multitude of insecurities came crashing down on me. Sasha smiled and said I was like a bride with honeymoon jitters. When Michael came to pick me up, I couldn't help but smile. He looked just like what I thought a man going to his yacht would look like. He had on white casual pants, a red polo shirt, and a navy sweater. All he needed to complete the picture was a captain's hat. I said my goodbyes and left.

"We traveled to Paris and then flew to Venice. Being in Venice brought back memories of when Jean and I had been there. I felt slightly awkward, but Michael reassured me that the same thing often happened to him. He and his wife Suzette had traveled extensively, and often a place would cause him to instantly picture her there. 'We've both loved someone else, and to try and deny it to each other or ourselves is wrong. They're gone from our lives, but not from our hearts or memories. We just have to go on with our lives. I believe Suzette would be happy knowing I found someone like you.' he told me.

"Yes, I agree Jean worried about me being so much younger than him and actually told me he wanted me to find someone."

"The scheduled boarding of the ship was not until seven in the evening. Michael and I walked along the canals, exploring the city. It was a warm, bright, sunny day and the canal waters twinkled back the sun's light, often blinding us in its brightness. We stopped and bought fruit from a delightful outdoor vendor. He was a short pudgy man with a roly-poly shape that reminded me of Humpty Dumpty. It was actually his voice that drew us to his stand. He was singing about his vegetables as if he were on the opera stage. All you could hear was this deep Italian tenor announcing he had the finest green peppers, bright red tomatoes, and delicious fruit. The combination of music and advertisement was interesting, but it was his voice that called to you as it echoed off the canal walls.

"After buying the fruit, we gradually made our way toward the ship. As we reached the docks, I saw the beautiful white ship with its blue smokestack with a golden C engraved on it. Near the boarding area, the ship's immense size created a white wall that almost blocked out the sky. With butterflies in my stomach, we boarded the ship and were escorted to our stateroom. It was an outside cabin with a balcony. The porter brought in our bags and Michael offered him a tip. As I looked around what would be my home for the next week, I was surprised at how much I was looking forward to this trip. I was filled with excited anticipation. We decided to go up on deck to see the ship depart. We stood at the railing as the ship pulled out of port. The sun was just setting. The sky filled with a multitude of shades of red, orange, and purple and its rays cast a golden glow on St. Paul's Cathedral and the entire Venice skyline. Even though my nerves were on edge, the sudden beauty of the scene brought a sense of peace into my heart.

"Returning to our room to dress for dinner, we found that our bags had been unpacked. All my clothes were hung in the closet, and opening a drawer revealed all my finery was placed neatly inside. I glanced over at Michael and he smiled back at me and remarked, 'I think I will take a stroll around the deck.' I was moved by his attentive understanding. He knew that I was still nervous and uncomfortable in undressing in front of him. I quickly dressed in a tea-length royal blue flowered wrap dress. I was seated at the dressing table touching up my makeup when Michael returned. I watched in the mirror as he came up behind me and caressed my shoulders. After changing in the bathroom, Michael returned and again I watched as he came up behind me holding a jewelry box in his hands. He leaned forward, kissed my neck, opened the box, and placed a teardrop sapphire on a silver chain around my neck. I gasped at its delicate beauty and watched as the light caught and sparkled off the stone. I finished putting on my earrings and placed my mother's sapphire dinner ring on my finger and stood up to express my thanks. Kissing Michael softly on the lips, he drew me closer, and the kiss deepened, causing my insides to exchange the nervous butterflies for a heat that spread throughout my body. Michael broke the kiss and commented that if we continued we would miss dinner, though he wouldn't mind if we could pick up where we left off when we returned. We left the cabin laughing like children, and all through dinner, the looks that passed between us were filled with silent messages. I felt like a bride on her wedding night walking arm and arm around the deck, looking at the golden moon laying a shimmering path across the water."

"Upon entering the stateroom, a bucket of champagne and glasses were waiting for us. The pop of the cork exploded across the room as the champagne bubbled up and over the bottle top just like an erupting volcano.

Michael poured two glasses and after giving me mine, he raised his and said, and 'To the loveliest lady I know and love. May our journey together start tonight, and may we be blessed with smooth sailing now and in the future.' He tapped his glass to mine, took a sip, and then leaned over and gave me a quick kiss. We talked over the events of the day as we finished off the champagne. I then went into the bathroom and changed. I glanced in the mirror and almost didn't recognize myself, but standing before me was a woman dressed in a black lace peignoir set with silver white hair cut short and eyes that were sparkling with excitement."

"With some trepidation, I re-entered the bedroom. Michael was out on the balcony smoking a cigar. He flicked it away as he turned to me and said, 'Mi Bella' in a soft whisper. Placing his hand behind my head, he grazed my lips as he murmured, 'You're beautiful.' His soft kisses rained over my face, and he returned gently to kiss my lips. Like a flower, I opened slowly to welcome his kisses, which became more ardent as his tongue delved in and danced with mine. There was a stirring in my stomach, a smoldering fire that his kisses were fanning into a roaring flame. While his kisses were occupied with my face, his hands had begun to explore my body. I couldn't help but thank myself for all the exercise routines of the past. As his kisses deepened and began to travel past my neck, he slid the strap of my peignoir off. Gently fondling my breast, his tongue circled my nipple, and his teeth pulled, causing me to gasp in pleasure. My back arched, trying to get closer to ease the ache building up inside me. I felt as if at any moment I would burst up in flames. Michael rose over me and his thrust was met with a glorious cry of welcome. We entered the dance, each meeting the other's movements until we established a rhythm that brought me to a climax. Soon after, Michael followed and we lay satiated in each other's arms. I drew a chuckle from Michael when I said, 'I might not be able to walk tomorrow.'

"The next five days were filled with sightseeing during the day and romantic dinners in the evening. Our first stop of the cruise was Bari, Italy. There was only a four-hour time allotment to do any sightseeing. We walked to the church of St. Nicholas and toured the interior. I found its gray walls and small windows made the church dark and dreary and wasn't that impressed with the bony skeleton encased in glass. We meandered down the narrow cobblestone streets, stopping at a local butcher shop. It was fun using a combination of signs and pointing to purchase cheese, grapes, a sliced pepperoni, and a loaf of bread. Michael purchased a small bottle of wine. As we walked back to the port, we sat on a stone wall with the harbor filled with ships at our back. We munched on our impromptu lunch, enjoying the view and the comings and goings of the people in the square. Eventually we made our way back to the ship."

"The next two days we visited the ruins of Ephesus and the city of Istanbul. In Istanbul, we left the ship early and Michael haggled with a taxi driver to take us around the city. Our first stop was the Topkapi Palace. It was the primary residence of the Ottoman Sultans and their harems for over 400 years. We toured beautifully decorated rooms. I admired a huge pendant with a diamond in the center the size of a large egg. The sultan's chair, with thousands of jewels inlaid on all sides-pearls, rubies, sapphires, and turquoise-stood out against a red velvet background. I found it interesting that the most guarded object in the palace was the partial skull and arm believed to belong to John the Baptist. Michael and I discussed all that we saw as we traveled to the Blue Mosque. There is simplicity in the beauty of the Blue Mosque, from the view we had gazed at upon entering the harbor the night before, to seeing the beautiful blue tiles inside on the walls and ceilings as we entered. We were given plastic bags to put our shoes in. As I walked through, I was moved by the impressive interior. Everywhere you looked, from the intricate gold gates that were decorated in Arabic style to the stained-glass windows that sent light blue beams of light shining down on the floor, to the people reverently praying on prayer rugs, all I saw impressed me."

"We left the mosque and after putting our shoes back on, Michael and I made our way across the plaza where street vendors, were trying to sell their wares. We entered the Aga Sophia, which we found to be quite stark in comparison to the Blue Mosque. The church had plain walls with a few mosaics. We were told of a legend about sticking our thumb in a hole worn in a pillar which would bring us good luck and a safe return. We ended our tour with a stop at The Spice Bazaar, and then visited The Grand Bazaar, which is one of the largest and oldest enclosed markets in the world. Our taxi driver told us to write our entrance spot down, for many foreigners got lost in the vastness of the market. The interior was separated into squares and had sixty- one streets, with each square having many vendors selling similar souvenirs. When you turned a corner it would look very similar to street you were just on. With over 3,000 shops, the vendors expected you to haggle over the price of the item you planned to buy. We learned that each day over 250,000 customers entered the marketplace. Michael and I enjoyed arguing with one particular vendor over the price of some lovely silk scarves. We exchanged price bids at another shop and finally bought some beautiful plates with a design similar to those we saw in the Blue Mosque. After purchasing a few other small gifts for friends and family, we asked a policeman for directions to our entrance. Safely outside, we made our way to our waiting guide, loaded the car with our packages and traveled back to the ship."

"That evening we sat at the captain's table and then went gambling in the ship's casino. After several enjoyable hours of play at the blackjack table and then slot machines, I left a happy, but exhausted traveler and made my way back to our cabin. My pocket jingled with all the coins, and upon entering the cabin, I filled the tub with bath salts and settled in with a sigh to the soothing comfort."

"After dressing in a new deep purple peignoir set, I was sitting at the dressing table brushing my hair when Michael returned. Smiling, he placed a kiss on my shoulder and dropped a large amount of coins in my lap. 'A wonderful night spent in enjoyment and pleasure. I feel as if I have won the big prize.' Michael gazed lovingly at me as this was said. Speaking his native French he continued to express his feelings and his love for me."
'Mon ami, votre beauté qui m'étonne et m'a apporté beaucoup de chance ce soir à mes gains à la table. Aussi vous avez mis une lumière in ma vie j'ai pensé que j'avais perdu. Vous êtes une femme à l'intérieur et je veux express mon amour pour vous. Veuillez vous hare mon lit avec moi Ce soir?' ('My friend, your beauty amazes me and has brought me much luck tonight in my winnings at the table. You have put a light in my life I believed that I had lost. You are a beautiful woman inside and out, and I want to express my love for you. Please will you share my bed with me tonight?')

"I thought nothing could outdo our first evening together, but Michael was incredible in his quest to fulfill my needs. Gasping for breath, I cried out as his hands brought forth my first climax of the evening. We acted like young lovers as we explored each other's bodies for the rest of the evening. Falling into a deep slumber, I awoke to the sound of seagulls outside my window. With a smile, I made my way to have breakfast with Michael."

"The next few days were spent exploring Olympia and Athens. Michael shared his knowledge about each of the city's history and points of interest. We enjoyed climbing up to the Acropolis as much as shopping in the great shopping plaza. Michael's attentiveness toward me made me feel very treasured. I had to learn not to show him I liked something because when I did, the item appeared at the dinner table or on the bed as if he was a magic genie. I never thought that I could love someone again after Jean, but the affection between Michael and me began to blossom into a different kind of love. We had a natural companionship that enabled us to discuss any subject. Enjoying our differences of opinion as well as finding out we had much in common made our conversations lively and often filled with laughter. We also shared a great love for our families and also for the arts. By the end of the cruise, we had gone from a caring relationship to a deep and abiding love. "After the cruise I returned to Bellaire only for a very short time. Michael had asked me to move in with him, and I graciously accepted. He had a lovely cottage by the sea, and I immediately fell in love with the ocean view out his kitchen window. The cottage was located in Honfleur, a seaport town located eight miles north of Deauville. The house overlooked the harbor, which always had a vast array of colorful sailboats docked along the quays. The interior was open and airy, but it was the exterior gardens that surprised and amazed anyone who came to visit. Michael was an avid gardener. He had a beautiful rose garden with more than forty different varieties. They ranged from a long-stem red rose that was the size of a teacup when in full bloom to a short-stem white rose that was delicate in size and fragrance. I quickly developed a favorite: a yellow rose of medium size that opened to a creamy center. It had a lovely scent and I would often cut one to put in a vase to place on my bedside table. In addition to the rose garden, there was an herb garden, a vegetable garden, and several perennial gardens that provided colorful blooms to adorn different tables in the house. When we weren't traveling, every morning Michael was out working in his gardens. After doing my morning routine, I would walk out onto the patio and offer to help. Most mornings he wouldn't need any, and I would sit in the sun with a cup of coffee and Ballerina on my lap watching him move among the plants. Michael had planted a garden around the patio that had flowers to attract butterflies. There was many a pleasant morning watching for butterflies and recording their size and color in a little book. I had purchased a book to help me try to identify them. Often we were surprised with a hummingbird visiting the flowers. They were amazing little creatures, with their small bodies and tiny fluttering wings.

"We would sit down to breakfast and plan out our day. During this time Michael began to show me his diverse investments, and I began to learn how to invest in the stock market. At first I would do it on paper, watching and marking its progress for a month or two. Eventually Michael convinced me I was ready, and I purchased my first group of stocks. I nervously watched the up-and-down progress, and I gradually built up quite a portfolio. I didn't know it then, but these investments would come to my rescue in later years.

"In October the family gathered for LJ and Yvette's wedding. Irene and Leslie arrived with their whole family. I was enchanted with my great-grand- babies and amazed at how the family had grown. There were fourteen people that came from the U.S. We miraculously found rooms for all of them.

"Irene and I spent a few hours together discussing the events of the past year. She was still active in the protest movement against the war and had just participated in a march on Washington, D.C., that encompassed over half a million people. We discussed her two young boys. Peter was ready to come to Paris, and I promised to contact my friends and get him a placement.

"Bermont and Sasha were busy checking on the final touches for the wedding, but there still was plenty of time to sit and talk about what was happening in and around Bellaire and their children's lives. The conversation flowed among us, filled with laughter and comical antidotes about the coming and goings of all the grandchildren. Irene and Leslie entertained us with stories of a music festival called Woodstock that was held in New York. Irene had taken both Peter and Richard and drove over to the festival, where they were joined by over 400,000 other teenagers. The boys really enjoyed the music, but the lack of sanitary services, drugs and out-of-control crowds created havoc. The boys actually enjoyed themselves. Irene hadn't while it was happening, but was full of funny stories now that she had survived it. She was 68 years old but she didn't look it, especially when she was dressed in her t-shirts and peasant skirts, along with her multiple pierced ears and short cropped hair. When standing next to her boys, she looked more like their older sister that their mother.

"On the day of the wedding, Michael and I drove over to Bellaire. The day was cold, but the sun was out. Bermont and LJ were on the front steps to greet us when we arrived. Greetings were called out as the whole family gathered together and pictures were taken. Jan was struggling to keep the girls from getting messy and let out a sigh of relief when it was time to leave for the church. We all made our way to the pews, and LJ and Leo left to go to the front of the church. Soon organ music played 'Ode to Joy' as the attendants walked down the aisle. Dressed all in pink, they carried white roses tied with yellow ribbons. We all rose to watch as Yvette came down the aisle in a stunning gossamer gown of white silk covered in lace and pearls. Her eyes shimmered with tears as she passed. The ceremony was traditional, and soon the minister was telling LJ that he could kiss his bride. Then we were off to the reception, where good food and great company made for an enjoyable evening. Everyone gathered to throw birdseed at the couple as they departed for their honeymoon.

"I spent the next several days talking with and catching up with the comings and goings of all the grandchildren. It was good to have babies around again, and I spent hours enjoying their company and playing with them. As always, the week went by too quickly, and the U.S. entourage had to head home. We said our goodbyes and I promised to visit next year. Elizabeth, who was four months pregnant, wanted me at the baby's baptism, which was in the beginning of May. As Michael and I had plans to go to the Kentucky Derby, I said the two events should coincide.

"With the new decade starting in 1970, many new faces would appear in the family. Elizabeth had a daughter that she named Mary Ann. Peter came to France; he was extremely excited with his new job working with the Paris Ballet and his idol, Rudolph Nureyev.

"In late April, Michael and I flew to the U.S. We visited with Irene and Leslie and participated in the celebration of the baptism of Mary Ann. A picture was taken of the four generations of girls, with me in the center; Irene, Joan, and Victoria on my left, and Elizabeth holding Mary Ann dressed in the family christening gown, with her sister, Karen beside her,"

"We left Watch Hill and traveled to Kentucky to attend the 100th running of the Kentucky Derby. Bermont had asked Michael check out a horse named My Dad George for possible stud services. I was excited just to be at the derby, but I was also interested in the first woman jockey to participate in the race. Diane Crump was going to be on a horse named Fathom. We went and placed our bets, then made our way to the viewing stands. I found the atmosphere in the stands to be quite disorderly, with spectators heavily drinking and being very boisterous. I had dressed in my black and white outfit with its matching wide-brimmed hat with the black feathers and a brand-new pair of spiked heels. Many times Michael had to catch me from falling, as I was pushed by someone trying to get somewhere, and they were not looking where they were going."

"The horses were led around the track and guided into the starting gate.

Each jockey was colorfully dressed in their different color silks, and the horses pranced and stepped sideways, showing their excitement over what was to come. We waited with anticipation for the announcer to say, 'And now they're off.' When the race started, the roar of the crowd was deafening. As the horses exited the gate, several horses bumped Dust Commander, the horse I'd bet on, and tried to block him in the back. Soon the exciting atmosphere had me cheering loudly for my horse to win. He began to advance on the inside of the pack for the first half-mile. Continuing to gain ground at the final turn, he emerged between two horses, and galloping down the final stretch, he surged forward and crossed the finish line. My Dad George, who seemed to be slow at the start, followed Dust Commander over the finish line. Michael was excited, and he was looking forward to negotiating breeding him with Bellaire horses. High Echelon came in third running an amazing race after being forced to come from the outside. The rest of the pack made their way over the finish line. I stood marking my program as each horse passed. I loved all the different names: Silent Queen; Admiral's Shield; Corn off the Cob; Personality; Terlarge; Holy Land; who tripped and fell, but got up and finished; Rancho Logos; George Lewis; Robus Bug; and Naska. Diane Crump came in 15th."

"We made our way to the betting area to collect our winnings. We then headed back to our hotel room to get ready for dinner and our meeting with the owners of Dust Commander and My Dad George. After some negotiation, we came to an agreement to breed the following spring.

"The next morning we left Kentucky and traveled to New York. I had made arrangements to visit with my friends at the theater, and Michael was meeting with the computer company executives. In 1969 the company had developed a cell battery and they were working on a video game. He came back to our rooms excited about the new technology, and we discussed what to invest in and how much. He was quite excited about a thing called e-mail that was being developed but wasn't completed yet.

"We finished off our trip by returning to Seagull's Perch and the wedding of Karen to Dr. Ronald Gauthier. Ronald was a veterinarian for small animals; Karen had met him while doing her internship for college.

They were planning on opening a veterinary hospital after Karen graduated from Johnson & Wales University in 1971.

"In a simple A-line gown with tiny daisies forming a ring around her waist, Karen carried a bouquet of daisies in her hands and a crown of daisies in her hair. She looked like a woodland nymph walking down the path to the beach. She walked through the aisle of chairs filled with family and guests to join Ronald at the edge of the shore; they exchanged their vows with the sounds of waves and seagulls in the background. Everyone stood and clapped as they were pronounced husband and wife and exchanged the traditional kiss. They walked up the aisle together. The family and guests followed them back up the path to enjoy an informal reception on the back lawn. With tables heavy with an array of food and wine, the party continued until well into the night. Everyone danced and exchanged family news with each other. I enjoyed watching everyone enjoy themselves, especially Victoria. She danced around the room in her fancy yellow dress, never stopping for a minute to rest. She had used up so much energy that she fell asleep on a wicker chair on the porch. Jan picked her up and carried her inside to bed. Michael and I joined in the festivities and enjoyed the music, but then getting tired; we left the youngsters to their merriment and retired to bed also.

"We returned home just in time to welcome LJ and Yvette's baby boy, whom they named Joshua, into the world. A beautiful chubby baby with the Le Blanc green eyes, he was the joy of his grandparents. At his christening, Peter came, bringing with him Charles Wentworth III; it was obvious that they were a couple." Varvara paused. "Peter loved that boy. Such a handsome young man, so sad, he died so young. Varvara seemed to be thinking out loud; then she continued.

"Peter kept us entertained with stories about the Paris Theater and members of the Paris Ballet. He absolutely loved holding Joshua." Varvara's voice softened and she paused as if thinking and then continued. "Often during his visit, his beautiful baritone voice could be heard singing a lullaby to the baby. He was missed when he left to go on tour with Nureyev in Australia."

"As Varvara continued to reveal her past, it was often told in a shaky quiver-and even more so lately-that it caused the family to be quite concerned. As she began talking the next day those who listened weren't sure if it was the subject or her health that caused the shaky and disjointed speech, but still Varvara continued on.

Turning Point

Jan, Victoria, and Angelique all were talking with Varvara's nurse about their concern with Varvara's deterring health and her struggle to breathe while telling her story. After checking with the Dr., she informed them to just take it slow and give her plenty of breaks. They all gathered to hear her as she started again.

"In November we learned that Charles De Gaul had passed away. It was a somber time that brought back memories of World War II and how it had changed our lives." Varvara's voice drifted. Everyone struggled to hear her thoughts: Jean … so proud … to be part of De Gaul's staff. Aurele … and Irene … baby … yet what courage. Lost too soon … Leslie, the handsome American. Yves dashing back into our home. Worries … little fuel … shortages of food. All the destruction … the losses." As if startled, she looked around the room and then continued. "His funeral had many dignitaries in attendance. At the end of the service, the bells in the churches all over France tolled.

"The early '70's didn't affect our lives that much. Michael and I followed the dressage competitions around the French countryside, watching Leo and Jacqueline compete against each other. Jacqueline's mother and her sister had come to terms with Michael's and my relationship, and we often sat in the stands together. It was obvious that there would be a family connection with the developing romance between Leo and Jackie. In early December, we learned of the death of my godmother Mathilda Kchessingke. It saddened me not only because of her loss, but it also was the end of an era. The Paris ballet was no longer made up of ex-Russian Ballerinas. We attended the funeral and I said goodbye to one of the last links I had to my mother."

"The year did end on a happier note with the birth of a baby girl to Karen and Ronald. They named her Sally.'

"During the following year, both Leo and Jackie tried to qualify for the 1972 Olympic Equestrian Team but were not successful. Michael arranged for us to go to the equestrian events anyway, and there were seven of us that arrived in Munich. We traveled to the Nymphenburg Palace; it was the original summer palace for the Bavarian rulers. The palace was a vast stone structure with red roofs. All equestrian events were to be held there. While we were there, we toured the court stables. Antique carriages and sleighs once owned by King Ludwig V were on display. As we walked through the exhibit, we marveled at the intricate work and impressive craftsmanship that was evident even in some of the oldest vehicles. Along with the carriages, there was a collection of Nymphenburg porcelain on display.

"We were disappointed that the French Equestrian Team didn't win any medals, but we thoroughly enjoyed the competitions. While we were attending the equestrian events, a tragedy was taking place at the Olympic village. Such a waste … They died so young … Evil men exist everywhere." Again, Varvara seemed to be speaking her thoughts, but then she snapped back into her story.

"We learned that Israeli athletes were taken hostage by a terrorist group. Eleven athletes and coaches, along with one German police officer, were killed during a failed rescue attempt. Five of the eight terrorists were also killed. It was a very sad and quiet group that returned home to Bellaire."

Stephanie called a halt to the filming. Everyone in the room looked at Varvara's nurse with worried expressions.

"I will take Varvara upstairs and get her settled. Call Dr. Simon and let him know what is happening."

It wasn't even a half-hour before Dr. Simon came. He did a thorough examination of Varvara and joined the family gathered in the great room.

"Varvara's heart is just wearing out. It's not pumping correctly, which causes less oxygen to get to the brain; this causes the confusion and makes her tire easily. She knows that she has only a little time left, and I know that getting these memoires done is really important to her. Take each day as it comes. If she tires, stop, but don't smother her. She always has been an independent woman."

Stephanie came back the next day and Varvara began talking.

"In February Irene called to tell me her baby got married on St. Valentine's Day. I wasn't surprised-Richard had introduced me to Christina when I was in the U.S." Varvara stopped talking and sat quietly looking out the window, and then she began talking again. "Though just teenagers, they had a special spark and every time I talked with him, every other word was Christina this or Christina that." Again, there were a few minutes of silence, and then she began again. "I got a chance to talk to them both and wished them much happiness. Irene reminded me of the upcoming celebrations being held in July, and checked to see if we were all going to come."

"My favorite American holiday is the Fourth of July. In 1976 the holiday was celebrated in a much grander scale because it was the bicentennial year. For months all my phone conversations with Irene's family were about the plans being made for the fourth. Even in Europe there was talk about the tall ships race and the planned Parade of Ships that was to sail up the coast and arrive in Newport. Irene and Leslie were busy planning a large family reunion. Michael and I, along with his daughters and their families and Bermont, Sasha, and the boys came, to the U.S. The whole family gathered on the beach for a huge cookout. As usual, tables were filled with food and beverages. A huge bonfire was lit in the evening. We all sat around it and watched as the sky filled with a multitude of colors from the fireworks. The following morning we made our own little parade of cars as we traveled into Newport to watch the ship parade. Tim, Jan and Peter were sailing amongst the ships on the family sailboat, the Ballet Slipper II."

"The rest of the family gathered along the shore to watch the ships' parade. It was a pretty awesome site just looking at the ship's three masts with their big puffy sails. The ships had just come from a race and they represented several countries including Russia, Argentina, England, and the USA. After leaving Newport the ships would travel up to Boston. It was a joyful time with the whole family gathered in one place. I watched over the entire group proud of the family Jean and I had created. It was a happy event that we all enjoyed.

"In early January, Michael came down with a terrible sore throat. His hacking cough echoed throughout the corners of the house and seemed to shake the very bones of his body. Taking him to the doctor and after several tests, we were told he had lymphoma. Unfortunately, it was throughout his body and nothing could be done. It seemed as if in a day, my once strong and healthy companion became a weak and fragile shell of himself. With the help of medication, the hacking cough left, but in its place was an awful wheezing sound as Michael struggled to get air into his lungs. He made it through that winter, but it was obvious that Michael's condition wasn't improving. We couldn't go anywhere without his oxygen tank, and

Michael just hated it. He'd rather stay at home and we slowly stopped going out. His daughters and grandchildren visited often and brought a brief reprieve of laughter into our lives. I painfully watched his struggle for breath for six long months and tearfully said goodbye in late spring. I walked out onto our back patio and thought how ironic it was that the air was fresh and filled with the sweet aroma of Michael's roses. As I walked about the garden, I arrived at Michael's favorite rose, and as I reached up to cut off a slightly opened bud, a single drop of water spilt from its petal. It was as if his roses were crying at his passing. The ever-efficient Michael had everything arranged, and after a small gathering of family for a brief memorial service, he was laid to rest beside his beloved wife."

"I spent several months grieving over the loss of Michael. Walking through our home, I would often turn to tell him something only to realize he was gone. In late summer Irene called and insisted I come to the States for an extended visit. Though I protested, even Bermont added his encouragement for me to go. So I came and again found peace along the Atlantic shore."

"In October of 1977, Nureyev went to New York to film an episode of the Muppets. Irene came into the great room and told me in an excited voice that Peter and Charles were coming to visit and were bringing Nureyev with them. After they finished the filming in New York, they drove up to spend the weekend at Seagull's Perch. They arrived just in time for dinner and kept us entertained with stories of how the filming went. Swearing us to secrecy because the actual show would not air until January of the next year, we heard about the six hours of filming it took to record just the dance scene with a large pig. Loud laughter could be heard echoing off the walls of the dining room as they told tales of Miss Piggy attacking Nureyev with kisses in the steam room. I sat at the table enjoying the camaraderie, and then we moved to the great room to have coffee in front of the fireplace. I couldn't believe how rusty I was in my attempt to speak Russian with Nureyev, but it soon came back. We talked of the old country, and he expressed his need to return to Russia to visit his mom. I told him that I would pray that he could soon have that wish granted."

"For the rest of the weekend, different members of the family came and went. They were all interested in meeting Nureyev, but also, in spending time with Peter and Charles, who didn't get home very often. It was during this time that I noticed that Charles seemed to tire very easily. Peter said he had had a cold for several weeks and that's why he was tired. It seemed as if they had just arrived and it was time for them to go. Wishing them well, I told Peter and Charles that I would see them in the spring at Easter."

"In 1978, on January 23rd, I sat in in the family room with a group of the grandchildren and watched The Muppet Show. Knowing what was to happen, as each scene appeared on the TV, memories came back of that dinner spent with Nureyev, Peter, and Charles the October before. I continued to follow Nureyev's career which had Peter and Charles traveling back and forth across the ocean."

"Richard and Christina had a son they named William. Elizabeth's son Nicholas married Safiya. There wasn't much else that happened that year … Hmm … Large unemployment … dollar not worth much … lost some money. … Oh, Irene's favorite car, the Beetle, was stopped being made. She was so mad. Who has her last little Bug?" Varvara looked around the room. Karen's youngest daughter, Alycia, at just sixteen, spoke up and said she did.

Varvara nodded. "Good. She would like that her granddaughter was using it."

"At the end of the year, I returned to my home in France."

"1979 wasn't much different than ` 78. Irene was still very involved in politics and we had many discussions over the changes that were happening all over the world. In January, the Cambodian government fell. It was discovered that during the Khmer Rouge regime over 1.5 to 2 million people were killed. Mass gravesites were discovered in fields that were soon called the "killing fields." Irene was very upset that another, genocide had happened."

"We talked often, and she was always informing me about something: The Iranian government was taken over in February by Ayatollah Khomeini, Margaret Thatcher was voted the new British prime minister, and the Soviet invasion of Afghanistan started in December. She was quite pleased about Thatcher and also about Mother Teresa wining the Nobel Peace Prize.

"We entered into the new year of 1980 not knowing that events that would happen in this year would be like a sculptor with a chisel carving away the past to reveal a new and different world." After she finished talking, Varvara bowed her head and let out a long sigh. It was getting more difficult for her to talk, and Stephanie called it a day. A tired Varvara was guided out of the room to rest.

Stephanie and Angelique exchanged glances as Varvara left.

"I'm worried about her. Her energy seems to fade much faster than when we first started. I'm worried we won't finish this," said Stephanie.

"I am too," replied Angelique. "She gets frailer each time I see her. Yet I know how determined she is to finish this and to see me get married. I have to go tomorrow to make the reception hall arrangements. I'm wishing the days away and yet there is still so much to be done."

Angelique was as anxious as a racehorse at the starting gate when she woke up on Saturday morning, knowing she was finally going to see the restored Ocean House. Plans had been made for Varvara, Jan, Victoria, Angelique, and Vari to go to lunch at the new restaurant inside the hotel. After lunch, Victoria and Angelique had an appointment with the wedding coordinator to discuss the reception and to reserve rooms for some of the guests and wedding party.

A handsome valet attendant warmly greeted them as they exited their cars onto the circular driveway. As they climbed up the circular stairs, more staff stood and said, "Welcome to Ocean house." A doorman held the door for them and they entered the foyer. A concierge welcomed them again, asking what he could help them with.

Angelique, in her enthusiasm, answered, "We're here for lunch. I'm getting married. I've wanted to see the inside for so long! I can't wait to look around!"

Smiling, he directed them toward the restaurant at the end of the hall. "I feel like I'm going back in time," said Victoria.

"This reminds me of the opening scene of the Titanic," whispered Angelique in awe.

"Oh! I know just what you mean. When the doors opened to the staircase," replied Victoria with a smile.

As they slowly moved into what they later learned was called the living room, they admired the décor. The walls were painted a soft yellow, and the hardwood floors were impeccably polished. Glancing left and right, they noticed several small seating areas. One, on the right, had a large coffee table with a chess board set up on it. A baby grand piano was behind the couch. Large white and blue pots filled with plants were so many feet apart on each side. On the left side, there were more comfortable seating arrangements: A cushioned bench lined with an assortment of colorful throw pillows in shades of blue and yellow, above which large windows provided a panoramic view of the wraparound porch, the sweeping lawns, and in the background the Atlantic Ocean. At the end of the bench, there was a huge fireplace made of tan stone. Arriving at this, they were greeted by the hostess, and guided through the bar area, which also echoed the blue and yellow theme with bar stools covered in blue leather.

They entered the restaurant and were seated at a large round table covered in white and gold linen tablecloths. The high cushioned chairs were quite comfortable. A young waitress dressed in a yellow plaid shirt and white apron came and took the lunch order. Another waiter filled the water glasses. Every attention to detail was met. While seated, the women admired the cobalt blue lanterns hanging from the ceiling and the view of the ocean. Jan was pointing out to Vari Block Island and Mantauk, New York.

They all enjoyed a leisurely lunch, and then Jan took Varvara and Vari home, while Victoria and Angelique met with the wedding coordinator, Mary DeVizia, who gave them a guided tour of the hotel. They were shown a deluxe oceanfront room, which had painted walls in a soft yellow. The king-size bed had a plush pillow top European feather mattress. Angelique chuckled and said she'd need a ladder just to get into it. There was a large flat-screen TV on one wall and a fireplace on another. In front of the fireplace was a sitting area that included a couch, chair, and coffee table. Classical music played softly in the background. The impressive bathroom drew a gasp from Victoria as she glanced from the deep white marble tub, to the black and white tile, to a small flat screen TV. White shutters were open to reveal an opening, made to look like a window, which allowed you to see right into the bedroom. A small balcony was off the bedroom and you had a partial view of the ocean.

Leaving the guest suite, Angelique commented on the beautiful artwork hanging on the walls. Mary said that throughout the building, there was over one million dollars' worth of art, a large portion owned by the owner of the hotel.

Continuing with the tour, they were shown conference rooms, the restored elevator, and the private member club. Walking down a spiral staircase, they entered the OH! Spa. A number of services were listed in an elegant pamphlet. They walked through the fitness center and then were shown the heated saltwater pool. From there, all that was left to see were the reception rooms. Back in Mary's office, they went over all the particulars, choosing the dinner menu and exchanging information about vendors and the florist. Both Victoria and Angelique were impressed with the thoroughness to details. Driving home, they discussed all the plans that had been made and were even more excited about the upcoming wedding.

As Varvara entered the room the next day, everyone was surprised by how refreshed she looked. The tired lines around the eyes were not so prominent, and she seemed to have more energy. Angelique kissed her cheek and noted how good she looked.

Varvara smiled and replied, "I had a talk with myself and decided I needed to finish things here, and I am going to do it."

Angelique laughed and said, "If anyone can do it, Mémère, it would be you.

You've always set an example of how to stand strong against any odds." So the filming began again.

"The day had started out just like any other day. I remember the sun was shining. We had just finished our work for the morning and were enjoying a much-needed cup of tea, when the sounds of the telephone ringing disrupted the quiet peace we had been enjoying. Bermont rose to answer it. We overheard his response.

"Oh, my God! ... No. I understand ... Yes, we will be on the next available flight ... No, and I'll tell her ... I can't believe it ... Okay, yes, as soon as we can!' Bermont sadly walked into the parlor to the questioning faces of Varvara and Sasha.

"'Irene and Leslie took off this morning for their trip to Nova Scotia,' Bermont said. 'Their plane disappeared off the radar and it's believed they crashed into the ocean. The Coast Guard is out searching, but so far nothing has been found. That was Jan on the phone. We have to call Peter in Paris. I'll arrange for a flight. It doesn't look good, Mom.' Bermont choked out the last words as tears filled up his eyes."

"Within hours, we were on a plane heading for the U.S. The flight seemed extremely long, as my fears and worries prevented me from resting. The six-hour flight felt like twenty as we touched down at New York's LaGuardia Airport. Gathering up our things, we made our way out of the plane. Bermont had called to check if there was any news while we went and waited for our luggage. He reported nothing had changed. After a two-hour drive to Watch Hill, an exhausted group entered the great room only to be surrounded by the family already in attendance. After a few moments Jan, quietly updated us with what she knew.

"'The Coast Guard believes that they went down somewhere close to Martha's Vineyard off the coast of Cape Cod. They haven't found any evidence of the crash or the plane. They've been searching for it the last twenty-four hours and nothing.'

"Elizabeth's husband Harrison spoke next. 'We double-checked that plane before they took off. Everything was top-notch. I don't understand any of this.' Visibly shaken, he walked over to stare out the window.

"There was conversation amongst the children telling me about how happy Irene and Leslie were the day before. Excited to be going away, they had dinner with the family and said their goodbyes. They had planned their flight to get them to Nova Scotia around seven p.m.

"'Jan said, 'Mom and Dad gave me a kiss goodbye. Mom said she would call when she got to the hotel. I told them to have a safe trip.'

"I responded, 'I know it looks bad, and we have to prepare ourselves for the worst, but still pray for a miracle. We can hope that they can still be out there somewhere.'

"The shrill of the telephone ringing was like a gunshot, causing everyone to jump and then freeze in anticipation of the news that it might bring. Jan picked up the phone and the family listened to the one-sided conversation.

"Yes, I understand. …Okay. …Yes, we're all here. …Yes, they just arrived. … Okay. …Yes, right away. …Thank you. …Goodbye."

"Hanging up the phone, Jan turned and, with tears filling up her eyes, she told the family what she had just heard.

"'A piece of the plane washed ashore on Coast Guard Beach. Also, some pieces were found floating near there. The Coast Guard hasn't found any sign of Mom or Dad.'

"With this news, there was a haunting silence that was soon broken by the sound of people crying.

"Most of the grandchildren were too young to understand and were playing quietly on the floor in the great room. Victoria, at nine, knew something was wrong when she heard the crying. She made her way over to her mother and asked what was happening. Jan quietly told her of the news they just heard.

"There was no news for the rest of that day and evening, nor 'til late afternoon of the following day. The Coast Guard called again and informed Jan the status of the search was changing from search and rescue to search and recovery. More pieces of the plane were washing ashore on Cape Cod, including a suitcase and a plastic bag of Irene's vitamins and pills. On Thursday, the main part of the plane was found. It was confirmed that both Irene and Leslie's bodies were in the plane. Divers were sent down to recover the bodies.

"It was a devastating blow to the whole family. A small part of each and every one of us had been hoping for miracle. Now faced with reality, it was difficult to accept that they were really gone.

"I was looking out the window at the beach when I heard Peter speak up that he remembered that his dad had mentioned liking 'Amazing Grace.' This started a discussion about the funeral. We made a list of items that needed to be done and divided them amongst ourselves."

"I called Smith's Floral Shop and spoke with them about the flower arrangements. Irene had loved yellow roses, and Leslie's favorite flower was a carnation. Using the flowers, I ordered casket covers for each of them. I then ordered large arrangements for the children and great-grandchildren.

"The children informed me that Leslie wanted to be buried in his uniform. The girls went to Irene's closet and chose a beautiful blue wool suit that was a favorite of their mother's. Taking both outfits, Bermont drove them over to the funeral parlor.

"Jan contacted the caterers and ordered platters of sandwiches and a buffet of hot food to be set up in the great room in preparation of the dinner after the funeral. It was an exhausted group that came together in the evening to check in and make sure everything was completed.

"I remember that I left the group and made my way to my room. I was followed by the sound of Ballerina's claws tapping down the hallway. That night I tossed and turned for several hours and then went down to the kitchen. The house was eerily silent, and as I approached the kitchen, I found the lights were already on. As I entered, I saw Bermont sitting holding a cup of tea in his hands.

"'Let me make you a cup of tea, Mom. So, you couldn't sleep either? Every time I close my eyes, scenes of Irene and I flash through my mind. I even thought of Aurele and how much I still miss him. Now both are gone. How do you do it? You have gone through this more than I. It feels as if someone has stuck a knife in me and cut away a piece of my heart.'

"'It never gets any easier," I replied. 'The only way I know is to have faith that they're in a better place and I'll see them again when it's my turn to die. I also believe that they are watching over us. Do I miss them? Yes, but I go on honoring them by living life to the fullest.'

"'I understand, but right now it just hurts too much.'

"Finishing my tea, I patted him on the shoulder and made my way back to my bedroom. This time I fell into an exhausted slumber, only to wake in the early morning hours.

"I entered the exercise room and wasn't surprised to find many people already there. After doing a series of stretches, I felt better and joined the others at the barre to start the morning dance routine. Doing the ballet moves didn't distract me from pondering what the rest of the day would bring.

"The day seemed to drag by slowly, but eventually it was time to go to the funeral parlor. Then, time seemed to be on fast-forward because the next thing I knew I was standing amongst the children greeting people as they passed and expressed their condolences.

"The next morning, I sat numb throughout the funeral services, barely hearing what was said or even the beautiful hymns that were sung. Sitting in the limo, we entered the graveyard and proceeded down the gravel driveway to the gravesite, which was located along the riverbank. There was a light breeze coming off the water, and the sun's rays cast a golden glare. Standing with the family during a brief gravesite ceremony, I looked up and saw a lonely seagull fly over our heads. We all then made our way back to Seagull's Perch. Friends and family seemed to stream through the house. The doorbell kept ringing, bringing the delivery of baskets of fruit, plants, and flowers.

"I remember watching it all transpire. I felt like I was looking at a scene being played out before me. I was numb with grief. I felt detached from what was happening. Days went by before I started functioning normally. Jan had received a call from the lawyer asking to come and read the will. The family again gathered in the great room to hear what the will said. There weren't any surprises. The children equally inherited the estate. The problems were in the death taxes and in the upkeep needed to maintain the house. Not a single child of Irene and Leslie's was able to take care of it. All eyes seemed to turn to me, asking for guidance. After much discussion between me, the children, the lawyer, it was decided that I would pay the taxes and buy the estate. It took several months to iron out the details, but I soon found I was the owner of Seagull's Perch.

'Thinking of my loss of Irene, my sadness nearly overwhelmed me. I was lucky that there were so many things that needed my attention, and it prevented me from wallowing in self-pity.

"I needed to return to France to take care of things there. Bermont and Sasha already had ownership of Bellaire, but I had to pack up my belongings in the cottage in Honfleur. I had offered the cottage to Leo and Jacqueline, who had been living in a tiny apartment near the horse training facility where Leo worked. They were both excited to be able to have a home of their own. I'd like to think that Michael was smiling down at my decision because Jacqueline was secretly his favorite and having her living in his home made sense. Now that both my homes in France were taken care of, all I had left were some business dealings in Paris. While in Paris, I visited with a few ballet friends who were still living there. On the last evening, I had a lovely dinner with Bermont's family. Joining us were Peter and Charles who had returned from the States. It was their lighthearted banter reminding us of funny stories involving Irene and Leslie that made the evening pass smoothly. As we were reminiscing about them, a sense of peace filled my heart. Irene may be gone from me physically, but I really carried her with me in my memories and in her children. I was going to America, and my new role would be the head of Irene's family.

"Adjustment to living in the U.S. was fairly easy. While I had been in France, Irene's girls had emptied out Irene and Leslie's suite. The first few months were spent working subtle changes to the décor to make the rooms my very own. It was also during that time that we had several family meetings to discuss the future of the different businesses that were left in limbo at their parent's death. The charter service was still running and was fairly busy with the upcoming summer season. Richard, who already was an established pilot and had been working under Leslie, wanted the chance to keep it going. We worked out a six-month trial period and then a payment plan for him to slowly buy the business for himself. El' Pointe, Irene's dance studio, would continue to be run by Elizabeth. She asked me if I would step in as advisor, filling Irene's shoes, and I agreed. The first few months were not easy as I tried to fill the huge gap in the family. I could only show my confidence in their ability to run the family businesses. It took a while, but we slowly adjusted to our lives.

"Watching the children grow was a constant joy for me. At the age of 86, I had seven grandchildren, nine great-grandchildren and six great-great- grandchildren. The older children filled my days with every sport imaginable, and the babies just brought me a source of peace as I held them in my arms and rocked them to sleep." Varvara stopped talking and just gazed around the room, pausing often to stare out the window. It was decided that it was a good place to stop filming for that day.

When Varvara started talking on Monday, she began talking about Peter and Nureyev. "In the early 1980s, Peter and Nureyev's dance troupe was in Berlin and Vienna. Then in April, they came back to New York to dance with the Martha Graham Dance Company at the Metropolitan Opera House. The boys came home to see me whenever they could, but the tour kept them traveling back and forth across the ocean until September of 1983. It was then that Nureyev was appointed the director of the Paris Opera Ballet. Peter and Charles were happy to be able to find an apartment and settle in one place. I didn't know it then, but Peter had kept me from knowing how ill Charles had become.

"It was during this time I began hearing rumors from my friends in the ballet of a strange new disease that was causing an illness that couldn't be controlled. Soon the AIDS epidemic would sweep through the arts community with a force of an invading army. This devastating disease would cause the loss of many talented people. Peter kept us informed of our friends and coworkers that began coming down with this illness. It was during one of these phone calls that Peter admitted that Charles was suffering from AIDS. Both he and Peter were tested. Charles' test was positive, and though he was HIV-positive, Peter didn't have AIDS. I was in constant contact with Peter, urging him to bring Charles home to Seagull's Perch. They always refused and they stayed in Paris.

"In 1984 I went to Paris, my usual trip to visit with friends and see the latest ballet. I was looking forward to seeing Peter and Charles. I was slightly concerned because of the last few conversations with Peter. I knew that Charles' condition was failing. Peter had been telling me everything was okay, but I didn't believe him. Upon arriving in Paris, I was shocked at Charles' appearance—or, I could've said, disappearance. He had been a tall, muscular, built man the last time I saw him, and now he was all but skin and bones. He had deep dark circles under his eyes; his cheeks were sunken in; his body was just a mass of skin and bones. Even his hair that was once always impeccably styled and never out of place was now sticking out in all directions. Often he would have to bend over because of a terrible hacking cough that would start deep in his chest and have him gasping for air by the time it was over. It was obvious that he was in the last stages of the disease. I was appalled at the change.

"Sitting in the kitchen with Peter, I asked. 'Is there anything that can be done?' Sadly with eyes filled with tears, he shook his head no. 'He's really weak and the doctors don't have any more answers. This dammed disease has taken several of my friends already, and Mémère, I don't want to lose him!" Peter sat down and sobbed.

"I sat down beside him and patted his shoulder, 'Life hands us all burdens that seem too heavy to carry. I'm sorry this is happening, and I'll do anything you need. Do you want to bring him home to Seagull's Perch?'

"No. Charles doesn't want to take a chance of giving AIDS to anyone in the family. That's why we haven't been coming to visit over the last two years. I have missed all of you.'

"At the time, no one really understood how the disease was contracted. I asked. 'Is there anything I can do for you here?"

"Thank you, Mémère, but all that can be done is being done. It's just good to see you.'

"I heard the sound of shuffling feet slowly making their way into the room, heralding the arrival of Charles, whose appearance still caused a shock, when he finally appeared in the doorway. He slowly moved and sat down next to the Peter. I had stood to assist him, but he gently shook his head in denial of the help.

"'Hello, Varvara, welcome back to Paris. Thank you for your concern for me. I overheard you ask if there's anything you can do. I wish that you would take Peter out. He hasn't left my side for weeks.'

"'Peter started to protest, but Charles held up his hand. 'I think you need a break! I can handle being alone. Take him out and enjoy a quiet dinner together.'

"I looked between the two men. Even now, the love they had shared over the years was evident on their faces as they looked at each other."

"Saddened and at a loss for words, I nodded my head and Peter accepted my invitation to dinner. It definitely was a somber air when we sat down to dinner at the restaurant. Peter let out a sigh as he sat across from Varvara.

"'I sometimes find myself wishing it all would end, and then I'm appalled with myself because it's like I'm wishing for his death!'

"I sadly smiled at Peter, as I said 'When Michael got sick, I was trying everything in my power to cure him. Then when I knew he was dying, I had a mixture of emotions. Sometimes I wanted Michael to be at rest, especially when he was struggling to breathe and obviously in pain. Then I wanted to keep him with me and prayed that he would hang on. So I know how you are feeling. Just be there for him and let him go when the time comes.'

"The conversation continued over dinner. Peter told me that Nureyev had come down with AIDS also, but he was still in the beginning stages of the disease. He mentioned a few others in the ballet world that I knew that also had the disease. After dinner, we roamed the streets of Paris and then returned to the apartment and a waiting Charles.

"I don't remember much of the rest of that trip, and I returned home to the States. Sadly, Peter called two months later with the news of Charles' death.

"After burying Charles in England at his family's estate, Peter flew home and stayed with me at Seagull's Perch. Peter tried to console himself for weeks with many bottles of Jack Daniels. No amount of talk or persuasion from any of the family could penetrate his depression or sorrow. He finally received a call from Nureyev asking him to come back to work. He decided to go mainly because his idol had asked him to. Before he left, he and I had a conversation about what Charles would want him to do with his life. Peter told me about one of the last conversations he and Charles had before Charles' death. He told me that Charles had said, 'Don't stop living because I and others have died from this disease. Live and live with a purpose. Continue on for all of us. Fight for a cure. The solution is in research. Find it, so others won't go down this road that was chosen for us.' He said that just before he died.

"I advised Peter to listen to Charles' advice and go back to work and also added that I would donate money to have research done to look for a cure for AIDS.

"A few months later, Peter called and issued an invitation to go with him and Nureyev to Russia. Nureyev had been denied entrance into Russia for several years. Learning that his mother was ill, he had petitioned the Russian government to allow him to return. When he was finally granted a visa for him to return, plans were made for him also to perform.

"I flew in to Paris and joined Bermont and Peter along with the entourage traveling to Russia. As I boarded the plane, I was filled with a mixture of feelings. My nerves were taut with anxiety over who I would see after being away for 67 years. I was excited to be returning; it was an opportunity I never believed I would have. I was anxious to show Peter and Bermont all the places I knew when I was a child. I was also worried that some things would not be there anymore.

"After arriving at the airport, I was surprised that I didn't have an emotional reaction being back on Russian soil. As we traveled to our hotel, I stared out the window in wonder at all the changes that had taken place over time. St. Petersburg had become a modern city. I had left when the streets were still occupied by horse-drawn vehicles, and now they were filled with the modern chaos that comes from beeping horns, wailing sirens, and heavy traffic coming and going in the busy streets. We arrived at our hotel, and after settling in our rooms, we met for leisurely dinner and discussed what was happening the following day. Plans were in place for us to visit the Marjinski Theater and school. An itinerary had been planned for us by the government, and our movements were somewhat restricted. It was my hope to be able to visit my mother's grave and to go back to my old apartment. We talked with our guide, and she said that she believed we could do all the things that I wanted to do. We retired to our rooms for a much-needed rest. The morning sunshine streamed through my hotel window when I awoke the next morning. "I dressed for the upcoming day's journey. Bermont and Peter met me in the hotel dining room. A lovely breakfast was served as we waited for our guide to appear. There were butterflies in my stomach as we approached my old dance school. The large oval-shaped building was now painted a soft green. Upon entering, the echoes of the past took me totally by surprise as memories flashed through my mind so quickly it made me stumble at the dizzying pace. Sounds of childhood laughter echoed in my ears as I remembered friends walking down the hallways with me. Nathalia Krussovska, Alixandra Danilova, and Sonia Wojcikowska, my three good friends' faces, flashed across my memory, and their little girl faces seem so real as if they were really there at that moment.

"Tears filled my eyes as we walked through the backstage of the theater. It brought back memories of Mama sitting and mending costumes and talking with her friends, laughing at some joke only they understood. I really felt her presence as I walked through the old building. I told Peter and Bermont the stories behind my memories. They laughed at my childhood antics and comforted me in my moments of sadness. We left the theater knowing we would return to see Rudolph Nureyev on Friday evening. I asked to go to my old apartment, only to find that it was no longer there. It had been replaced with a modern building that was now used for businesses. We continued until we reached the Alexander Nevsky Monastery. The cemetery contains the graves of some of the giants of Russian culture, including Tchaikovsky, Dostoevsky, and Glinka. As we entered the graveyard, we walked to a quiet corner and found Mama's grave. Placing the bouquet of white roses on her grave, I tearfully talked to her about my life and the extended family she would have been so proud to be a part of. It was a tired group that returned to our hotel at the end of the day, and after quick dinner, we retired to our rooms.

"Upon awakening the next day, we realized that there was a storm outside. A heavy wind pushed rain so hard it was pounding at the window; you could almost imagine that it was asking you to be let it in. After breakfast, our guide arrived with a white minivan to take us to Peterhof, Peter the Great's summer palace and its gardens. The first building that confronts you is the enormous yellow and white palace. It is beautiful, and at both ends there are towers with golden turrets. Peter likens them to golden onions. Totally ruined during World War II, it has been restored to its original splendor. We took the guided tour throughout the palace, seeing its ornate central staircase and beautiful grand ballroom. The ballroom had gold-encrusted trim and large mirrors. Bermont's favorite room was the small oak office, while Peter's favorite room was the Chinese study. It had red silk wallpaper and Oriental furniture. My favorite was the turquoise throne room. Of course, that was a given because it was in my favorite color. We then made our way out to the immense gardens. Thankfully the rain had stopped. Walking across a checkerboard patio, you reach a white railing and looking beyond it gives you a panoramic view of the formal gardens. The gardens extend out the back of the palace with miles of walkways that lead you to spectacular sections that feature statues and fountains- over 200 in all.

"The oldest part of the Peterhov gardens was finished in 1724 and is found in the lower park. This garden is protected by a man-made rampart on top of which is a three-meter-high stone wall. The flowers are protected from the harsh sea winds, and blooms are full and beautiful in early spring. This garden is called the Garden of Eden's; it also holds Peter's Orchard with cherry and apple trees and many statues. The garden of Bacchus, which has many fountains and statuaries, is next to the orchards.

"Continuing our tour, we went to the upper gardens, which were completed by Peter's daughter, Empress Elizabeth, who continued her father's work.

These gardens, which are just beyond the entrance to the park in front of the Grand Palace, have three extensive alleys that end in front of the palace. Each alley is surrounded by formal flowerbeds and beautifully trimmed hedges. Catherine the Great commissioned the first landscape garden, called the English Park. Inside this park there once was a building that was called the English Palace, which was often used as a guesthouse for foreign diplomats. It was destroyed during World War II. During Nicholas I's reign, the Peterhov gardens again were extended to include Alexandria Park.

"As we entered the aviary and I followed a path, my heart began to beat faster when I realized I had come to the garden of my childhood memories. It was, for a moment like I had traveled back through time. I could hear the childhood laughter, as I led Peter and Bermont to the steppingstones of my childhood. We played on them like we were children until we found the trick stone. I shouted with glee when the bench was sprayed with water. I looked over to Bermont and Peter, and they were looking back me with an expression of delight and laughter. I'm sure it wasn't often that a 79-year-old woman played on the stones or took so much pleasure and joy out of the trick to water the bench. For me, it gave me back a moment of my childhood, and it was a very moving experience and one I'll never forget. On the way back to the hotel, Bermont and Peter constantly teased me about playing in the garden. It was a jovial group that returned to the hotel, and it was good to see Peter laughing again.

"After the gardens of Peterhov, I didn't think anything could impress me. But I was wrong, for the next day we traveled to Catherine's Palace. It is located in the small town of Pushkin, about 17 miles south of St.

Petersburg. The palace is a huge building over 2,000 feet long and is painted a bright blue with white trim and gilded with gold. Bermont found out there were over 200 pounds of gold on the building. The palace was a gift from Peter the Great to his wife Catherine in the early 1700s. Like Peterhov, Empress Elizabeth increased its size, hiring the famous Bartolomeo Francesco Rastrelli, who was responsible for decorating the palace in the Baroque style. Catherine the Great was responsible for the interior of the palace, and it was done in a more Neoclassical style. In the northern corner there are five onion domes, which are on top of the palace chapel. When you enter the grand ballroom, you get the feeling that you're really small. Its immense size, over 150 feet long, seems even bigger because all the walls are mirrored and there are two tiers of windows on each side. The ceiling is covered with frescoes, and the floor is done in pattern parquet. If this wasn't impressive enough, we soon walked through the Amber room, where the walls are decorated in panels of pure amber and surrounded by fancy gold trim. Each room that we entered had its own individual style. My favorite was the green dining room, which was decorated with Roman motifs. It reminded me of one large cameo.

"I don't think either Peter or Bermont were as impressed as I was, and I believe they had had enough of touring palaces. There was one last place I wanted to go to, and we left Catherine's Palace and made our way to The Church of the Savior of Spilt Blood."

Varvara paused in her story to tell those who listened that most people recognize this church, not only because of its fancy and ornate exterior, which includes several fancy onion domes, but also because it is seen on almost every advertisement to tour Russia.

"Closed down after the Russian Revolution when religion was outlawed, it was once used as a cabbage storage facility," she continued. "After years of neglect in 1970, a restoration project was started. The interior of the church is breathtakingly beautiful. All its walls are covered with mosaics, each one an incredible depiction of the story of Christ from his birth through the Last Supper. Each depiction is done in incredible detail using mosaics of every hue and color, much like an oil painting. Your head is stretched and twisted as you look up and around the whole interior of the church. As we exited the church, we realized we had been in the church for over an hour; our necks were sore from looking up at the whole interior. We all expressed our feelings of being overwhelmed with the beauty of it all. Then, realizing how late it was, we rushed back to the hotel and dressed for the ballet.

"I wore a long silky silver gown by Dior and felt very special, flanked by two gorgeously tuxedoed gentlemen: Peter and Bermont. My butterflies returned as I entered the auditorium and took my seat. I remember glancing over at Peter; he was wringing his hands and his forehead was creased with worry.

"'Mémère, I worry he won't be able to complete the performance,' Peter had said.

"I remembered I had reached over and patted his hand and then spoke softly. 'I know Peter, but I think he needs to dance again here. It's the fulfillment of his lifetime of achievement. I'm sure he'll be okay.'

"Suddenly the music from the orchestra swelled and the ballet began. I admitted to myself that Nureyev wasn't the spectacular dancer that he was in the beginning of his career. I remembered his vitality and energy that I had witnessed and been impressed with when I had watched him dance in Paris. It was obvious to those who knew him that his illness had taken its toll. The people in the audience still showed him their appreciation with their applause, and the ballet completed without incident. There was a reception after the ballet where I got to talk with a few of my old friends who had remained in Russia.

"Though the trip was memorable, I was glad when I entered the plane to return to the U.S. Approaching the driveway of Seagull's Perch, a sense of peace filled my heart. It was almost as if the house was welcoming me home."

Another day of filming came to a close. All who had listened had questions about the trip to Russia. Fifteen-year- old Juliane, Karen's granddaughter, looked up on her i Pod St. Petersburg and its tourist attractions. Scanning the list, she found Peterhof and Catherine's Palace. Everyone gathered around her as she showed picture after picture of all that Varvara had just talked about.

"Wow isn't it beautiful."

"That building is so big"

"Look at those gardens."

"It is amazing."

For over an hour the children looked at all the information they could find. The adults marveled at their easy use of the i Pod. Jan brought up the fact that already, the telling of Varvara's story was making the family more aware of their ancestry.

The next day, everyone got settled and Varvara started speaking again. "You all know Victoria, and the next part of my story involves her.

"Not everyone handled Irene and Leslie's death well. For Victoria, having lost her grandparents brought on feelings of anger and resentment. Being an only child she had always been the center of Tim and Jan's world, but also had spent much of her childhood at Seagull's Perch with her grandparents. She withdrew into herself and over the next two years became more and more rebellious. There were constant arguments over her attire and attitude. She stayed out late, skipped school, and her grades dropped.

"The only thing she didn't stop was her dancing. She had incredible talent and was the featured ballerina in several performances in Providence Theater, including the lead in the Christmas musical The Nutcracker. She was looking forward to going to Paris to study the summer she turned 16.

"In the spring of that year while out with a group of friends, there was a terrible car crash in which two of the boys died and Victoria was critically injured. Suffering from a broken pelvis and her left leg shattered in several places, Victoria's hopes and dreams of becoming a prima ballerina were over. It would be months before she would be able to walk, and the repercussions of that night would affect her life for years to come.

"I watched as the happy Victoria we once knew turned into a depressed and even more rebellious teenager. Due to the pain the injuries caused, she was prescribed pain medication. I constantly worried about the road she was heading down. I caught her several times taking alcohol out of the bar. No amount of talking could reach her, and when we tried, it only increased her rebellious actions.

"She began seeing a boy named Marc Bursell. From an affluent family, he had money to spare and spent it on Victoria. Her life revolved around him. We heard he threw large wild parties at his family summer home. There were rumors that he was into selling drugs. We saw very little of Victoria during those months, and we were shocked when we were informed that she had married Marc right after she turned 18.

"After the marriage, they settled into an apartment in Westerly. They weren't there very often. They would stop in at Seagull's Perch announcing they were off on a trip to the Bahamas or Jamaica. Victoria looked thin and withdrawn. Her laughter was brittle and held no joy.

"The subject of Victoria was a constant worried conversation between Jan and me. It was shortly after Jan had arrived for her annual summer stay when Victoria stopped over to share the news she was pregnant. She didn't seem all that excited. Her pregnancy wasn't easy, and twice she was rushed to the hospital because she was so dehydrated from her morning sickness. For most of her pregnancy, she could hold nothing in her stomach, and instead of gaining weight, she lost pounds.

"Our worries continued. Victoria didn't seem happy, and we wondered about her relationship with Marc. Though outwardly they seemed the perfect couple, I always felt uncomfortable when he was around. We heard he had a terrific temper, and I noticed that Victoria would cringe whenever he raised his voice. In April of 1986, Victoria gave birth to a beautiful baby girl she named Angelique.

"The birth of Angelique seemed to bring out the old Victoria we knew. She seemed happy and doted on the baby. But the happiness seemed to be short- lived. Soon there were signs that the marriage wasn't going well. We began to worry all over again because Victoria would show up with Angelique and have dark circles under her eyes and often a bruise on her arm. She once sported a black eye that she told us she got falling out of their boat. She soon began asking us to watch Angelique so she could go out with Marc during the evening. After several months she dropped off Angelique on a Friday night and we received a call on Saturday morning that she was in Jamaica with Marc and could we take care of Angelique for the week.

"When they returned, Victoria looked more exhausted than ever and announced that she was pregnant again. This second pregnancy was much easier for Victoria, and after nine months she gave birth to Marc Junior.

"For months we would only occasionally see Victoria and the children. Usually we received a quick phone call asking us to watch the two children and Victoria would breeze in and quickly leave. We again began to hear rumors of all-night parties and Marc's wild behavior including having been arrested for drunk driving and disorderly conduct.

"On an early summer morning, at about 1a.m., I was awakened by the sound of screaming. Running downstairs, I was joined by several family members to discover Marc, trying to drag Victoria out of the house. Tim stepped up and removed Victoria from Marc's grip. We heard the hysterical Victoria tell us of Marc's brutal attack on her and how four-year-old Angelique tried to intervene. Marc had struck out at her, and Victoria said that this was the final straw. We found out later that she had been in an abusive situation almost from the beginning but wouldn't tolerate the abuse turning on her children.

"In all the chaos, with Victoria hysterically crying and Marc yelling apologies and promises that he would never do it again, I asked where the children were. Victoria told us that she had bundled them in the car. Jan and Tim ran outside and gathered up a tearful Angelique and the sleeping baby Marc and brought them inside. Marc was told to leave and did so after much yelling, realizing it wasn't getting him anywhere.

"After Marc left, it was decided that both Victoria and Angelique needed to be checked out at the hospital. Tim and Jan went with Victoria and Angelique while I stayed home with the baby. When they returned, Angelique was sporting a bright neon pink cast on her left arm. It was 4 a.m. everyone retired to their rooms only to be awakened by the sound of pounding on the door by Marc at 7 a.m. insisting that Victoria and the babies were returned to him, Marc threatened to take Angelique to court as an unfit mother. He was spouting off about her drug addictions and alcohol problems. Later we would learn there was some truth to his words, but at the time, my anger over the whole situation got the better of me. So before anyone could stop me, I marched out onto the front porch and confronted Marc.

"You're quite sure you want to take Victoria to court, Marc?" I asked. "Angry and red-faced, Marc came right up to my face and replied, 'Yes, I'll take her precious babies from her and she'll never see them again.'

"'Well, you listen up for just a moment. I've been worried for over a year about you and Victoria's relationship. I have documentation of your activities over the last few months, including the X-rays that are evidence of your breaking Angelique's arm!'

"Marc began to interrupt, but I continued. 'So this is what you're going to do. You're going to get off of my property. You will be hearing from Victoria's lawyer as to the terms of what the future will be. You will not at any time have contact with either of your children or Victoria without another adult from this family in attendance. Finally, if I ever in the future find out that you have laid a hand on any of my family, I will make it my sole mission to have you arrested and punished to the full extent of the law. Now go!'

"Shaken, I walked back into the house and slammed the door, only to lean back and collapse against it. I looked up into the admiring eyes of Jan and Tim, who clapped silently over the performance.

"Over the next year, Victoria and the two children established a home for themselves in the apartment over the garage. Victoria struggled to get control of her addictions as she dealt with the gossip over her separation and Marc's behavior. We were told that he continued holding wild parties and was seen often cruising around town with a young girl in his yellow convertible. There was sadness when we were informed that both Marc and his passenger were killed in an accident, leaving Victoria a widow at the age of 25 with two little children.

"With Marc's death, Victoria's depression increased, along with her drinking. There were days when she would not come out of her room, or she would disappear for a week or two. Her behavior caused me to have concerns for the children. Angelique and Marc were constant visitors to 'the big house' as they called it. They were a source of joy to me. Angelique, at four, began doing the morning dance routine with us. It was apparent even at that early age that she had incredible talent. When Victoria saw Angelique dancing, she started enrolling her in talent and beauty contests, and even though Angelique obviously didn't like performing, they were soon into a routine of pageantry and dance competitions. No amount of caution or advice from me or Jan was heard, and Victoria continued to push Angelique. We watched Angelique strive to please her mother by winning prizes and crowns. Victoria seemed to be able to control her drinking better when she was dragging Angelique from pageant to pageant. When Angelique won, she would be praised, but often this was followed with criticism about what she could do better. When she did not place first, Victoria would spend days having Angelique go over her routine. The pressure she put on Angelique to be better was extreme. Nothing was ever good enough. Even during competition there was always a criticism coming from her mother. Whether it was her leg wasn't held long enough in the air, her turn wasn't fast enough, or her head wasn't held at the right angle, Victoria found something to criticize Angelique about. Both Jan and I tried to intervene on Angelique's behalf, but our words fell on deaf ears. Many times after competitions, Angelique would come home and visit with me. Telling me all about her day, she would not mention her mother. I would hear stories about other dancers or something funny Marc had said. It was like we had an unspoken agreement, that talking about Victoria was off limits.

"As Angelique and Marc grew, Victoria's obsession with them increased.

Where Angelique got criticism, Marc got smothered with love. He was the adored little boy. It's surprising that he wasn't a spoiled brat. He took everything Victoria did in stride and from a very young age started protecting his sister whenever he could from his mother's needle-sharp tongue. He became Tim's shadow and followed his grandpa where ever he went. Tim was retired from the service, and his days were free. You could hear him quietly explaining things to Marc about how things worked. They were constantly working on some project out in the garage. Marc's interest in horses had Tim taking him to his great-aunt's farm where he began to learn dressage. Angelique joined Marc whenever she could and secretly began to learn dressage, too. There was a huge confrontation when Victoria discovered her secret. It was only when she saw how good Angelique was on a horse that she changed her tune and began a new obsession with having both her children put into competition. This only added more pressure on Angelique, and I constantly worried about her. My only hope was that Tim, Jan, and I provided both Marc and Angelique the stability and acceptance that they needed."

The filming stopped. Varvara looked over at Victoria, who had tears rolling down her cheeks, and Angelique was patting her shoulder… They both smiled and assured her that everything was okay. Victoria was saddened at how her past actions had caused so much anxiety for Angelique. She turned to tell Angelique how sorry she was, but Angelique told her that they had put the past behind them.

The next day Varvara picked up the telling of Marc and Angelique's childhood.

Turning Point

"As Marc and Angelique went from children to teenagers the relationship between them and their mother deteriorated to the point that they rarely spoke to each other. When they did, it was usually an angry confrontation with much shouting and no one listening. Though Marc had stopped doing dressage competition and begun to show interest in breeding; Victoria still demanded Angelique to continue. I found it very sad that Angelique could not find a way to enjoy her dressage routine in competition, but she never could stand crowds. There was a special bond between her and her horse which she had raised since she had watched him being born at her aunt's farm. She had named him Midnight-Magic. For those of us that watched her perform, we couldn't help but notice her grace and beauty as she circled the ring, and it was because of this that she constantly came home with blue ribbons. When she was not competing or training in the ring, she was in the dance studio, going over her routine for her next dance competition. If it was possible, she was even more graceful and had a delicate beauty when performing on pointe.

"When Angelique finished high school, she chose to go to Johnson & Wales University. A happy young lady stood before me waving a paper announcing she had been accepted. I knew it was a huge step in her growing up and being on her own." Varvara stopped as if to catch her breath for a minute. "I'll continue on," she said.

"The next year it was proud Marc waving acceptance papers to Quinnipiac College that stood before me. I felt a twinge of empty-nest angst, but was so proud of how grown up both children had become. Their college years brought a maturity and independence streak out in both Marc and Angelique, much to Victoria's dislike. She still struggled with trying to control their lives, and her behavior would soon cause a break in her relationship with Angelique." Varvara suddenly stopped talking. Filming for the day was over. Varvara's nurse took Varvara back to her room.

"She's tiring more quickly now. We are barely getting an hour's worth of taping done," Stephanie said as she, Angelique, Marc, and Yves set out together for dinner at the Mystic Pizza. Made famous by the movie bearing its name and starring Julia Roberts, it was known for its good food and great atmosphere. There was plenty to talk about and the conversation flowed, about the upcoming wedding, Varvara's story, her health, and general plans for the future. It was during dessert that Stephanie spoke up and asked a question.

"I know from listening to Varvara's story and a few outside conversations how you and Yves were split up, but I guess I'm just nosy and want to know what happened to you when you got to Paris. Sorry if I'm being rude and you don't have to answer if you don't want to. My curiosity gets me often into awkward situations."

Angelique glanced over at Yves and then laughed at the comical worried expressions on both Marc's and Stephanie's faces.

"After I went to Paris, I was quite depressed," Angelique said. "I had already informed the Paris Ballet Troupe that I couldn't accept to go on tour with them. I did accept the job offer to teach at the school, and I settled into a small flat within walking distance from the academy. I contacted Marc and my uncle instructing them to have Midnight-Magic shipped home as planned.

Marc knew someone who was looking for a trained dressage horse and made the arrangements for a two- year lease. I spent my time teaching during the morning and roaming through shops to find odds and ends to decorate my apartment."

Yves asked, "Why didn't you just go out and buy what you needed?"

Angelique's face flushed a little as she answered him. "I had vowed that I was not going to touch another cent of my inheritance and prove to myself that I wasn't the spoiled rich girl my mother had portrayed me as. I would live off of what I got paid. In the beginning, it wasn't as easy as I thought it was going to be, but soon I was having fun and I found out I have a natural flare for what's known as shabby chic.

"It was during that winter that I seemed to get the flue more often, and the headmistress called me into her office to discuss her worry over my weight loss and general health. I never worried about my period because they weren't often there. I had a few dizzy spells but attributed them to the stress of my mother's calling me every night. I assured the headmistress, I was fine, and we began talking about the next week's classes when I fainted right at her feet. The doctor was called in and I was informed that I was in a delicate condition. It took me awhile to comprehend what he was saying. I'm not sure who was more shocked when I just started laughing. I just didn't believe him. I went and purchased one of those pregnancy tests and in my bathroom watched that strip turn blue. The tears came first, then the anger, and then in the stillness of the night, the determination that even this, I could handle. A lot of questions were running through my mind. Should I stay in Paris or go home? Should I go to the farm and tell Yves? Could I go back to the U.S. and keep my vow not to use money I hadn't earned? Would the school fire me or let me finish out the year? Some answers came quickly. The headmistress called me back into the office the next morning to inform me I would no longer be employed at the end of the school year. Within days there came a knock on my flat's door and upon opening it found Mémère and Marc standing arm and arm and smiling down at me. Marc was on his way to the farm for the summer, and Mémère, though she would never admit it, was there to check up on me. I always suspected that the headmistress had contacted her to let her know about my condition.

"Ushering them inside I watched as they took in my surroundings. Marc, being a typical brother, said it was the size of our bathroom at home. Mémère just took everything in and then commented on my good taste. Over a cup of tea, we discussed the family's comings and goings and then Mémère asked when I was due. I never have seen my brother's head whip around so fast or his face turn an awful shade of gray."

Marc interrupted, Angelique's tale, defending himself that he had no hint that there was a possibility of her being pregnant. Laughing, she continued with her story. "Mémère wanted me to return home, and I assured her that that would not be happening. I informed them that I had been in contact with an old dance friend who was in need of a teacher for the next year and that there was a small apartment attached to the studio I could use. I assured them that I was in good health and would be returning to the States at the end of the term, which was in about a week and a half's time. That evening I had a talk with Marc about his upcoming visit to the farm. I explained that I didn't want him to tell Yves about the baby. After extensive arguing, he agreed to do it my way. He also promised he would be home in time to be there for the baby's birth. He didn't keep either promise."

Marc, again laughing, told Stephanie about his arrival at Bellaire and Yves' offhand comment that he wasn't sure he could handle another summer dealing with a spoiled rich kid. "My fist just swung out and connected with Yves' jaw, knocking him to the ground. In my anger, I told him just what I thought about him abandoning my pregnant sister."

"Yves, rubbing his jaw, said Marc had a powerful left hook. Then he continued the story, telling of a long discussion held with Marc. "I had made plans to go see Angelique after that weekend's horse show. Fate stepped in and I was seriously injured saving a little girl who wandered into a horse's stall."

Angelique told of her hearing of the accident and going to visit Yves in the hospital. She was told by the nurse that Yves was refusing to have visitors. "I asked her to check to make sure that included me. She returned telling me that Yves told her himself that he didn't want to see me. Devastated again, I returned to my plans and flew home. I had just enough time to unpack and organize my apartment, before I needed to start teaching. My life was beginning to have some kind of order. I had a pretty normal pregnancy until I was about eight months. I started to retain water, especially in my ankles. It became difficult for me to teach my classes. I went in for my regular check and immediately was rushed to the hospital. Marc had just left on a business trip back to France and I thought I was going to have to have the baby all alone. I didn't know it then, but both Ann and Marc had promised Jan that she would get called if anything started happening. Grams and Mémère showed up and Grams came into the delivery room with me. I had Vari, and even though she was tiny she was in perfect health. I stayed in the hospital four days, and Vari stayed in two more before I brought her home. I decided to name her after the two women who had always been there for me. Three weeks later, after Marc had returned, she was baptized Varvara Jan Haroutunian. Marc had gotten the family christening gown from Varvara, and he and Ann are her godparents. Grams and Grampa Tim along with Mémère came. If you saw how many gifts were loaded in their car it was surprising they made it," said Angelique laughing again.

Stephanie thanked them for telling the details of their past and the rest of the evening was spent talking about the upcoming wedding.

Angelique and Stephanie met again the next day as they attended the filming of Varvara's story.

"Around the end of the 1980s into the early 1990s the changes in computers gave me the opportunities to keep in touch with the families on both continents. When instant messages came out, we were able to talk daily with each other. Then shortly, or so it seemed, Skype provided face-to- face communication. We could see the families and how they grew. The beeping sound called me to my computer every day. Sometimes it was Bermont needing information about some horse, or Joshua calling to show off his new baby girl, to actually having several family members connecting together to make decisions about any number of the several businesses we were involved in. Skype would become even more important in the next several years.

"It was the summer of 1991 and Jan had come to stay. Timothy had brought her and was leaving for his six-week summer tour of duty the next morning. Sitting on the porch with Tim, I commented on how tired Jan looked. Timothy replied, 'She hasn't been herself lately. She's having a lot of digestion problems. She has a lot of gas, and by the end of the day she looks five months' pregnant. I'm really worried something is seriously wrong. Please talk to her about seeing a doctor.'

"I commented, 'I don't know if I can influence her on that. She's always had a stubborn streak. I know where she got that trait from. You couldn't budge her mother when her mind was made up, and if you tried, you were met by a determination that was stronger than a stone wall. I'll try anyway. Tim, don't worry.'

"It was later that week, as I stood at the barre, doing the morning routine with Jan and Angelique that I got a chance to talk to her. Angelique was giggling because Jan was passing gas as she went through the dance routine. It gave me the perfect opportunity to bring up the subject of her health.

"'Jan, something's not right.' I told her. 'I paid attention to you over the last week, because Timothy mentioned he was worried about you. As much as Angelique finds it funny, it is not normal for you to be passing gas as much as you do.'

"Jan was embarrassed even talking with me and tried to make light of it.

"'Jan you don't look yourself,' I told her. You're bloating by the end of each day. If you're not passing gas, you are in the bathroom. I seriously advise you to get checked out, if not for your peace of mind, for Tim's and mine.

"Jan was quiet for a moment and then replied, 'I have been thinking of calling a doctor. After listening to you, I'll call and make an appointment.'

"Two weeks later we made a day outing that included a visit with Dr. George. She ordered an ultrasound to be done the following day. It was with great trepidation that we entered the hospital. The ultrasound didn't last very long, and we left with instructions to call Dr. George immediately. Then came the dreaded news Jan had cancer. They thought her to be only in stage one but she needed a total hysterectomy. After hanging up the phone, we sat in shocked silence and then Jan spoke up: 'I'll need to inform Tim.' then she burst into tears. Gathering her in my arms, I tried to give some small form of comfort.

"News travels fast in a large family, and before the day was out, all of Jan's siblings were at the house offering support and help. Timothy arrived and Jan collapsed in tears in his arms. A scared and worried face looked at me over her shoulders.

"'We will take it one day at a time,' he said as he patted her shoulder. 'We can beat this. Everyone will have to do their part and we will get through this.'

"The family did just that. If something was needed, someone stepped up and filled the need. Mostly Karen, Elizabeth and I made sure Jan's needs were taken care of. It was a long and difficult time.

"A small family group waited while Jan was being operated on. It seemed we waited for hours when Dr. George finally came out to inform us she made it through surgery.

"My love of hats came in handy when Jan started losing her hair. At first she was upset and angry over the appearance of clumps of hair lodged in her hairbrush. I offered her my multitude of hats, and we spent a hilarious morning trying them on. Then we were joined by five-year-old Angelique. She began to entertain us with her own version of modeling, strutting around with hats that fell over most of her face. It was when she came out of the closet dressed in a slinky black tunic, with several strands of beads, a pretty pink feathered boa, six-inch high heels, and a large picture hat that made us break out in hilarious laughter. Our laughter drew Tim into the room. He couldn't help but laugh at the sight he saw. It was a memorable moment in a time that was mostly filled with worry and sorrow.

"We all teased Jan that with her hats and sunglasses, she looked like some movie star hiding out at Seagull's Perch. The toll on Jan was obvious. She always had an extra 20 pounds that she was forever trying to lose. She joked that the only good thing that came out of being sick was her trim new figure and that her hair, which had grown back, was now a beautiful silver gray. The next few weeks she regained strength and appetite, only to repeat the ordeal over and over. After the series of chemo was completed, we went with nervous anxiety to Jan's monthly checkup. My eyes filled with tears of joy when I heard the good news that she was cancer-free. We celebrated with an early dinner at the Victorian Tea Room. Jan still tired easily and we returned home so she could get some sleep.

"After all the treatments were completed Jan, went into remission that lasted a year. Then the symptoms returned and after a visit to the oncologist's, an early growth in the lymph nodes was detected. Before making a decision over how to battle the cancer again, we sought a second opinion at Brigham and Women's Hospital in Boston. They confirmed the cancer was back and offered an experimental program. There was extremely limited space left in the program, and Jan had to decide whether to go that route. There was one thing that Jan liked about the program and that was that the treatment could be administered at the local hospital. And so it was decided that was the route they were going to go.

"When they returned to Seagull's Perch that evening, the family was waiting for them. Everyone had been praying that by some miracle the doctors were wrong and the cancer wasn't back. Jan entered the family room and calmly announced the dreaded news: 'My cancer is back.'

"They all had expected the news, but hearing it aloud brought on feelings of frightened worry and concern. Everyone gathered around Jan and expressed their love and promised to be there for her in the upcoming months.

"Within weeks, she was scheduled again for surgery. Again a small group gathered in the waiting area anxiously awaiting Dr. George's news.

When she finally came, she told us she removed the small lump and the operation was successful.

"I don't know what prompted my concern, but I knew there was something more she wasn't saying. We learned later from Tim that during surgery, she had found the cancer had traveled and Jan wasn't considered in stage I, but actually stage III. In less than two weeks, she was scheduled for her first chemo treatment.

"Over the next nine months, she would have an eight-hour treatment every three weeks. The effects of chemo showed up almost immediately. Though she had pills to combat the nausea, she had trouble with it on and off during treatments. Of the five different drugs she was given, one caused her severe pain. She often kicked us out of the room during that treatment. I don't know what was harder -watching her struggle or knowing she was in pain and not being able to comfort her or help her. Jan spent a lot of time sleeping, and when the chemotherapy started, the reaction was a week of sickness, which left Jan exhausted."

Varvara paused in the telling of her story; as if lost in her memories, and then began talking again.

"It was one of those beautiful, clear, crisp, mornings when the sky is so blue and white puffy clouds look like they've been pasted in place. The air is so crisp that you can see your breath like fine smoke coming from your mouth. I was returning from my morning walk along the beach, and the colorful fallen leaves were crunching beneath my feet as I walked across the lawn. I quickly removed my gloves, scarf, and coat. As I was doing this, I was greeted by Timothy who offered me a much-needed cup of coffee. We sat in the breakfast room in companionable silence. After a short while I asked him what was on his mind.

"He then replied, 'Oh, I'm having a multitude of thoughts this morning, thankful that Jan survived through the last nine months, worried about what the future will hold, and angry that it made me feel so helpless. I'm used to being in charge and in control. I have lived all my life keeping everything orderly. Sometimes Jan and Victoria would complain that I was too military, but it was and is who I am. I feel like I've been in a battle where the odds were stacked against me and I didn't have the weapons to fight the war. I'm tired; I don't know where I'll find the energy if the cancer returns. I've never been so scared in all my life. Jan is my life. I've loved her from the minute I saw her, and I'm still scared I'm going to lose her. Sorry, I didn't mean to unload this all on you.'

"I patted his hand and reassured him that it was okay. 'Thanksgiving brings about so many emotions. I really understand what you are feeling. I go through many different emotions when I think about what I'm thankful for. You know that I believe God gives us the gift of life and that each day should be treasured. I lived a long life and have had my share of tragedies, but my faith and love of God has pulled me through the worst of times. Don't get me wrong. I have been angry at God many times, questioning why he allowed things to happen the way they did. You can't live to be as old as I am without that. In the end, it's about looking for those little things you can be grateful for. Your family, friends, or sometimes it's the sound of laughter from the children, which gets me through a difficult day. Other times it's just a quiet moment of prayer. I'm scared, too! I've had enough death and sadness, but life is about living and dying, and eventually we all come to the end. Let's hope that the future holds health for all of us and be thankful that the family has gathered together today.' At that Timothy smiled up at me and thanked me for listening.

"Standing, I made my way toward the dance studio where I could hear members of the family preparing themselves for our morning routine. My granddaughters, Peter, and Victoria were already warming up at the bar. Elizabeth and Karen were discussing the feast they would be preparing later that day. This caused me to chuckle to myself, thinking that some things never change.

"The day unfolded like any normal large family gathering, everyone pitching in to prepare the meal. Soon the turkey was stuffed and placed in the oven, and mounds of vegetables were peeled, chopped, and cooked. The sideboard in the dining room was laden down with desserts: pies, cakes, brownies, and cookies covered every corner, along with Karen's Choereg and Elizabeth's famous baklava. Soon the whole house took on the aroma of the turkey roasting and the all familiar sound of family banter and laughter. When the meal was ready and we all gathered together around the dining room table, Timothy spoke up and requested to say grace.

"'This morning, Varvara reminded me that life is a gift from God. I come with gratitude that I am sharing my life with my wonderful wife and family. May we look back and be thankful we had each other to share the road and look ahead to the joys that each day will bring. Let us be thankful for the food before us and treasure the company in which we share it. Blessed be. Let's eat!'

"As everyone started eating, I took a moment to look at all the members of my family and I was filled with awe. Life's challenges bring about many unexpected situations that can be turned into wonderful opportunities. Losing Leslie and Irene was a difficult time, but it gave me their family to watch over and care for. I was extremely grateful." It was time to stop filming for the day.

The next day brought the same group together and they settled right down to listen eagerly to Varvara.

"Living along the Atlantic Ocean for the most part was amazing and quite peaceful. Only occasionally did the weather give cause for concern. The winter of 1993 caused the whole eastern seaboard to worry. A winter hurricane later to be known as 'the storm of the century' was racing toward us with fearsome force. The national weather station started talking about a super storm as early as March 2. The storm lasted for more than seventy-two hours and spanned from South America up the eastern seacoast all the way into Canada. The storm had everything- high winds; heavy snow; thunder and lightning, and cold temperatures. The South was hit hard. Unsuspecting Florida residences were awakened by a storm surge pouring water into their homes: Forty-five people drowned. Not used to more than an inch of snow, both Tennessee and North Carolina received thirteen inches of heavy snow, which caused buildings to collapse. The Appalachian Mountain area was buried under two to three feet of snow, stranding tourists and locals. Washington, D.C. and New York City struggled to dig themselves out of over a foot of snow. Most of New England handled the storm okay. It was an unusual one, because it came so late in March. At Seagull's Perch, we watched the storm reports 'til the electricity went out. We hunkered down around the fireplace and pretended we were camping. For Marc and Victoria, at five and seven, it was an adventure, but the grownups worried as the windows rattled and the wind howled. We also were worried about William Clayton, Richard and Christina's son, who was on duty at the Coast Guard station. After it was all over, the statistics were amazing. A freighter was sunk in the Gulf of Mexico, losing seven crew members. The coast guard ended up rescuing two hundred thirty-five people off one hundred boats. There were almost sixty thousand lightning strikes across the U.S. and the term 'thunder snow' was used by some weathermen. Over three hundred people died. All airports from Halifax, Nova Scotia, to Atlanta, Georgia, were closed. Ten million customers were out of electricity, one-fourth of the U.S. population. It was an amazing storm and we were blessed that no harm came to any of us."

Filming stopped then for the day. "Varavara came into the room the next morning, carrying some papers and pictures on her lap. She explained to Stephanie that they were memorabilia of a trip to France in 1995. Several members of the family went for the 50th anniversary celebration of the battle of Normandy. There were ceremonies held in more than fourteen countries, commemorating D-Day, but culminated with ceremonies in Normandy, France, during the first week of June. The event brought veterans from fourteen countries to the French countryside for ceremonies and memorials. On June 6th, fourteen Allied soldiers waded in from a landing craft onto the beach, each carrying his nation's flag. Each man represented a country that made up the original invasion force. The original American 82nd and 101st airborne unit had parachuted on the eve of D-Day. Approximately forty of the original units joined more than one thousand paratroopers who came falling from the sky to land successfully again into Sainte-Mere-Eglise. There were only a few minor injuries, including a few sprained ankles amongst the seventy-to eighty-year-old veterans. The French press dubbed them the "Jumping Grandpas." Amongst the jumpers was Karen's son James, jumping in honor of his grandfather. He told us later that a few of the men remembered his grandfather and teased him about Leslie grabbing the most beautiful girl in France.

"I stood with family amongst the crowd in a steady drizzle while we watched two presidents lay wreathes on Utah Beach. President Clinton led a moving ceremony at Pointe du Hoc to commemorate the heroic efforts of American soldiers who died in the fight to knock out the six big 155-mm howitzer guns that were used to cover both Utah and Omaha beaches.

"The main ceremonies were held at Omaha Beach and at the American cemetery at Colleville-Sur-Mur. You can't walk through Colleville-Sur-Mur without it having an effect on you: ninety-three hundred crosses all facing west mark the graves of servicemen who died during the battles on D-Day. We placed a red, white, and blue wreath of flowers on Richard Clayton's cross at the Colleville-Sur-Mur, the American graveyard. It was touching to see all the veterans and their families walking through the hundreds of white crosses. Everywhere you turned, you could overhear stories being told about that day fifty years ago. We traveled to the shore and threw rose petals in the ocean in honor of Leslie and Irene.

"While at the ceremonies at Omaha Beach, we listened to countless stories from individual veterans. It was moving to hear the catch in their voices as they told of friends dying at their sides fifty years before.

"Approximately three hundred-fifteen veterans of the 9th Air Force division participated in a transatlantic crossing on the QE2. Amongst this group was the legendary journalist Walter Cronkite. At seventy eight, his voice still recognizable, he still commanded an audience as he shared his knowledge about the airpower and it's important to the success of D-Day.

"At the end of the formal ceremonies, a large group of family and friends gathered at Bellaire. We walked somberly to the family graveyard and placed a white flowered wreath on each of Jean's and Aurele's graves. Victoria, Karen, and Richard all had come from the U.S. with their children. Everyone said their own individual prayers and placed flowers on the graves. Bermont had invited veterans of the French resistance that had been friends of Irene and Aurele. There were two GIs that had served with Leslie and even an old gentleman who had served with Jean in the De Gaulle's camp. We left the gravesite and made our way back down to the main house. I was remembering all the loved ones I had lost during the war, as I sat down in one of the comfortable chairs arranged around a warm crackling fire. The day's dampness seemed to settle in every bone of my body. I was tired and sore. It wasn't often I felt my age but that day I felt every one of my ninety years.

"The warm breath of summer was soon upon us, and the start of the influx of tourists and vacationers began to fill the harbor with boats and the streets and stores with laughing patrons. The family gathered to get all the summer furniture out of storage and placed around the porches and down on the beach. Oh, how I loved the beach. It brought me peace and solitude every time I set foot on its sandy shore. Many mornings, after running through my ballet routine, I would grab a cup of coffee and make my way to the beach. For an hour, I would enjoy the sound of the surf and gather strength to face whatever came my way that day."

Over a month of filming had been accomplished when Memorial Day weekend approached. Filming was called to a halt, and everyone began planning for the three-day celebration. Family traditions that had been followed for generations were scheduled. The first was to happen on Saturday morning with the opening of the Flying Horse Carousel in Watch Hill. All the children twelve and under were gathered up and taken down to the harbor. This year there were nine, including a very excited Vari who was busy telling Yves all she knew about the carousel. With her brown eyes sparkling with anticipation, she let Yves buckle her in. Chattering non-stop, she talked about the black horse she wanted to ride again this year. At 10 a.m., the ride would open. Purchasing the nine tickets at $1.50 each, the price for an outside horse, Yves also asked for the information flyer. Angelique was browsing through the souvenirs that were being sold outside the ticket booth and decided to purchase a pink sweatshirt for Vari. Keeping a close watch over the nine excited children, they walked over to the white gates to wait for the first ride.

Yves was busy reading about the history of the carousel. He found it interesting that the carousel was believed to be left by a traveling carnival on the beach in 1883. It had been in use for more than 125 years and was believed to be the oldest continuously running carousel in the United States. It was the only surviving flying horse carousel. Yves was chuckling as he read about the first horse that pulled the carousel. It loved its job so much that during the winter, the horse would escape from the stable and make its way down to the carousel. When people woke up in the morning, they would find the horse circling the carousel on its well-trodden path.

As Angelique stood amongst the children, she told them the history of the twenty wooden horses that were made from carved spring rocking horses that hadn't been sold during the Civil War.

"They're very old; I rode the gold one for the first time when I was two and a half."

"Vari, my favorite is the gray one," said Victoria. "I rode him for the first time when I was two. That would have been in 1968."

Standing beside Victoria, Jennifer Green, Elizabeth's granddaughter, was telling her daughter, Erin about her first ride on the white horse with the yellow mane.

Yves stood studying the stone pillars that supported the wooden roof, which protected the carousel from the weather. The children were sitting on the stone wall that connected each pillar and supported a short white picket fence. He continued to read about how the horses were hung by rods attached from overhead sweeps with no platform underneath. The speed of the ride caused the horses to swing out on the rods, and that was why it was called the Flying Horse Carousel.

Suddenly, music from the player piano blasted out the "Battle Hymn of the Republic," and a loud cheer went up from the crowd as teenage attendants opened the gates and let the children in. There were squeals of delight as children sought and reached the horse of their choice. Angelique lifted Vari onto her black stallion. The horses had real horse hair for their mane and tail and leather saddles. An attendant placed a safety strap around Vari's waist and asked all adults to step outside. There was only one horse left on the outside, and this was grabbed by a tall boy who was shouting that he would get the gold ring for sure. As the carousel began to turn, gleeful laughter came echoing out from the children astride their horses. The tall boy began to collect silver rings from the slot, and he placed them on his horse's ear. He let out a whoop as he showed off the brass ring that won him a free ride.

Yves had finished reading the brochure and was examining the many murals that covered the sides in the center of the carousel. He slowly walked around the outside, looking at the paintings. He especially liked the one of the women dressed in old-fashioned-clothing standing amongst the dunes with the ocean in the background. Angelique quietly walked up beside Yves and told him her favorite was the one of the carousel horse flying over the kids playing on the beach.

All the children had had several rides and it was time to go home. Amongst tears and a few tantrums, the children were herded back into cars to return to Seagull's Perch.

A day on the beach had been planned. The group grabbed towels, coolers filled with drinks and food, and blankets and chairs and made their way down the path to the beach. The rest of the family were already there. Children were building sandcastles in the sand; some were already playing in the surf. An active game of volleyball was going on, with most of the family's teenagers and young adults participating.

Turning Point

Varvara was established in her chair with a brightly colored umbrella spread out overhead. A large group of chairs were placed about her, and several aunts and uncles were occupying them. Uncle Bermont was overseeing a group of men who were placing tubes in the sand in preparation of the family's annual fireworks display. There was also a large pile of timber ready to be lit for Sunday's bonfire.

The coolers were at the disposal of everyone to snack or eat at their leisure. The afternoon passed with pleasant conversation, hearty competition, familiar laughter, and camaraderie.

Making their way up the path toward the house, everyone was discussing the upcoming concert down in the harbor. Everyone was carpooling because of the limited parking space downtown. Knowing that it was a Beatles tribute band, most everyone was going, including Varvara.

The entourage took up a large area on the grassy knoll beside the quay. It was a perfect summer night, warm with no humidity. There wasn't a cloud in sight to interrupt the multitude of stars that filled the evening sky above. The band was warming up as everyone settled into their seats. Varvara was entertaining the grandchildren with stories of her flight to the U.S. with The Beatles.

Soon the sound of music filled the air as one song after another was performed. "Hey Jude," "Yellow Submarine," "I Want To Hold Your Hand," "Here Comes The Sun," "Michelle," and "A Hard Day's Night" brought people out on to the sidewalk to dance. Children were running in circles with glow sticks wrapped around their heads like halos. Others were sitting amongst the grown-ups holding sparklers. The band was exceptionally good, and everyone young and old had an enjoyable time.

Varvara looked tired, and when she returned to Seagull's Perch she wished everyone, "Blessed be," and wheeled off to her room.

The teenagers started setting up tables and chairs while the parents of young children guided them off to their rooms and tucked them all safely into their beds. A game night of Hand and Foot was prearranged for the rest of the evening. Angelique and Yves were a team and started their first game against Aunt Karen and Uncle Peter. Teams had already been drawn up during the day. It was instant elimination, and everyone was excited to get started. Laughter groans, and the sound of cards shuffling soon filled the room. After about an hour, the field of players was cut in half and seven teams remained. Angelique's team was going against Marc and Stephanie. There was boisterous bantering as the games continued. Joshua and Joan, visiting from France, were muttering in French as they lost the first two hands to Wayne and Victoria. Things changed rapidly and the last two hands went quickly and they came back to win. Three teams played each other and the winners were Juliane and Mary Ann. It was going on midnight, and Joshua and Joan bowed out. Marc teamed up with Stephanie and took their place to play against Juliane and Mary Ann and Angelique and Yves. The first two rounds were won by Angelique and Yves. The third hand Marc and Karen finished off, catching both teams with red threes in their foot! As a result there were no more than two thousand points, between the three teams. Many people had drifted off to bed but a small group watched the final hand. Marc was the first to open using all but two cards to make the required one hundred twenty points. Juliane couldn't play so Angelique laid her cards down, bringing her team real close to having the required elements to go out. Stephanie played all her cards and went right into her foot; she only had three cards left when she finished her turn. After another round of play, Marc laid down his last card. Tallying up the points, Yves and Angelique let out a groan when the scores were revealed. They lost the game by only one hundred points. Marc and Stephanie were the winners. As it was after 1 a.m. everyone made their way to their beds knowing that tomorrow would be another long day.

 The sunlight was pouring through all the windows as the silent house awoke to greet the new day. The kitchen was already a beehive of activity-potatoes were being cleaned and peeled to make a potato salad; coolers were being packed with drinks, boxes of chips and cookies, along with paper goods, all were ready to be brought down to the beach. Others were taking freshly baked muffins out of the oven. Their mouthwatering aroma permeated the kitchen and traveled out into the hallways, drawing people to breakfast like a magnet. Coffee and tea, along with juice and fruit, were placed on the sideboard for everyone to make their own breakfast. It was like Interstate 95 at 5 p.m. as waves of people came and went, grabbing breakfast and then joining the stream of people all picking up the supplies and carrying them down to the beach.

By eleven, the whole family was established on the beach. Varvara again was seated in her beach chair surrounded by other members of the family. Groups of spectators gathered around to watch games of volleyball and horseshoe competitions. Children were enjoying digging in the sand, building sandcastles, gathering seashells, and playing in the ocean. Teenagers and adults ventured deeper into the crashing surf to swim or ride the waves with their boogie boards. The smell of suntan lotion along with the scent of burning charcoal spread out across the beach as it grew close to noon and the grill was being prepared to cook the upcoming meal. Chicken, hamburgers, and hot dogs were soon piled high on a platter to be distributed amongst the crowd, along with assortment of salads: potato, fresh, macaroni, and Aunt Karen's famous orzo salad. A family favorite, the salad consisted of orzo noodles, English cucumber, grape tomatoes, feta cheese, shrimp, and basil tossed in olive oil. The tables were filled with several different kinds of chips and trays of pickles and olives. A pot filled with corn on the cob was set at the end of the table.

Mothers quickly filled their children's plates and soon everyone was enjoying the delicious meal. As with most family gatherings, there was the familiar banter and teasing going on. After everyone was finished, a small tent city was set up to accommodate all the little ones' nap time. Not only had the young taken advantage of a much needed rest, but also many of the older generations could be seen dozing in their chairs.

With people sleeping, the teenagers and many of the young adults went off to play in the surf. Angelique, Yves, Stephanie, and Marc set out for a long walk along the shore. Angelique's turquoise cover-up's pockets soon filled up with tiny shells and smooth sea-washed stones. As they were walking, they discussed the upcoming weeks and the final filming of Varvara's story.

"Varvara is almost finished; I have mixed feelings about that," Stephanie said. "I'm glad, because lately Varvara seems to tire much more easily. I'm sad, because I have become so involved in her story and it's going to end."

Marc smiled down at Stephanie. I will be glad because it will free up more time for you to spend with me."

Laughing, Stephanie said, "Who said that I would?"

Marc held his hands to his heart and looked pained at her response.

Angelique and Yves laughed at their antics. Stephanie and Marc were constantly teasing each other, but anyone watching knew there was a budding relationship between them.

Yves commented on how fast the weeks were flying by. "I remember at Easter telling Angelique that June seemed too far away, and now it seems like that was just a few days ago."

"Speaking of time flying, I think we better head back," Angelique said. "Vari will be awake soon, and I don't want her to wake up and find me not there."

The rest of the afternoon was spent enjoying the sunshine and participating in family activities. Everyone pitched in to bring all the remnants of food, beach paraphernalia and sports equipment back up to the house. As they were returning to the beach, the sky's colors turned from daytime blue to golden hues, touching purple and pink clouds. As the sun dropped behind the horizon, the sky quickly grew dark. Many returned with blankets, along with sweatshirts and jackets. All gathered around the large pile of wood that was soon set afire. From the bonfire, a few men lit torches and made their way over to the long fuses for the fireworks. Sparklers were lit and adults watched carefully until they burnt their way out. For the next fifteen minutes, children and adults oohed and aahed as they watched the sky fill with amazing bursts of color.

After the fireworks, the children and the older adults made their way up the path to the house and their beds. The rest of the family pulled up chairs and blankets close to the fire. Soon bongos, guitars, and a few violins began to appear. Clear voices were heard as they began to sing along old family favorites: "Kumbiya," "Michael Rowed the Boat Ashore," and a hilarious rendition of "The Bear Went Over the Mountain." The music and voices blended with the tempo of the crashing waves and echoed down the beach. As the evening progressed, songs from the Beach Boys, The Beatles, and Elvis were added into the mix. At each passing hour, the group got smaller and the fire dwindled. A few teenagers held out till the end and raked out the last of the coals before heading off to bed.

Memorial Day dawned with the sound of the sea coming through Angelique's bedroom window. She awoke to a small face starring right in front of her.

"Mommy, are you awake?"

Rubbing the last of the sleep out of her eyes, Angelique glanced over at her alarm clock, which revealed 6:50, and said, "I'm awake now."

"Mommy, I'm hungry! Hurry up and get dressed. I want to go down to breakfast! Where is Daddy? Are we going to go down to the beach?"

"Whoa! Vari!"

Angelique stumbled out of bed and made her way to the bathroom for a quick shower. Vari continued to talk all the time Angelique showered and dressed. She repeated her whole weekend's activities.

Angelique let Vari's continuous chatter roll over her as she finished getting ready for the day. Glancing over at her daughter, she had to burst out laughing at the sight of dishevelment before her. Vari's dark curls were tossed in all directions. She had put on a bright yellow shirt with hot pink shorts. Around her neck she had hung several different colored necklaces, and she completed the outfit with one blue and one green sneaker, each on the wrong foot. After a few minor adjustments, they made their way down to the dining room that was already filled with family.

Those who lived far away were quickly finishing the breakfast and saying their goodbyes. Others were having a more leisurely breakfast and planning out the rest of the day. Yves joined Angelique and Vari, and it was decided that another day at the beach was called for. Angelique had a list of items she needed to organize, so she grabbed her laptop and her file folder on the wedding and set out down the path toward the beach. Yves and Vari went off to build the biggest sandcastle ever, while Angelique settled into her beach chair and called her wedding planner. They reviewed the plans and the order of events. As she went through her list, she checked off florist, cake, horse and carriage, band, reception, flight, hotel.

After she finished with her planner, she called Stephanie. They began checking her list of pictures that she wanted taken during the wedding and reception. It amazed her how much work was involved in planning just one day.

Finishing in about an hour's time, she shut down her laptop, satisfied that everything was in order. She knew the last week before the wedding was filled with activities, but she believed her list for that week was well planned and she could accomplish everything. Her thoughts drifted to the surprise wedding gift she was planning for Yves, but she was interrupted by the sounds of delightful giggles coming from Vari. Glancing down the beach, she saw Yves and Vari were playing in the surf. Stripping off her sundress to reveal a trim one-piece in aqua, she flipped off her shoes and tossed her sunglasses on her chair and ran down to join them. The rest of the day was spent in a playful exchange between the three, bonding them closer into a family unit.

Tuesday morning the house seemed empty and hollow without the extended family in residence. Varvara was prepared to continue with taping and finish telling the final years of her life. There was a small gathering of women standing around Varvara waiting for the taping to begin when Angelique's footsteps echoed down the hallway. At that moment, Vari came skipping into the room and up to Angelique. "Morning, Mommy." After a hug and a kiss she looked around and said, "Morning, Gamma, Gram, Mémère."

The women all smiled and said good morning back.

Varvara said, "Not many people get to see six generations altogether in one room. I think I want a portrait of all of us. I will have to talk to Stephanie about it."

"I already have, Mémére, remarked Angelique. "It's on the list of pictures I want taken at the wedding. That will be a good time to do it."

"Yes, that would be, but I was thinking of a picture of us as we are now informal."

Jan smiled over at Varvara and nodded in agreement as she held Vari on her lap. "Its times like this I miss Mom. She would have enjoyed so much of this time we're spending together."

The mention of Irene seemed to sober the group for a moment, and then Vari spoke up. "Mémère, are you telling stories to us today?"

Everyone chuckled as Varvara ruffled Vari's curls and nodded yes. Later that day, Varvara did begin telling her story again.

"After dealing with the battle of Jan's cancer, life seemed to settle into a familiar pattern. Tim retired from the service. After some discussion, they both decided to establish their home in the side suite at Seagull's Perch. It wasn't that much of a change, because Jan had stayed so often. Marc and Angelique were so excited that their grandparents were going to be so close. Victoria didn't show much emotion either way, but welcomed them when they arrived.

"I tried to attend as many activities that the children were involved in. Soccer games, football, baseball, equestrian events, and the dance studio kept me pretty busy. At least once a year, I flew to France to catch up with the family there. It was the year 1996, and I had seven grandchildren, thirteen great-grandchildren, eleven great-great-children, totaling thirty-one in all. "Just as you think your life is complete and on a direct path, God sends you a curve you don't expect. Mine came when at the age of ninety-one, I found I had a new beau. During the summer months, we shared the beach with a small group of families, who owned cottages along the shore. One couple, Linda and Maverick, would sit together enjoying the beach. Many times I would bump into Maverick and Linda as I took my morning walks. Maverick, Linda, and I had many discussions over the years about her cancer. Having leukemia, she sometimes was too exhausted to attend a business dinner and asked if I would go in her stead. At first I felt uncomfortable, but with her assurance I started being Maverick's hostess. Linda and I would get together and share laughter as I told her stories about the previous evening's events. We became good friends and I was saddened by the news that the cancer had come back and she had lost her battle during the winter. Maverick didn't come to the beach that year or the next.

"In the early spring of 1998 while I was enjoying a brisk evening walk along the shore, Maverick came out and joined me. He filled me in on his loss of Linda and how it had taken him two years to adjust her being gone. Maverick said he was glad he returned to the beach because it filled him with a new sense of peace. I could only agree with him, for the beach brought those same feelings to me.

"We began meeting quite often in the morning and evenings. I soon learned that part of Maverick's personality was being a prankster. He had a caustic humor that he used on anyone he encountered. My laughter echoed across the beach as I watched him pull tricks on my unsuspecting family.

"The family began to tease me about a budding romance, but I was just seeing a comfortable relationship that provided me with a good companion who was on the same wavelength as me.

"Maverick and I were constantly having heated discussions about politics, the stock market, theater, and society in general. He was a conservative to the extreme, and I was way too liberal for him. That summer passed so quickly, and I was a little saddened when it came time for Maverick to close up his cottage and head back to New York.

"We said our goodbyes and promised to keep in touch over the winter.

"For the next several weeks, I found myself a little lost, especially on my morning and evening walks. I missed Maverick. I really hadn't realized how much time I had been spending with him until he was gone. Apparently neither did Maverick. In October, I received a call from Maverick asking me out to dinner. I accepted.

"Nothing shocked me more than the handsome extremely well-dressed gentleman that showed up on my doorstep that Saturday evening. I was used to seeing Maverick in a shirt and swim shorts, his wavy gray hair tossed by the wind or held down by a baseball cap.

"It was a different person holding out a bouquet of fall flowers. His hair was neatly combed, and he was dressed in a well-cut silk suit. I saw for the first time an extremely attractive man. I was quiet as he helped me into his car, but soon the atmosphere relaxed as Maverick's humor took hold and we laughed through dinner. Sitting enjoying coffee and dessert, Maverick brought up the subject of how much he had missed me and all the time we spent together over the summer. He wanted to know if I would consider being his hostess over the next several months, as he had several conferences and business meetings set up across the country. Scattered over several cities, it would involve several weekends of travel.

"Quite surprised by the proposal I honestly had to tell him I needed time to think and returned to Seagull's Perch with a lot of questions running through my mind and not quite sure what I was going to decide. In the end, with encouragement from Jan and Victoria, I went forward with plans to work with Maverick. I was healthy and fit, thinking that life is an adventure; I might as well join in. My travels with Maverick revealed the majesty and vastness that encompassed the whole United States. What started out as a three or four month job, stretched out over the next four years. I enjoyed the challenges we faced doing business together and the laughter and companionship that we shared.

"Very few people get to be the ripe old age of 100. Just before I reached that number I came down with a terrible cold. Normally, I would fight off a cold in a matter of days, but it was soon apparent that this wasn't the average cold and it wasn't going away. Jan brought me into the Dr. Simon's office and I was immediately put in the hospital. I had pneumonia and he was seriously worried. My room was soon overflowing with family as the news spread that I was ill. I questioned why they were all there and told them all to go home. I'm not ready to leave this earth yet. I truly didn't realize how dangerous my condition was. Over the next several weeks I was struggling to breathe and ran high temperatures. When I was finally feeling better Dr. Simon informed me that the pneumonia had taken its toll on my heart, and I would have to take it easy if I wanted to live longer. I chuckled at this comment and asked him how old he was.

"'He replied, 'Thirty-three.'

"I'm going to be one hundred years old soon. Do you really think I care when I am going to die. I have lived a full and productive life. I don't believe I have missed out on anything. I have no regrets.

"Overhearing the conversation as they entered the room, Jan, Victoria, Angelique, and Maverick protested. Jan told me, she still needed my wisdom to guide her through the running of the family and the house.

"'I'm not ready to step into your shoes.' Jan said.

"Angelique joined in with her own protest. 'You promised to take me to France after I graduate. What would Uncle Berm say if he heard you talking like this?'

"Maverick just fondly looked down at me, and said he wanted my companionship for a little while longer. The conversation was interrupted by a young man whose appearance brought a groan from my mouth.

"I can't give any more blood, my veins aren't strong enough anymore," I complained.

"The nurse just quietly drew two vials of blood and patted my arm. 'That wasn't so bad,' he said.

"No, you have gentle hands," I replied.

"Dr. Simon had slipped into the room and said in his jovial voice, 'What's this I hear about someone getting ready to die.' He peered at Varvara batting his long brown eyelashes and said, 'What would I do without my girl?'

"At this, I laughed, and said. 'Your wife might have something to say about that.'

"He bantered back, 'She has known from the very beginning that I had a love affair with a beautiful woman. She knew she couldn't compete so she accepted being second best.'

Turning Point

"Everyone was smiling as they watched the natural comradery between the Dr. and his patient. He started his exam, and watching his facial expressions carefully, Jan and Victoria exchanged worried looks.

"'I would like to order a few test, and then I believe you can go home,' he said.

"This brought a smile that quickly changed to a frown when he continued. '"You have to have complete bed rest for at least ten days.'

"I told everyone to leave the room. Angelique and Jan tried to stay, but insisted that they too must leave."

"'When the room finally emptied, I turned to Dr. Simon and said. 'Ok! Out with it, what's going on? What are these test you want to make me have? I want to know why you're so worried. The facts, and give it to me straight.'

"'Well … I can tell …' Dr. Simon looked over at Varvara and this time there wasn't a smile on his face.

"'Young man I have known you your whole life. We have always been honest with each other. So what I want to know is what's different this time? The truth boy, I just want the truth."

"'Varvara, the truth is that your heart is tired, plain and simple. It's a hundred years old, and is starting to show signs of wearing out. If you don't slow down and rest it's not going to last much longer.'

"How much rest, are we talking?" asked Varvara.

"'If I let you go home at least two more weeks complete bed rest. Do you thing you can do that?'

"I remember I nodded my head."

"'Continuing he said. 'I want you to start using a wheelchair instead of walking. The less strain you put on your heart the better.'

"How long?"

"'I can't answer to that right now. I want to take these tests and look at what the results are. Then I'll give you an answer. I'm suggesting we get you a nurse to watch over you. I would also recommend that you inform your family of your condition,' he looked over at Varvara as he said this.

"'No, no one is to be told this. They would coddle me up and not let me live my life! I'm not ready to die yet. There are some family issues that need my attention. No one is to know this. Understand?'

"'Understood.'

"That afternoon, the tests were completed and Dr. Simon returned to my room with the results."

"'Where is everyone?'

"'I told them to go home. That I was tired and I was going to take a nap. I'm sure Maverick and Jan are around here somewhere. Ok. What did the tests say?'

"'That your heart was damaged with this bout of pneumonia and it's slowly going to stop working.'

"'How long?'

"'There's no real answer to that. It depends on if you're willing to follow my instructions and how much rest you take. I would normally say two years at best, but knowing you, I'll say five. If you start taking care of yourself,' he added.

"'I'll take the five.'

"'Take care of yourself, old girl; I don't want to see you again for a long time,' Dr. Simon chuckled, and gave Varvara a hug.

Varvara was chuckling to herself as she finished relating the story. She looked around the room and said. "He was right. I have made it the five years, but I'm afraid it won't be much longer. I'm tired." So the filming stopped for the day.

The next day, Varvara was surprised to find a large gathering of the grandchildren waiting for her to come down to begin her telling about her life. Several of the boys began asking questions.

Mémère, you have lived so long. What are the biggest changes you have seen, and what affected your life the most?"

Varvara, thought carefully before she answered. "When you get to be my age you have very little that surprises you. I've gone from horse drawn carriages to jet airplanes and space travel. I began using candle light, and now have LED lights. I went from communication by letters to being able to talk and see people half way around the world. But the answer to your question is that the cruelty of men, and their incessant need for wars, affected my life the most. The Russian revolution cost me my mother. World War II cost me Aurele. Vietnam almost took Tim from us. Now we have these new-fangled Iran, Afghanistan, and Iraq conflicts and the war on terrorist that has brought fear, injury, and anguish into my life."

Varvara started telling her story.

"I remember I was sitting outside looking down at the beach on one of those crisp clear days when the sky overhead was a crystal clear blue without a cloud to mar its vastness. An early September morning, the surf was calm and even the seagulls were quiet. The earth seemed to understand something was about to happen. I was joined by Jan and we were enjoying the fall sunshine when we heard Tim shouting to us from the back porch to come inside.

"'A plane just crashed into the twin towers. Tim came and quickly pushed my wheel chair into the great room which housed a large screen TV that was revealing unbelievable pictures of the scene in New York. Suddenly, as we were watching, the announcer started screaming that a second plane had just crashed into the other tower. We all watched in shock as the news unfolded before our eyes. I realized that this was not an accident, but that we were under attack. Tim was on the phone trying to get information about friends and family members who worked or lived in the twin towers area. As the day unfolded family slowly began to find their way to the great room. As we continued to watch, we learned that the planes were out of Boston. Another plane had crashed in Pennsylvania and a fourth in Washington. Jan and I began to panic because Karen and Ronald were to fly out of Boston that morning to go to Europe and take an Anniversary cruise. It would be several hours before we knew they were safe. Unfortunately because all flights were cancelled they returned home, and had to cancel their trip. Richard came in and said he was at the airport and was told no flights were to go in or out until further notice. All his planes had returned except John Clayton's. He had flown to Block Island and was coming home on the ferry. Richard said they would have to go get the plane when the flight restrictions were lifted. We returned to watching the TV learning more about what was happening. Peter was in New York and by mid-afternoon he was able to get a call through to tell us he was ok. Karen and Ronald walked in and were surrounded with us all giving them hugs and talk of how thankful we were because they were safe.

"The day was spent watching the news. We heard reports updating information about the attacks. There was a sense of shock and unbelief that this was really happening. We finally shut down the TV and with saddened hearts went our separate ways.

"My early morning routine of having a cup of coffee while watching the ocean didn't provide me with the usual sense of peace. There was an earie silence to the sky. It was another crystal clear day but there were no sounds of the occasional airplane flying high overhead. All the little planes that usually flew out of the Westerly airport were obviously absent. It was as if even the seagulls knew something was wrong for they were strangely silent and didn't seem to want to fly. I returned from the beach to find family glued to the TV listening for further details surrounding the 911 attacks. We learned that a terrorist group called Al-Qaeda had taken responsibility for the hijacking. Nineteen terrorist boarded four planes and hijacked them. Two of the planes were flown into the World Trade Center in New York. A third plane had crashed into the Pentagon. The forth plane was supposed to crash into the White House, but the passengers resisted and the plane crashed into a field in Pennsylvania. The death toll rose to nearly 3,000 and the list of injured rose to over 6,000. All air traffic was suspended for three days. We learned about the heroism of the New York City's fire and police. The stories filled the news for weeks. Soon, I began to worry about the repercussions that the attacks would bring. The U.S. certainly wasn't going to sit back and do nothing. An ache filled my heart as war seemed to be looming over us again. There were several family members who were currently serving in the armed services and quite a few more in the National Guard. I naturally worried about what this would mean to them.

"The talk around the breakfast table was when not if the war was going to start, but when. In less than a month Afghanistan Operation "Enduring Freedom" began. On October 7 air strikes on Taliban and al Qaeda targets start and last for five days. On October 19 the first grown action is taken and within five months the number of grown troops more than doubles. Among the military deployed were Elizabeth's son and daughter. Nicholas was a member of the Air Force and Maryann a nurse in the Rhode Island National Guard. They both served two terms and came home safely. In 2004, Karen's daughter, Alycia was deployed to Afghanistan. As you know Alycia wasn't as lucky. She was severely injured by a roadside bomb losing her right leg just below the knee. She was treated at the emergency Surgical Center in Kebal. When stable, she was flown to Landstaht Regional Medical Center in Germany. She finally came home to the U.S. and was fitted with her first prosthesis at Walter Reed National Military Medical Center. Ronald, Karen, and I flew down to see her. Alycia looked like a tiny waiflike form in her big white hospital bed. In a deep depression, she barely acknowledged any of us. After a week of trying to reach her and failing; we went home and pushed for her to be transferred to the Providence VA Medical Center. We finally were successful and the family gathered to try and help her. Everyone was taking turns to visit her. Her brother and sister came as often as they could. Cousins came and went to try to not to leave her alone. Nicholas and Mary Ann came often and their visits seemed to help. They had an understanding because of the shared experience. She had physical and psychiatric therapy and her depression seemed to improve. It was almost a year when she finally came home. Still slightly depressed, she spent most of her time up in her room. Karen had come over to talk with Jan and me, about ideas of what she should do. We consulted with the therapist at Apple Rehab and her advice was to encourage her to get out. 'Invite her to join you for lunch, go shopping, and ask her to do something she did before she lost her leg. These suggestions might sound simple but it takes time for a person to adjust to her new life. She is also dealing with the loss of her friends and that can take years to adjust to. Be patient, and with our help we think Alycia will come around. She has come a long way already.'

"So the whole family pitched in and Alycia received many invitations. At first she refused but, eventually she began to do a few things with her cousins.

"I went to visit and had quite a talk with her. 'I'm old, I have lived a long and wonderful life, but wars rob people of fulfilling their potential. It's just such a waste. I think of all the mothers, fathers, brothers, and sisters that will never see their love ones again because they lost their lives over there. Alycia you are young and have a long future in front of you. Look at that future and decide to make something of yourself. We're not quitters in this family. We are fighters. I believe in you.' My little speech didn't seem to have much effect, so I patted her hand and went downstairs to talk with her mother Karen.

"When I walked into the kitchen I found Victoria having a serious discussion with Karen. Victoria turned and told me she had come because she had been in a similar situation when she was sixteen and thought she could relate to her. At that moment I was so proud of Victoria. She really wanted to help Alycia. She went up to talk to Alycia and I was hopeful she could work some miracle to break the wall of withdrawal and depression. It was surprising that in the next several weeks working along with the therapist's suggestions Alycia did become more like herself. It was at Christmas, during the annual family decoration party, that I finally heard her laugh. I knew she was getting better and I could stop worrying about her.'

Varvara paused in talking. Stephanie asked if she wanted to stop for the day. Shaking her head no, she began again.

"Ah… Christmas at Seagull's Perch…the day after Thanksgiving wasn't called black Friday by us, but maybe some of the men felt that way? We gathered early and usually Tim and Harrison went off in trucks to go get the Christmas trees. Of the four trees, one would be placed in the entrance hall, one in the family room, one on the front porch, and the last would be placed down on the beach. The teenagers and young adults took care of what they called 'their beach tree.' Each year picking a different theme they gathered supplies and spent the weekend creating ornaments out of an edible substance made up of wild bird seed, suet, corn meal, peanut butter, raisins, nuts, and chopped corn. They also strung popcorn and cranberries into long strands of garland. Apple slices and oranges added a touch of color. The themes ranged from their favorite sports teams to the popular movie of that year. You could hear their chatter and laughter spilling out from the kitchen as they used the blender to mix together the peanut butter and suet. The constant popping of popcorn and an occasional "ouch" as someone stuck themselves instead of the popcorn or cranberries were usually heard. They worked all day and had boxes of garland and ornaments ready for the decorating party that happened on Saturday.

The rest of the men spent all Friday hauling boxes from the attic and storage room and placing them in the room that they were labeled to go in. When Tim returned from getting the trees he took charge and set Santa and his sleigh on top of the garage. He also pulled out all the wreaths and got them hung up on every window and door. The two boxes of candles were all unwrapped, checked for a working bulb by Tim then given to someone to be placed in every window in the house. Every string of lights was stretched across the great room's floor. Each string was checked and broken strings were thrown away. This job was left to Harrison, Ronald, and Richard. The life size nativity was unwrapped and washed by Irene's three daughters before being arranged on the front lawn.

The tree in the entrance hallway was decorated with ribbons of gold and strands of pearls. White lights were draped on its branches and then angel ornaments were hung on every branch. The idea of an Angel tree came when Jan had made a complaint that she had nowhere to put or display the collection that she had amassed from angels given to her while she was ill. Jan had always loved angels. She had started the collection when she was given a delicate hand blown glass angel in memory of Irene and Leslie's death. That angel was always hung front and center each year by Jan. Many of the angels had special sentiments attached to them. All of the grandchildren and great-grandchildren had angels with their names on them and they were all hung on the tree. Many of the angels came from family members who came across them in souvenir shops. Bermont and Sasha sent an angel every Christmas to go on the tree. What had started as a small collection now covered a large nine foot tall tree. Tim complained every year it was getting harder and harder to find a good size tree. The tree was truly beautiful when completed. It always felt like it was welcoming whenever I entered the front door.

The tree in the family room had a very Victorian feel to it. White lights again were placed amid all the tree's branches. Lace ribbon and strands of gold beads were draped around the tree. Then crystal snowflakes and pale pink glass ornaments were unwrapped and placed on the tree. There was a box that had a collection of twelve Thomas Kincaid glazed ornaments. Large glass globes and boxes of delicate glass ornaments that had been in the family for centuries were carefully placed on the tree. There were a few special family ornaments including a wooden nativity that came from Armenia and a set of Russian ballerinas. A beautiful gold angel was placed atop the tree.

The tree on the front porch was the official family tree. Colored lights decorated each branch and all the ornaments were a vast collection of handmade ornaments that had been made over the years by the children. Candy canes and decorated sugar cookies that were made each year were also hung on the tree. It took all of Friday to get the four trees decorated and the wreaths hung up.

Saturday was devoted to placing over sixty nativities around the house. A large handmade one was arranged on the dining room sideboard. Each fireplace had its own original set. There were snow globes and icons. An antique, porcelain set from Italy, and an all-white clay set that came from South America found homes in two of the bedrooms. A Willow Tree Set was placed on the large oak desk in the office. There were small sets placed on tables and on bathroom counters. There were night lights and candle toppers. Every year I am amazed at how many there are and how easily they blend into the decor of each room.

Beside the nativities there were Santa's and snowmen, angels and carolers that were placed in and around the house. By the time we finished on Sunday we all were exhausted but very happy. We always finished the evening with egg-nog and Christmas carols. Every year I looked forward to the week-end after Thanksgiving. It sets the season's start for me. Again Varvara stopped talking. Sighing she looked over to Stephanie and stated softly "I believe that completes my story. Jan and you can add what's left after I am gone. Slowly she glanced around the room at all her love ones. Smiling she said her departing 'Blessed be.' and left the room.

The room was strangely quiet after Varvara left. Then Stephanie spoke to Jan and Angelique.

"There were times when I didn't think she'd be able to finish her story and now I find it sad that she has. I will miss coming here to hear her tales of the past."

"I believe she can rest now and stop worrying. I know she is looking forward to Angelique and Marc's wedding. I try to focus on that knowing she wants to be there. I can't help being sad that the signs are there that her heart is just wearing out." This came from Jan as she wiped tears from her eyes.

"I'm so glad I came home to experience all this with you.

My life has changed so much and I owe it all to her. I can only strive to be like her. She is one truly regal lady," said Angelique.

The next day was Saturday and Angelique had plans to tie up all the loose ends before her wedding the next week. As she walked down into the family room a large group of women shouted surprise. Angelique had no idea that a bridal shower had been planned for her. She glanced down at Vari who was jumping up and down. 'I kept the secret this time! She shouted out to everyone. And laughter filled the room.

Angelique sat down in the chair provided and looked at the pile of presents in awe. The next several hours passed in great comradery and teasing especially when some slinky nighty was lifted out of its box. Vari sat next to her mother with her grandmother Victoria on her other side and watched all the presents being unwrapped. She smiled at Angelique and said, "We are really going to be a family aren't we mommy?"

"Yes, dear we really are."

The following week flew and it was an excited Angelique who stood looking out her bedroom window on the eve of her wedding. There was a soft knock on her door. Varvara came in quietly and patted the side of the bed for Angelique to sit down.

"I have just come to give you my best wishes and blessing. I have said many times that you and Yves remind me so much of my own Jean. I have wanted to give you this special gift to wear on your wedding day." Angelique held out her hand and a strand of pearls fell into her palm.

"They were the first gift he gave me and I think he's smiling down on you and granting you his blessings too. Enjoy tomorrow and look only towards your future. Blessed be, my Angel, Blessed be."

Angelique and Yves' wedding day finally arrived with a picture-perfect summer day. The family all made their way to the church. Yves and Marc went off to the front of the church while guests were being escorted to their seats. Soon the church was filled, and music swelled with the first notes of the "Pachelbel's Canon." Varvara, looking regal in her wine colored gown with its embroidered lace jacket, was wheeled down the aisle by Maverick, and then came Pam, Yves' grandmother, dressed in a lovely pale pink chiffon dress. Linda wore a gold and black sequined sheath, and was escorted by Yves' dad. Jan, elegant in her royal blue gown with its sequined trim came down the aisle her chiffon skirt floating softly down to her feet which had sequined slippers that matched her top. Victoria, her tall willowy frame was shown off to perfection in the emerald green gown she had chosen at the shop. She had bought a shawl of the same material to cover the fact that the gown was backless. There was a mischievous twinkle in her eyes as she walked down the aisle on the arm of Wayne. Stephanie and Yves' sister Safyia came next. Each dressed in the pale yellow, strapless, tea length dress. The maid of honor was Angelique's best friend since the fifth grade; Ann was dressed the same as Stephanie and Safyia except Ann's was a beautiful shade of apricot and had the added straps she had requested. Vari drew a lot of laughter as she came skipping down the aisle throwing out rose petals from a basket. She was dressed in the apricot sundress and a ring of flowers sat amongst her curls on top of her head.

There were several gasps and ahh's as Angelique appeared at the back of the church holding on to her Grampa Tim's arm. The wedding marched swelled out from the organ as she made her way slowly down the aisle. Tears shimmered in her eyes as she looked towards the front of the church to where Yves was waiting. To Yves she looked like a fairy princess with the beads of her gown shimmering in the reflecting candlelight. Her face glowing with happiness she smiled as she walked past the pews. She touched the pearls that were around her neck as she passed the front pew and mouthed a thank you to Varvara for letting her borrow them. Finally, joining Yves at the altar, the wedding ceremony began. The preacher talked about how Yves and Angelique met; their troubles and their coming together. She talked of their strong faith and charged them with relying on that faith in the future. Their voices strong and clear could be heard exchanging their wedding vows. After exchanging wedding rings and given a final blessing they were pronounced husband and wife. Amongst loud cheering and clapping they exited the church holding Vari's hands between them. On the steps of the church all the wedding guest opened small envelopes they had been given as they entered the church and released a butterfly into the sky. Soon butterflies were flying everywhere. The wedding party made their way across the street to the park for pictures and waited for their time to be included in the photo shoot. Victoria came up behind Varvara's chair as she was talking to Vari and overheard their conversation. "Mémère look!" Vari's voice was filled with youthful excitement.

Varvara was watching the adorable child as butterflies were dancing around them. A beautiful yellow and black one circled Vari's head and then flew to light on Varvara's hand.

"On the wings of butterflies your love ones will send you their love." Vari came and stood beside Varvara's chair.

"Who is sending us their love, Mémère?"

"I don't know child, but it doesn't matter who, just know that someone is. After I am gone, whenever you see a butterfly you will know that it is bringing you a message of love just to you from me."

Tears were falling from Victoria's eyes as she witnessed the scene before her. She quickly brushed them away as the photographer called them over to take pictures. Little did anyone know that in a few days' time, that overheard conversation would bring comfort to the whole family.

After all the pictures were taken, the family all headed to Ocean House for the wedding reception. Ocean House, located on 1 Bluff Ave. in Watch Hill had been Angelique's dream location for her reception. Ever since she could remember she had an attachment to the classic Victorian style hotel. An immense yellow structure, with white railings surrounding its porches, it sits high on a bluff and overlooks the Atlantic Ocean. On a clear day you can see both the Montauk and Block Islands. It has its own private beach and its lawns and gardens accentuate its grandeur. In its prime it was the summer house for the rich and had been the setting for the silent film American Aristocracy staring Douglas Fairbanks in 1916. After falling into disrepair it was bought and demolished in 2005.

The hotel was rebuilt and over sixty percent is a replica of the old hotel. In the new hotel there are forty-nine guest suites and twenty-three residential suites. The suites were selling anywhere from two to seven million dollars.

Angelique had grown up with a fascination for Ocean House. As her limo drove through the harbor it stopped at the quay to drop off Angelique and Yves. A white wedding carriage was awaiting them to take them the rest of the way to Ocean House. The carriage driver helped them into the carriage and with the words "Step Up" they were on their way. Excitement and happiness bubbled up inside Angelique and burst forth in a series of giggles and laughter as they turned up the hill to head toward the hotel. It was hard not to be filled with awe when you approached the beautiful structure. Yves and Angelique admired its impressive elegance as they stepped out of the carriage.

Angelique had worked so hard on her wedding day and had hoped everything would go smoothly. She smiled as she approached her wedding party standing outside the reception hall. The party was in full swing as the bands drum roll called attention to each pair of groomsman and bridesmaid entering the hall. Finally amongst cheers and whistles Angelique heard, "For the first time, I'm proud to introduce Mr. and Mrs. Yves Haroutunian!"

As prearranged they went right in to their first dance. The first notes of "It's your love" by Clint black floated out as Angelique and Yves circled the floor. Soon all the bridal party was invited to join the happy couple. Uncle Bermont and Victoria danced together and Maverick was rocking Varvara's chair on the sidelines. Vari didn't need a partner as she just danced and weaved her way through everyone. As the dance finished everyone made their way to their seats as dinner was beginning to be served. Marc stood up and raised his glass as he began his toast.

"Angelique and Yves, I've waited a long time for this day. I don't know anyone who loves someone as deeply as you two love each other. It seems like the struggles you went through to get to where you are have only strengthened the bond between you! Angelique, my angel, I am so glad your finally happy, I love you so much! Yves, from enemy to the best friend I could ever ask for and now you're my brother. May each step you both take into the future bring you joy, laughter, and love. Blessed be. Lifting his glass he raised it again and said, 'to Angelique and Yves!'" Throughout the dinner conversation flowed along with the clinking of spoons on glasses. After dinner Angelique and Yves cut the cake. It was almost hard to destroy the ornate sandcastle wedding cake. They exchanged feeding the cake to each other and laughed when Vari came running up wanting her personal share. While the cake was being served the band began to start playing and soon everyone was up and dancing. Young and old danced together. Everyone was enjoying themselves and sharing in the couple's joy. Varvara sat in her chair and viewed her extended family as they celebrated on the dance floor. She found it amazing that she and Jean now had thirty-seven descendants. It was hard to imagine that the frightened girl that left Russia was now the center of a family that was spread out over two sides of the Atlantic Ocean. She reflected back to the fortune told to her by the gypsy at the train station. Life would come in threes: three men in her life, three homes, and three children. Her life would split in two and she would live in two worlds: France and the United States, one old and one new. She would have a long eventful life: one hundred and five is a pretty long life. Varvara chuckled to herself at this thought. As the evening was nearing its end everyone was saying good bye and wishing Angelique and Yves many blessings; they were staying in the hotel overnight. Victoria was guiding Vari over to say goodnight as she was returning with Varvara to Seagull's Perch. Stephanie and Marc were the last to leave and Angelique hugged Marc and thanked him for his heartfelt words. Finally, the happy couple made their way to their room. Angelique let out a squeal as Yves lifted her in his arms to carry her across the threshold. Smiling and gazing into his eyes they began a sensuous kiss that lasted for some time. Placing her on her feet, Yves continued to spread kisses across her face and nibbled at her ear. He muttered a minor complaint at all the buttons he was trying to undo. While occupied with Angelique's dress, Angelique began her own disassemble of Yves' tie and was trying to undo the studs on the front of his shirt. Soon, reveling in the soft curls of his chest, she quickly nipped at his nipple causing Yves to gasp and mutter something under his breath. It was Angelique's turn to gasp, when Yves kisses traveled to the dainty white bra that he just had exposed. His kisses soon reached her creamy white breast that was held firmly in his palm as he teased her nipple with the slight shadow of a beard on his chin. He continued with little nips with his teeth and Angelique gave out a groan as his warm mouth finally entrapped her breast. Thoroughly enjoying himself, he gasped himself, when Angelique's hand slipped inside his pants and firmly grasped his manhood, which quickly responded to her soft but messaging fingers. Their foreplay continued as they worked their way out of their wedding clothes. Each stared at the other and fell onto the large bed to continue exploring where they had left off. After completely satisfying her every need Yves rose over Angelique and entered her fulfilling his needs and soon collapsed at her side. Smiling he whispered words of love and promises as he kissed her smiling lips. They both dozed off for a while. Angelique woke to the popping of champagne and a smiling Yves said, "Hello, wife would you care to join me in the soaking tub." Smiling at him she climbed out of bed and slipped into the steaming tub. Taking a glass from Yves, he filled it with champagne and filling his own he joined her in the tub. Raising his glass and tapping the rim of hers he began a toast.

"To my lovely wife of several hours, I offer this pledge to you. From this day forth, as we begin our new journey together, and knowing the history of our past mistakes. I am vowing to always listen to your opinions and never disregard your wishes. You and Vari are my first priority. I swear to you that I'll always listen to you and work by your side to raise our daughter. I didn't believe in miracles before, but having you again in my life feels like a true miracle. I will love you and honor you for the rest of my life." Yves again touched his glass to the rim of Angelique's glass.

Teary eyed, Angelique responded. "That was a beautiful speech and I will value the sincerity in which the words were said. I too, have a tendency to pinch myself to make sure this is real and I am not dreaming. I have loved you since the moment I set eyes on you. I feel blessed that we have arrived at this point and are starting a new beginning together. I will love you for all time. It seems appropriate to give you one of my wedding gifts."

Reaching to the shelf behind her head Angelique picked up a small brightly wrapped box and handed it to Yves.

Yves carefully began to unwrapped the small but heavy box, and upon opening let out a sigh. He gently lifted the beautiful pocket watch and opened the lid. The engraved message said:

"I will love you for all time!'

Angelique told him it was her great-great- grandfathers, "Mémère had given it to her, for him.

"I will treasure it. Thank you."

"In the spirit of giving gifts, I have one you don't have to unwrap. Mémère must have been in a giving mood, because she said for me to tell you to keep the Safire ring you are wearing. Angelique picked up her hand and glanced at the heirloom that had been in Mémère's chest since she travelled from Russia so many years ago. Tears were rolling down her cheeks as she looked up at Yves.

"This makes me happy and sad at the same time. I know we are going to lose her, and I am not ready to let her go. I'm so glad we got her story finished … hiccupping…" she laughed. "No more champagne for me."

The next morning, Angelique said to Yves, "Let's get dressed. We are meeting Uncle Richard at the airport. I can't wait to get to Block Island. The bed and breakfast place is amazing and I'll show you all my favorite spots."

It seemed that time flew, because they soon found themselves seated in their seats with Uncle Richard telling them that he had the ok for takeoff. Yves admired the ocean view from his window and as quickly as the flight started the plane banked to make its approach to the island airstrip. Landing with a soft bump, the plane rumbled to a stop. Angelique's chatter with her Uncle ended with a reminder to pick them up at four on Wednesday.

They made their way to the Inn at Old Harbor and began their stay. Their days were filled with sightseeing on rented scooters. They went touring the two old lighthouses, shared ice cream sundaes at the Ice Cream Place, explored the only brewery on Block Island called the Mohegan Café and Brewery, and renting two horses they went riding along the shore at sunset. They took long walks along the beach finding seashells and a fairly large sand dollar, which they saved to give to Vari, when they returned. Evenings were spent enjoying the fine cuisine of the islands restaurants. On their last evening, Angelique surprised Yves with another wedding gift. Over the dinner table she handed him an envelope. Questioning, he looked inside, and a gasp escaped as he read the document he held. His eyes scanned the papers, and his hands shook as he read he was granted the ownership of the filly- Twilight, sire: Midnight-Magic, dam: Morning Star. After some time, he glanced at Angelique. Overwhelmed by her generosity and at a loss for words he ravished her mouth with kisses and asked, "How did this come about? Marc never said anything to me about this breeding. There are no words that are adequate to show my gratitude. Are you sure?"

"I called Uncle Bermont myself just before I left Paris and asked if there was a possibility of breeding Midnight-Magic. His reply was that he'd been examining the bloodlines to approach me to consider the same thing. We agreed and the insemination was completed with Twilight being the results. Morning Star is due any day with the second foal, and I gave up my share of it, for full share of Twilight. Now, I give her to you. She can be the start of your stake in the new stables you and Marc are starting together."

Yves thanked her again. Reminding her, that she was part of the business, and the rest of the evening was spent talking and planning their future together.

The days flew by, and too soon, they found themselves standing at the airport watching for Uncle Richard and the plane to land.

Arriving home to an excited Vari, who loved her sand dollar, and asked a million questions. She chattered away about all the things she did while they were away.

Entering the sunroom, they found Victoria and Jan enjoying a cup of tea. They spent the next hour sharing all they had done on the island. Angelique inquired after Varvara. Jan told them that after the excitement of the wedding she has been very tired and was resting up in her room so she could join them for dinner.

Laughter and squeals of delight were heard coming from the dining room as the family enjoyed their dinner that evening. Varvara was looking lovely, but Yves and Angelique noticed a subtle change in her breathing. They exchanged questioning looks with Jan and Tim. As soon as dinner was over Varvara returned to her rooms and the family began a discussion about her condition.

"Each day she seems to get weaker," Victoria stated

"We knew this was coming but, I'm not ready, never will be," said Tim. "I've talked with Dr. Simon and there is really nothing we can do, but keep her comfortable," Jan stated as she sat wiping tears away. Then added, "She's lived a long life and now her heart is just tired.'

It was a somber group that went off to bed that evening.

The next morning Varvara was at the breakfast table and turned to Tim and asked, "Could you bring me down to the shore. I'd like to sit and enjoy the sound of the surf and seagulls one more time. I checked and it's going to be a warm enough today."

Startled, Tim only nodded his head.

That afternoon a small family group started down to the beach. Tim carried Varvara. The mood was somber as they walked the path only Vari chattered happily about going to the beach. Reaching the sand, Tim gently placed Varvara in her beach chair. "Thank you my dear." Varvara voice was frail and raspy. She sat in her chair and looked at her family and then the ocean. Again, she found a sense of peace filled her. Her nurse hovered closely with a worried expression.

Everyone on the beach was aware of the situation and soon other family members appeared stopping to say a few words with Varvara.

After about an hour Varvara asked to be returned to the house. Tim again carried her up the path. Reaching the great room he gently placed her in her wheelchair. He was frightened by her pallor and shallow breathing. The nurse swiftly took Varvara to her room and got her comfortable in her bed. She stepped out of the room to a small impatient group awaiting her report. With tears filling up her eyes she told them, "I feel we should call Dr. Simon now and get the family here as fast as you can."

Dr. Simon arrived and with sadness he confirmed what everyone knew was happening. He assured them she was comfortable and in no pain. "It's just a matter of time." He couldn't get the words out and keep up his professional composure. With tears brimming over he just shook his head. "I'm going to miss the old girl." Victoria patted his shoulder and thanked him for all his care of Varvara.

The great room was filling up with family; aunts, uncles, cousins and friends all stood around waiting their turn to say their good-bye's.

Maverick stood by the window while family members came into the room to say their goodbyes. After a while he came and spoke to Jan that he couldn't bear to stay anymore. Choking on his tears he leaned over Varvara and whispered softly spoken words of love and finally said farewell. Victoria stood up and assisted the grief stricken man out of the room.

Out in the hallway Bermont, who had already said good bye to his mother; guided Maverick downstairs to join the rest of the family sitting in the great room.

Angelique quietly entered the bedroom and looked down at Varvara. Tears quickly gathered in her eyes as she gazed at the frail beauty lying in the bed before her. She was so still and Angelique thought she looked like a porcelain doll. Varvara's breathing was very shallow often there were seconds of time where she would pause from breathing. It was a curious pattern that was hard to get use to and frightening to observe. Angelique's thoughts came in flashes of memories of times shared with Varvara. She kissed Varvara on both cheeks and whispered a prayer. Angelique acknowledged that the time was near and taking one last look and a whispered, "good-bye" she left the room. Tears streaming down her face she walked directly into the waiting arms of Yves who himself was having difficulty controlling his own emotions. The two walked back into the great room and joined the others in reminiscing and telling stories about Varvara.

It was hard to believe that only a week had passed since she was happy, laughing, and enjoying herself at Angelique and Yves wedding.

Victoria and Jan were still sitting at Varvara's bedside. They had not left her since she had returned from the beach. The hours passed slowly, but soon there were signs that her life was ending. A tiny tear escaped from one eye.

Victoria wiped it away with a special handkerchief that had been lying on her pillow in preparation. Her breathing came in deep heavy gasps and then after a deep sigh she was gone. Varvara became a peaceful beauty with a look of serenity permanently frozen for all time. Choking on her tears Victoria hugged Varvara. Kissing her cheeks and telling her she loved her Victoria left the room. Jan followed suit and they both walked toward the great room. The sound of fireworks bursting in the sky made them look out the window. "How appropriate that her life ends with a grand celebration," Victoria thought. She turned and joined the family gathered together and gave them the news.

"She's gone."

The news brought more tears and silent prayers. There were even sighs of relief that Varvara was now at peace. Varvara had made all the arrangement for her funeral and all the details were quickly carried out. She was taken away by the funeral director, Mr. Belanger. He informed Victoria that he would be cremating her on Monday. The funeral was to be at 11 a.m. on Wednesday. The church was filled with family and friends and the organ played all Varvara's favorite hymns. 'How Great Thou Art' and 'Amazing Grace" were sung by the choir. Marc read the 23rd Psalm and Angelique read Corinthians II. The choir sang Alleluia. Uncle Bermont spoke the eulogy talking about his mother's life. How Varvara had just completed her memoires and had enjoyed having her family surround her. How happy she was at the wedding of Yves and Angelique. Mentioning highlights of her life made the family laugh and cry. It was a beautiful tribute to his mom. The choir sang a French Hymn and the minister's final blessing was in French. 'La fève de Se, fève de Se bonne par un dieu bénissent. Se Bonne, Se Bonne.' After the service the family went to the memorial garden and planted a large lilac bush in Varvara's memory. Leaving the church the family returned to Seagull's Perch and made their way to the beach. Each family member was given a small box filed with Varvara's ashes. After saying the Lord's Prayer the minister said a final blessing and each member threw the boxes out to sea. A flowered wreath was placed in the sand where Varvara used to sit. The family slowly left the beach making their way up to the house. Jan, Tim, Angelique, Yves,

Victoria and Vari were the last ones to leave. Vari in her usual exuberance went skipping ahead of her parents. She was out of sight when Angelique heard her voice talking to someone. When they came around the bend in the path they found Vari holding in the palm of her hand a beautiful yellow and black butterfly. With her face filled with wonder and joy Vari looked up at her parents and said, "Mommy and Daddy look! Mémère is telling us "good-bye!" as these word were said the butterfly took flight. The group stayed there and watched until the butterfly disappeared from sight. They all heard Varvara voice say, "Blessed be."